Room At the Top

CLEAN ROMANTIC FICTION

PACIFIC AVENUE
BOOK ONE

KRISTIN BILLERBECK

Praise for Kristin Billerbeck

"Billerbeck's best novel yet—smart and witty with wise insights about sisterhood and family."
—Colleen Coble
USA Today Bestselling Author

Praise for Kristin's Earlier Works:

SHE'S ALL THAT
Christian chick-lit star Billerbeck has moved on from her popular Ashley Stockingdale trilogy with an engaging new novel that features struggling fashion designer Lilly Jacobs and her two best friends, Morgan and Poppy . . . Snappy dialogue and lovable characters make this novel a winner."
—*Publisher's Weekly*

A BILLION REASONS WHY
The characters and breezy plot lie in this fun, romantic romp by the author of "Trophy Wives Club" series will please fans of Christian chick lit authors . . ."
—*Library Journal*

Foreword

Dear Reader,

I'm a fourth-generation Bay Area native. The Pacific Avenue Series is based on my own whimsical version of San Francisco. The one I remember fondly from my childhood. The place where Friday nights were spent cruising the hills and praying we had enough gas to get home. To this day, I can expertly get out of San Francisco as quickly as possible — I learned this "gift" from rushing to make curfew.

I've taken a lot of creative liberties to bring back the magical place where I learned to master my independence and the stick shift. In other words, you won't find this Pacific Avenue in the City, but I do hope you'll find characters that you can recognize from your own life.

Chapter One

"Money is a mirror to the soul. Protect your heart from its temptations." Those were my mother's ominous words as I headed to the reading of my grandfather's will. My *grandfather*—it was hard to give him such a heartwarming title when I'd never met the man.

Apparently, absenteeism was genetic because I'd never met my father either. The idea of entering a room filled with people who were technically family while still absolute strangers didn't sit well with me. The vengeful Italian part of me (probably the part that could be ruined by money) wanted to blow off this appointment like a dandelion's tender seeds. However, the practical, college-debt-owing part of me was much more reasonable.

Gia, my fearless twin sister, boasted no such worries. She flipped her long, dark hair and parallel-parked her Mini with ease in San Francisco's Financial District. "Let's do this!"

I sighed heavily.

"I don't know what you're worried about, Sophia. These people are nothing to us. If we get something from the will, we smile, say thank you and cash the check before they decide they've made a mistake. It's not like they want us in their lives."

"Don't you worry taking their money puts us in their lives?"

"Who wouldn't take free money? Working in the non-profit sector has ruined you. Seriously. You spend too much time with people who can't manage their lives."

"What if the money is a payoff? You know, to ensure we don't sully their bloodlines?" I rolled my eyes. "You know, with our commonness."

"We'll just have to slime them then." Gia laughed. "Besides, even the royal family now has an American, so it's totally trending to bring on a poor relation."

"Only rich people still live in their own version of the caste system."

"Think of it as winning the lottery," Gia said. "Maybe we'll get a buck and get to play again. Or maybe you'll have enough for graduate school for a few of your urchins. Isn't that your dream? Educate the world, restore families in the process. This should make your social worker heart go pitter-patter."

I frowned at Gia. She knew my Achilles' heel and how to wield it. "Don't be condescending. *We* are the urchins in this scenario. All we need is a blanket and a cardboard sign: *Will keep your dirty little secrets for money.*"

"Sophia, you and your righteous indignation. We don't have the luxury of righteous indignation. Get practical for a minute. Besides, we're not doing anything wrong. We were summoned to this place by the great king himself." She shrugged. "Before he died, of course."

"Really?" Even Gia's blasé comment about our grandfather-in-name-only made me feel guilty. He was dead, after all. Disparaging the dead felt like one of those great mortal sins my Nonna was always scaring the life out of us with as she crossed herself.

"You feel guilty because you carry the weight of the world on your shoulders. It's not up to you to fix everything that's broken, Sophia. The world is broken." She engaged the emergency brake and faced me. "Our family is broken. It's not our job to fix it.

We're all just doing the best we can in life." She tugged on the emergency brake again. "Come on, let's get this over with."

I followed after her. "It's hard to believe our father is doing the best he can, considering we haven't met him."

"Touché."

I looked up at the looming building in San Francisco's Financial District. The wild parrots of Telegraph Hill flew over our head and squawked maniacally as they disappeared over the mountain. "That has to be a good sign, no?"

"Maybe unicorns will fly out of the bank building. What do you think that means?"

"You don't have to get nasty," I told her. Gia dealt in facts and historical data. I had a more ethereal view of life—as if we were all here serving a greater purpose. It was the source of most of our disagreements.

She was my polar opposite in every way besides looks. Even that was up for question. We were identical twins, but she was elegant and fashionable while I usually resembled something out of the laundry hamper. Or perhaps a librarian after an overnight binge-reading marathon. Gia wore contacts while I preferred hiding behind horn-rimmed glasses, which gave off the impression that I was the more intelligent of us, but that wasn't true either. Glasses made me feel invisible so that I could watch people and ponder their actions. While pondering this, I nearly ran into my sister who stopped at the edge of the curb.

"What?" I asked her.

Gia hugged me so tightly my glasses pressed into my cheeks. It was awkward and completely out of her character, but I understood her meaning. *We belong here. Shut up already.* I nodded to let her know I was ready and clutched my cross necklace for strength.

"They have far more to lose when the world finds out about us." Gia swiped the cat hair from her black slacks and reached for the long gold bar that served as a door handle. I wanted to feel as confident as she did, but the idea of my father being in that room —a man I'd never met in person—took my breath away.

Gia took my hand. "If we get more than five dollars, I'll buy you a mocha."

"You're so generous, Gia."

"If it's more than five thousand, I'll buy you that mocha in Italy." She winked.

"Now we're talking." I'd worn my best suit, a shabby number that I'd picked up at the second-hand store for my first social work interview. Though I'd never noticed before, now I saw that it had loose threads and pulls in the fabric. "I suppose I need enough to buy a new suit."

Gia looked down at my skirt. "You look beautiful. Far better than our plastic sisters in their designer duds."

Bless her. I didn't feel beautiful. Dressing up wasn't a natural state for me. There were the women, like my heiress stepsisters, who could put on a pair of white slacks and sashay about like runway models without wearing a drop of what they ate that day. Maybe they didn't eat. Maybe that was their secret. If I didn't have a spot of something or other, I probably had starved myself that day and I definitely hadn't been to work.

"You really don't need to buy second-hand stuff, Sophia."

"I hate to spend money on clothes. Working with kids, it's such a waste." I stopped in the foyer of the grand building and looked around. "Maybe when my school loans are paid off."

"You'd have an easier time spending money on yourself if you didn't have that natural guilt reaction to everything. Nonna and her Catholic guilt sure did a number on you." She drew in a deep breath. "We're stalling. Let's do this." She reached for another vertical gold bar and yanked.

We entered the law office, which was an old bank—highly appropriate considering the circumstances. Like in a dark theater, we stood at the entrance, blinked wildly and allowed our eyes to adjust. Instinctively, I felt all attention on us as if we were in a stage spotlight and couldn't make out the audience. Me, with my dingy skirt with tears at the hem, and my wild black curls which I hadn't bothered to tame that morning. I wished I'd gotten up early and straightened myself out.

The room with its aged, cavernous style dripped of old money. Great white pillars soared into the elaborately carved golden ceiling and two mahogany staircases snaked down from the upper level and met on the grand mosaic tile floor. I half expected all of the women to be wearing fox stoles and flapper dresses.

I recognized our half-sisters Quinn and Brinn Wentworth from the society pages of the *San Francisco Chronicle*. They sat poised at the far table in fancy white suits as if the backs of their chairs were rattlesnakes that might strike at any moment. They ignored our entrance as if a mere burst of wind opened and shut the door and deposited two invisible spirits. Their straight blonde hair was professionally highlighted and their complexions luminous. They were the kind of girls who, in high school, wore pink on Wednesdays and made girls like me miserable.

Gia pushed me toward the guy in the suit who looked official. "Gia and Sophia Campelli. We're here for the reading."

"Of course, Ms. and Ms." He stood and led us to two of the chairs in a semi-circle facing the large wooden table at the head of the room. Our names were written in elegant script to show us our seats. "Welcome and please sit down. Can I get you anything to drink?"

Gia raised a brow at him as if to say, *are you serious?* He promptly darted his eyes away. I suppose working at the fine art museum, she was around more cultured people on a daily basis than I was because she was utterly fearless. If I possessed an ounce of her confidence, I'd be a seasoned school psychologist right now instead of a fledgling flunky assistant-almost social worker who worked in a state agency.

Our half-sisters looked down their straight noses at us. *Interlopers*, their expressions read. Well, who could blame them? Their father—our father—wasn't a man of character. Gia and I offered proof of what a tool he was. Bradley Wentworth had never married our mother, his high school sweetheart. Gia and I were older than his "legitimate" offspring, but rumor had it we weren't alone. A chair was still vacant with the name *Alisa Alton* neatly written in the same script was further proof.

"You were right," I whispered to Gia. "There must be another sister." Alisa was supposedly younger than all of us and confirmation that our father strayed yet again. He obviously had a hard time with the concept of self-control and monogamy. The holy state of matrimony clearly didn't curb his wandering ways.

The society pages said Alisa was born after the "legitimate" blonde daughters, who were the offspring of the illustrious Chelsea Whitman Wentworth, our father's wife. Chelsea and our father were conspicuously missing from the reading. Their absence made me feel rejected all over again, as if they couldn't be seen with the great unwashed and probably had their own reading of the will.

It dawned on me how the room was littered with the "sins" of our father. What a trail of destruction one man had left. Our mother, his first love, cast off like an old coat when she had the audacity to become pregnant. With twins no less. As if she'd done this all by herself. She had raised us by herself. We saw our father on weekends—in the Sunday paper once in a while on the society pages but never in person. He always smiled that bogus dentist grin he boasted with his Stepford wife and daughters beside him —their clothing designers' names printed under their own.

I shifted uncomfortably in my chair, willing this bizarre event to be over so I could get back to work. I supposed my grandfather had left me some trinket to know he was willing to concede his son had parented us, and for the first time I felt unmistakably angry. What had these people contributed to society that others worshiped them? They were born rich. *Congratulations, you won the birthday lottery.*

"Sophia, wipe that scowl off your face," my sister hissed.

"Don't give them the satisfaction." We settled in at the table across from our "sisters" and waited for the circus to start.

A man suddenly captured my attention as he peered in through the window of the foyer. He was tall, broad-shouldered, and desperately handsome in an old-school Hollywood way like Charlton Heston or Steve McQueen. He did not belong in the typical cache of Silicon Valley techies. This guy was legitimately different, and I was instantly intrigued.

"Who is that?" I whispered.

My sister followed my gaze. "How would I know? Honestly Sophia, stop fidgeting." In reality, she didn't want to admit she couldn't see him because she was too vain to wear glasses and her contacts didn't work that well.

I kept my gaze focused on the man in the foyer. His presence was angelic, but it was probably only the sunlight behind him, not an actual halo— although I wouldn't bet my life on it. "If they ever had Archangel Michael in a movie? That guy should play him. Doesn't he look exactly like that painting Nonna has in the kitchen?"

"Have you lost your ever-loving mind?"

"Probably," I said. "But I have to do something to entertain myself. This place is like a morgue. I'm going to call him Michael."

"You do you, Sophia," my sister snarked.

Out in the foyer, an elderly man handed "Michael" something before the old guy shuffled into the room and sat at the head of the large table—which looked more like a church altar than a desk.

"If I had a type," I nodded in satisfaction. "*Michael* would be it."

"You are certifiable," my sister said.

I watched the handsome warrior angel exit onto the street. I could have sworn the room became visibly darker. I sighed aloud.

Chapter Two

The old man stared at each of us "Wentworth heirs" knowingly, as if he held all of our secrets in the papers before him. He tapped the stack against the table's surface and looked up at us slowly. His tired gray-blue eyes were warm, and I wondered if he'd come out of retirement just to read his friend's will. *Well, I actually wondered if he rose from the grave, but that seems improbable.*

"I have here a letter," he said in his austere manner.

I supposed it was an austere occasion, but something told me he used that voice when he was announcing he wanted something from the kitchen.

"Our father isn't here yet," Blonde Number One said.

She had a very angular face with a long, elegant nose that she kept pointed permanently to the sky, but in earlier pictures her face seemed rounder, and I found myself preoccupied with her relationship with cosmetic fillers. Every move she made seemed posed and practiced in the mirror.

I knew her name, of course, but Gia and I preferred to call our society sisters, "Tweedledee" and "Tweedledum."

The old man told them that dear old dad wasn't invited, and it was time to get on with it. Then the two sisters glowered in our direction as if we had something to do with this decision. Gia rolled her eyes, clearly done with the entire debacle.

A flash of light illuminated the grand room and in skipped a spritely girl who brought with her an aura of bright colors. She was lithe and agile and made me wish I'd spent my youth with a more carefree attitude rather than locked down in libraries with my nose in a book. She flittered like a ballerina and danced across the tiles as if she never touched the ground. She wore ripped jeans, a crop top that showcased her taut abs, and a bulky cardigan sweater that seemed to swallow the rest of her whole. She'd been blessed with the Wentworth blue eyes and cascading blonde locks, which was braided in a Bohemian style.

"Hey!" She waved, unaffected by the ostentatious decorum of the room or the situation. "Alisa Alton." She pressed her fingertips to her chest. "Am I in the right place for the reading?" She spun around and took in all the surroundings. "This room is lit!" She pressed her hands together. "I feel like I'm in church. Hey everybody!" She met each one of us with direct eye contact. "I mean, seriously, don't you all just want to cross yourselves?" She pulled out a cell phone and snapped a picture of herself. "I'm so Snap Chatting this! My friends are going to crap a brick!"

"Miss Alton." Mr. Trunkett peered up over his glasses, clearly annoyed with the lot of us by now. "Have a seat and please put your cell phone away. There will be no recording of this meeting. We must get started. In the future, I'd appreciate your prompt arrival to any scheduled meetings. Is that clear?"

"Yes, sir!" Alisa slouched into a chair like a high schooler who thought her teachers were privileged to have her show up for class. She was childlike. I couldn't tell how old she was, but maybe twenty at the oldest. Our father had clearly been a busy dude in the breeding department and if he'd wanted a son, different mothers hadn't helped his cause. The man made girls.

"As you may or may not know," Mr. Trunkett mumbled. "I was a good friend to your grandfather. He was more than a scion of industry. He was a good man who had integrity and a generous nature. In this day and age, that combination is very hard to come by and I'll miss him greatly. I imagine the entire City of San Francisco joins me in that thought."

"We can only hope that's true," Gia whispered in my ear. "Show us the money."

Blah, blah, blah, I thought. This was just more PR to make us believe something that wasn't true. This family was garbage and no matter how much money they threw around to make it seem otherwise, they weren't *good people*, as my Nonna would say.

Mr. Trunkett cleared his throat again, clearly annoyed by all the feminine energy in his midst. He began to read the paper in front of him. "'To my granddaughters. Though I have never met three of you, as my life winds to a close, I am recalling the infamous words of your grandmother. She was a wonderful woman. A godly woman who never spoke ill of anyone in all the years I knew her. She used to tell me that nothing was more important than family, and I never understood what she meant until now that I face my Maker. When we lost our firstborn son, Wyatt Wentworth the Second, Amelie, your grandmother, was never the same . . .'" Mr. Trunkett paused as if to honor his friend's lost son.

As a social worker, this should have broken my heart, but I found myself strangely stoic. Losing their son didn't give them the right to excuse all their other son's sins.

Gia and I stared at each other. Our image hadn't changed of our mogul grandfather who denied our mother. We still saw him as little more than Scrooge McDuck sitting behind his great wooden desk counting his money.

Mr. Trunkett continued. "'Amelie made me promise when she left this earth that I wouldn't forget to put family first. I did not forget, but I was never good at those details that came so naturally to her with her sweet nature and consideration of others. My skill set was in making money and that's where I gravitated.'"

"Cry me a river," Gia whispered.

"'Amelie would say that you girls are my true legacy. Not the shipyards, not the many buildings named after me or the money I leave behind. I am compelled to try and piece this family back together again.'"

Gia squeezed my wrist so hard I cried out.

Mr. Trunkett looked up. "Is there a problem?"

"Just how much money are we talking about?"

"Let me finish." He narrowed his eyes and cleared his throat one more time. "'I have left my entire estate to be divided amongst the five of you. My son has made many mistakes that I ignored for the duration of my life. It is now that I make amends. Sophia, Gia, Alisa, I regret never meeting you and for my part in the crimes against you. I can only say at the time, I believed it to be the right course of action.'"

"Grandfather didn't write that," the first blonde said. "He would never say that about our father."

"He would and he did," Gia said in a flat tone. "Is that it?"

Gia obviously failed to understand the man just said we were going to get money. A lot of money. Me, with my shabby skirt, was awarded the same amount as my designer half-sisters with their perfect skin and tailored outfits.

"'There is one stipulation I have to my will.'"

Gia rolled her eyes and whispered, "Here it comes, the tragic fine print."

"The five of you must spend one year living together within the walls of Wentworth Mansion and remodeling it to current standards.'"

We all gazed at each other as if different animals in one round zoo. The idea of living with Tweedledee and Tweedledum in a confined space made me itch.

Mr. Trunkett continued reading. "'One thing I've learned in my long life is that relationships cannot be mended in absentia. You must work on creating relationships or they wither and die like an untended orchid. I realize what I ask of you must seem selfish, as I was not capable of such sacrifice and scandal myself. I must confess that I do not wish to control you from the other side of the grave. I wish to restore our family to that which it might have been had Amelie lived. It's the best I can do at this late hour and I ask for your forgiveness and understanding.'"

The five of us "sisters" stared at each other. *Live with them?* I didn't even want to have a drink with them. Blonde One looked as vain as any Kardashian, but without the substance and helpful makeup advice. Blonde Two was like Skipper, her less attractive sister who seemed twice as entitled. Alisa just seemed twitchy to get out her phone. The one thing we all had in common was that none of us saw this coming. We were never going to be a family. There wasn't enough money in the world.

Gia stood abruptly. "I think we're done here, Sophia," she said to me. "Thank you, Mr. Trunkett, but my sister and I aren't willing to give up our freedom. This won't be happening." She looked at the old man and our stepsisters. "I'm very sorry for your loss, but it doesn't concern us. Thank you."

"Miss Campelli," Mr. Trunkett said to Gia. "Do you have a question for me?"

"Our mother reminded us before we came that money is the root of all evil. I suppose this means the three sisters can split the money between them. That should be good for them."

I knew my sister. I knew she could walk away from this money without looking back. But something kept me bolted to the chair. The idea of what that money could do for kids in the foster system resonated with me. Maybe I'd never need my doctorate, which I'd put off because I couldn't afford it. Maybe this money could do even more than a costly degree could.

I stared at the lawyer. "Wait a minute, Gia. How much are we talking about, Mr. Trunkett?"

"Is your soul worth their money?" Gia said aloud so that everyone in the room heard her commentary. Like always, she wasn't going out without saying her piece.

"In all likelihood, with stocks split and the business valued, we're in the range of two billion each," Mr. Trunkett said blandly. "With another small percentage going to your grandfather's philanthropy work with cancer research."

"*Billions*," I said to Gia. "That kind of money isn't even real. Think of the families I could restore! We could get help for Nonna and Papa—"

But even I couldn't comprehend the amount. Why would any one person need so much? It made me a little sick to my stomach to think my father could have rescued us at any time from the financial peril we lived in, the hours my mother worked, the jobs my Papa took—all because of one man's greed and my mother's blasted pride.

"Is that what your soul is worth?" Gia hissed under her breath. "It's blood money."

I pushed her into a corner and continued to whisper. "So, take it from them." But even as I pressed her, I wondered if she was right. Looking at my two "sisters," it hadn't seemed to help them any.

"I'm pretty sure I could keep my soul and pay off my student debt. Think about the kids at the center I could send to college! Not to mention Mom selling that thankless restaurant. She deserves a rest, don't you think?"

"You're inviting that man into our life if you take this money," Gia said. "How do you think Mom will feel about that when she worked how many jobs to keep us clothed and fed? I know it's tempting, but this is our mother we're talking about."

Catholic and Jewish mothers had nothing on Gia when it came to guilt induction. I failed to see her point. It seemed like an easy answer to our troubles as far as I was concerned.

Mr. Trunkett pulled off his glasses. "If the five of you will not agree to the stipulations, all of the money will go elsewhere. Your grandfather was quite confident that you girls would have a lot in common once you had the opportunity to meet."

Somehow, I doubt that. I had about as much in common with these women as I did with pigeons on the street. But I could suck it up for a year to solve my family's woes. Thanks to the gentrification of all of San Francisco to the tech dorks, why shouldn't we fight back with a little old money? I could be as bougie as the next person given the right amount of cash.

Gia always said there were no ugly people, only poor ones who couldn't afford plastic surgery.

"Are we talking about our house? Wentworth Manor in Pacific Heights?" Quinn asked. "Gawd, that place is like a morgue. I couldn't wait to get out of there."

"Yes, that would be correct," Mr. Trunkett mumbled as if speaking was too trying for his old age. "Quinn, you know where you'll be living."

"It's my father's house. That's where my parents live now," Quinn replied.

"It's not your father's house," Trunkett said. "That's where you'll live. Your parents can remain there if the will's terms are met, but you will need to move back in, and I've seen to it that your old rooms are ready for you."

Plucky young Alisa raised her hand. "I don't care where we'd be living. Except does it have good WIFI? Because my Instagram feed is on point. I need to be able to take pictures and post."

Trunkett fixed her with a baleful glare and exhaled like an emptying air mattress.

"I have over 100,000 followers," she said to Trunkett as if to justify herself. Something told me the old man had no idea what Instagram was, much less cared about her followers. Then, she looked around the room at each one of us and homed in on me. "You should totally follow me. I give fashion tips, makeup advice, and home decor ideas. I'm Instafamous."

Quinn scoffed. "Brinn and I have more followers. You'll be fine. The mansion is enormous, built at the turn-of-the-century for some crazy lady." She looked over at Gia and me, as though we were something she couldn't rid off the bottom of her designer shoe. "You'd never really have to see us if that's your choice. Let's get this over with. Where do we sign?"

By her tone, she let us know it would indeed be her choice to avoid us, her riffraff sisters.

The old man straightened the papers before him. "There is the added requirement of a weekly Sunday dinner and a business meeting to go over corporate decisions regarding the philanthropy and the redesign of the house. Your grandfather believed in charitable responsibility with wealth."

"We know nothing about business," Alisa said as if she needed to tell us that. Obviously, Warren Buffet wasn't following her on Instagram.

"All of the details are in the paperwork along with your contact information. I suggest each of you meet with a lawyer and each other to discuss. If necessary, we'll reconvene in one week's time and set a required start date."

"Start date?" Gia shouted. "You make it sound like a prison sentence."

"You can meet with each other and discuss your options in detail. I guarantee you that it will be much more elegant than a prison sentence," he added with disdain.

"When would we have to move in?" Brinn asked.

"Brinn, you'll have to leave school for this. You can return to UC San Diego when the year is over and revive your studies. Your father and mother, since they are still in the house after caring for your grandfather, will be allowed to stay if certain stipulations are met. Quinn, you can leave the high-rise apartment and move back in at any time."

Peachy. We'll live with our dad now that we're thirty. There really is no such thing as a free lunch.

"My sister is getting married." Brinn looked us over to let us know we were not getting married.

"No," Trunkett said. "There will be no marriages allowed within the year's timeframe. There's a list of requirements that you'll find in your packets. If you have any questions, you can contact me at my office. Your grandfather was very specific. He knew that unification would not be easy, and he wanted to make sure he did everything he could to ensure the family legacy."

In our family, we call that a control freak.

Quinn's blue eyes went wide, the tip of her perfectly winged black eyeliner rose. "This is ridiculous. I can't have my life dictated by some ancient piece of paper. My grandfather loved my fiancé and I can't believe he wants us to wait!"

Mr. Trunkett shrugged. "I suppose you'll have to mention that to your sisters when you're deciding what to do, but all I can say is that a year is not a difficult time frame." The old man's weary eyes looked at each one of us, perhaps deciding which one of us would have the most difficult time sacrificing for billions. "Your grandfather knew this wouldn't be easy, but he thought it was the best way. He believed there was no gain in life without hard work and sacrifice. You'll all have to work together if this is the future you choose."

All for one or none for all. That's what it came down to—do as I say, not as I did. Grandfather, for all his greed, hadn't changed one iota, even if he did hide behind his saintly wife. He thought he could buy his mistakes off and let others take the consequences that he'd found too hard in life. Wasn't that the way the world felt? The rich got richer and the rest of us paid the piper.

My sister Gia stood, brushed herself off casually and walked toward the door without looking back. For all my pious beliefs about showing up that morning, temptation pulled me under far too quickly, like a surprise riptide. To be honest, I was ready to sign on the dotted line and call U-Haul to collect my things. While Gia strutted out the door without any regrets, I gripped our packets close to my chest and chased after her. Who thumbed their nose at the idea of being a billionaire? *It's only a year.*

Chapter Three

Gia was still ranting when we got into her little Mini. "What our grandfather—and I use the term loosely—failed to comprehend about the Campelli segment of his granddaughters, is that we have lived our entire lives without money being handed to us."

"You're right," I said, as if she needed any encouragement. I braced myself against the dashboard as she shot in and out of the Financial District traffic.

"I love that he thought after a lifetime of ignoring our existence, he could make us dance like puppets when he dangled some cash in front of us."

Perhaps she was getting carried away. "Gia, seriously. It's a couple billion dollars. Aren't you being a little hasty?"

"Did he have any idea what it cost for a single mother to raise twins in San Francisco? Does he think paying us now makes up for the days that we didn't have shoes that fit us to walk those blasted hills to school?"

"I mean, we came home every night to Nonna's homemade pasta and a three-story Victorian house, it's not like we were homeless—"

"We could have been for all he knew!" she snapped.

"Yeah, but he's dead now," I reminded her as she whizzed in and out of traffic like she was starring in the next *Fast and Furious*.

Gia's expression softened and she slowed down for a stop light. "I'm sorry the old man is dead. Truly I am, but I'm not living in that morgue of a house. To me it's like indentured servitude, *do what I should have done, and I'll pay you to atone for my sins*. I'm not his Jesus, Sophia. He should have gone to church and lit a candle like Nonna does." She looked into her rear-view mirror, "Is that guy following us?" She flew through the next yellow light.

I turned around. "If he was, you lost him." I faced her. "What if our grandfather truly wanted his family restored?"

"Don't get pulled into the romance of this, Sophia. Not all families were meant to be reunited. You know this. Some people are bad news. Why do you always have to see the good in people that might not be there?"

She was right. Even I had trouble believing that the scion of shipping suddenly grew a heart. For all Grandfather's talk of his beloved Amelie, there was no mention of a first wife he abandoned as our mother had been. There were family secrets too grotesque to speak of in mixed company. Maybe some things were left in the past and Gia's anger would serve us both well.

"I know what you're thinking." My sister's voice cracked. "But our father never even tried to see us. Not once in all of our thirty years. You don't think that has something to do with the fact that neither one of us dates or has ever considered marriage? No amount of money from our grandfather can fix the sins of his son."

"His son didn't inherit all the money, Gia. *We* did."

Gia wasn't as strong as she appeared. Her demeanor had visibly changed when she saw our two "princess" sisters acting like heiresses in their designer clothes. We missed out on being *legitimate* and that would never go away. It's one thing to be discarded by your father; it's quite another to see him as father of the year, treating his other children like royalty.

"You don't have to convince me," I told her. "You're right. I know you're right. I'm not giving up a year of my life to live in a creepy old mansion. I'm not Jane Eyre for goodness' sake." Though I had to admit, inside, all I wanted to do was restore our family and fulfill my grandfather's dream. It seemed hypocritical to not want that for my own family when it was my life's work.

Gia sighed. "I'm so relieved, Sophia. I wanted to make sure we were on the same page. You've got a lot of student loans," she reminded me. "I saw how tempted you were in there. Who wouldn't be? But taking that money makes what our dad did to us okay. I am ready to forgive him, but that doesn't mean I want to meet him or be around him."

"I'm not tempted enough to hand our lives over to that brood." I sounded stronger than I felt. "We belong with Nonna and Papa, and they're not getting any younger. They're our family." I had hoped to quell that rising temptation in my soul. I'd be completely out of debt and able to do social work in expensive San Francisco guilt-free.

"I knew you'd come to the same conclusion," Gia said. She had that way about her. She'd talk me into things and then make me believe they were my idea all along. I'd have to get alone in my room to know how I truly felt on the matter.

"If we don't take our share of the money, Sophia, our sisters don't get their share either. Did you miss that part?" I saw a glimmer in Gia's eye. While I may have had a vengeful side lurking within, Gia's was far closer to the surface and much more likely to take definitive action.

"Don't kid yourself, Gia. They have lawyers. It might take them awhile, but they'll figure out a way around the will. In fact, I can just see us spending the year in that gilded cage and ending up with nothing."

For a brief moment, I imagined a life where I could literally purchase anything my heart desired. I'd love to try on wealth for size, at least for a season. I'd buy a sparkling new gown at Saks, designer heels in Union Square (with lessons on how to walk in them properly). "What if we could do better with the money? I mean, do our vapid sisters need another round of Botox?"

"I can't believe you're saying this, Sophia. You, of all people! You've spent a fortune on education for a job that pays diddly-squat. Since when does your sainted self believe it's okay to accept charity?"

"Since it's not charity. It is rightfully ours and if nothing else, it reminds our so-called father that we exist. Maybe Mom will finally be able to move on. We were given this money. We're not taking what isn't ours."

"You're going to bring Mom into this? Fine, you can explain to Mom why we're moving in with a guy who abandoned us like an incurable disease. Oh, and the man who broke her heart. You tell Mom that she can take care of Nonna and Papa alone while they get frailer by the day because we have to jaunt off to Wentworth Manor."

I sighed. I was no match for Gia—nor her reasonable arguments. As much as I hated my father, I was curious about him and I was sickened that he was the main reason I was tempted. I wanted to prove to him what he'd missed by disowning us. I wanted to show him my mother had succeeded with us. *He* was the failure, not her.

"Rich people always win, Sophia. The rest of us are collateral damage."

Gia may have been a pessimist, but she was probably right in this instance.

* * *

Gia pulled up to our three-story Victorian house in the North Beach neighborhood of San Francisco. North Beach used to be the Italian section of San Francisco, but now it was quickly being taken over by the encroaching Chinatown and even a few Greek restaurants. Nonna and Papa didn't seem to notice. They still shopped at the little corner market for all their meat, bought their produce off Vinny's truck and drank Chianti from the local liquor shop. Every week their Italian friends gathered in the small dining room for Sunday dinner while Frank Sinatra crooned in the background. The men yelled about politics, sports and religion. The women gossiped in the kitchen over the hot stove, and the rambunctious children ran through the house like it was their own private playground. There were fewer of them now as the years ticked on, but the warmth remained.

My grandparents' decaying three-story home was the lone holdout in a neighborhood of upscale lofts and transformed apartment buildings. The house itself was probably worth upwards of four million for its location, but it looked like something out of a horror movie, and we couldn't afford to sell it. Bringing it up to code might come off the profits, but the problem remained that they would never be able to afford California real estate taxes on a new property.

My Papa worked in the trades, and household upkeep was not on his general list of things to do. Doorknobs fell off in your hand, tile crumbled under your feet, and ratty rugs from 'the old country' caught on your toe as you walked past, but no home was warmer or more welcoming. Papa believed in the old way of doing things and saw no reason to change. At eighty-five, I supposed he could do as he liked.

When Nonna and Papa went away for weekends on the gambling bus to Tahoe, my mother snuck workers in to fix the big issues, like plumbing and sparking electrical wires. Once she deemed it safe, she left it the way my Papa demanded, and we all continued as before. Papa wanted to live out his years in his home and he'd earned that right. The three of us spent our incomes maintaining the large structure, grateful for the low tax base and its convenient location. Only a multi-millionaire could afford such a location.

"We could fix up Papa's house," I said sheepishly to Gia in one final ploy for the money.

Once we parked the car on the street, the curtain snapped

shut and Mom rushed out the door. She was a tightly wired, fiery little spark plug of a woman. Marred by the guilt over the sin of her youth, she'd never married and spent her life taking care of her restaurant and all the strays who worked for her. She never hired one person without a story that would make us tear up. Then it became her personal mission to help them start over. Most of them never left. Gia says Mom was the original social worker in our family—I just got paid for the job.

My mother's staunch faith haunted her like an apparition that never left her side. She spoke of nothing but grace but couldn't seem to offer herself any. She went to Mass every day and lit candles for nearly every soul she came into contact with in a day. It was a wonder the church hadn't burned down in her piety.

"Is everything okay?" Mom cupped her hand around Gia's cheek. "Did you see them?"

"Bradley wasn't invited." Gia understood what my mother was really asking.

"I thought you were going to text me. I couldn't go to the restaurant until I heard something."

"Don't get excitable," Gia said in her cool manner. "We were a few blocks away; it was faster to come home than to have you try and find your glasses to read a text."

"With Gia driving, it was always faster to come home," I said.

"Anyway, he left us everything," Gia said casually. By the look on Mom's face, this wasn't even in the realm of possibility in her mind.

Mom dropped her hand to her side. "Come on, did he leave you enough to take me out to lunch? It's crab season and we could walk down to Fisherman's Wharf." To my mother, that was the ultimate luxury—to be able to eat with the tourists.

"Mom, she's not kidding," I said. "He really did leave everything to his five granddaughters, plus a hefty sum to cancer research that we are collectively supposed to manage. Oh, and redesign his house. He wants us to work together. Like a family."

"Five," Mom's voice lowered. "So, the rumors are true then.

There's another daughter out there . . . another baby mama." Mom's expression fell and her olive skin tone took on a sickly pallor. She so wanted to believe in her first and only love, even if the false hope destroyed her every day. It broke my heart. If that money could make my mother move on from her false reality, I'd donate every cent.

"You'll be happy to note that his youngest makes the older two look like Rhodes Scholars," Gia said.

"Gia, she can't be more than nineteen. Give her a break," I said.

Our mother didn't look a day over thirty-five. She had long, dark locks of hair that spiraled in an unnatural, cartoonishly beautiful way. The fact that she still cared anything about what Bradley Wentworth and his father did made us both crazy. Whatever she saw in Bradley we failed to observe in his pictures. He wore a fake tan and boasted Chicklet teeth—and didn't seem to do anything for a living than show up to charity balls. If he hadn't been an heir, he'd be selling used cars on Van Ness and probably charming women with rubbish stories of his imaginary accomplishments. *In essence, our father is a complete tool.*

Love made no sense. It had destroyed my mother, and because I was so much like her, love scared me. I believed in the good of the world and that no one wanted to hurt another. Who knows where we'd all be if not for Gia's daily reality check? Something told me I'd never be married, and I worked as though I knew this to be true.

"Let's go get some crab, Mom. They'll be open by the time we walk down the hill," I said. "We'll treat."

"You'll be rich." Mom stared at the filthy sidewalk while she imagined us off in a world she felt she couldn't enter. I saw the fear written all over her face, that we'd abandon our upbringing for a different life. Once again, Gia had been right.

"The money just comes with strings we're not willing to tie, so we got nothing," Gia said matter-of-factly. "On a happy note, neither will the princesses. Does Nonna have leftovers? I'm starving."

"Mom wants crab," I said through gritted teeth.

As I grabbed the doorknob to the front door, a light blue Prius drove up and parked in front of our driveway. My mother was about to yell that he couldn't park there, when the tall elegant man, my archangel from the foyer, stepped out in a dark, well-cut suit. He was so tall, in fact, I wondered if he had to bend himself in half to fit into his ridiculous vehicle. His bulging muscles strained at his suit and I tried to size him up, but immediately looked to Gia for her more realistic reaction. His hair was dark blonde, cropped close to his head and he seemed to stare at my sister, which allowed me to scrutinize him further and examine his chiseled jawline at my leisure. His eyes were the blue of a Sierra Mountain lake, but they had a severity to them that I couldn't read.

"Gia?" he said.

Her eyes narrowed but she said nothing. What struck me most about him was that he clearly had no trouble telling the two of us apart. His eyes captured the smile he wore, and they were at odds with his appearance. Underneath the business image, he looked more Montana cowboy than San Francisco tech nerd, as if someone had dressed him up and sent him on a foreign mission field. Something about him made me feel invisible as I drank in his delicious, gallant details. Manly men had gone away with the man bun in San Francisco. With all the high-tech employees and their backpacks being bussed into town, it was difficult to tell who was heading to work and who was off to middle school. The only way to actually distinguish them was their company badge as it hung off their belt loop.

"Are you qualifying for a race or just in a hurry?" he asked Gia with a sparkle in his eye. I thought I saw that halo behind him again, but it was just the sunlight bouncing off a car's side mirror.

"Have you been following us?" Gia asked, her eyes suspicious. She had a way of stating innocent questions as a threat.

Mom stepped between us and the handsome stranger. "Who are you? What do you mean by following my girls?" Her eyes glared at him in a menacing fashion. "We're not like most Californians. We keep guns and we know how to use them."

We do not keep guns. Nor do we know how to use them.

The man stepped back and lifted his palms. Though built like a gym rat, he clearly realized the bone-chilling threat of an Italian mother.

"Trust me, I mean your daughters no harm. I'm only here on business and then I'll be on my way." He held up two manila envelopes. "See? Business."

"Well?" Mom said. "See to your business then and be gone with you. You're about two minutes away from a parking ticket."

The man wore the air of confidence, but my mother reduced him to a sputtering fool. Our mom, *the terminator.*

"I was supposed to give them something after the reading, but I failed at my task because it seems your daughter's car runs on jet fuel."

"Does that mean yours runs on squirrel power?" Gia asked him. "How can anyone take you seriously in that car? Seems as if you'd need a sunroof just to stick your head of that tiny thing. I'd advise you to get another car. Or maybe take Uber. It can't be good for a man's reputation."

He cocked an eyebrow, "I'll take that under advisement." He handed Gia an envelope. "You've been served, Miss Campelli."

For a brief second, he looked at me directly with a mesmerizing gaze that held me in place until I realized he held another envelope and meant to serve me legal papers of some sort, too. I saw process servers all day long at the Regional Center. How could I have missed the clues?

His gaze stopped feeling so special at that point. Rather than act like a normal person and take my envelope, I ran. As though Forrest Gump's way of handling conflict might work for me in this instance. First, I ran into my grandparents' house, then I burst out of the back door and into the alley behind the house and up a one-way street the wrong way, so that he couldn't follow me in his tiny vehicle. I didn't have any clue where I was headed, but I kept running.

Granted, I had no inclination that the server was following me at all, but running was my solace. It's what I did when I needed to block out a child's palpable pain as a social worker or forget a mother's tears. When I ran the hills of San Francisco, nothing mattered. The steep inclines rendered me so tired that I thought of nothing else but the elusive oxygen that I craved.

When I finally stopped at the top of the hill to catch my breath, I knew that somehow my life would never be the same, whether we took the money or whether we didn't. Money brought the cockroaches out of their dark hiding places and there was little doubt that the gorgeous man in his business suit was a false front for the insects who'd been waiting for the reading of the will to activate.

Considering that my sister and I still had no money, I failed to see who might sue us at this juncture. But something inside me, probably that vengeful, money-grubbing side again, hoped he looked half as good as the angelic messenger.

Chapter Four

After I ran up Telegraph Hill to the base of Coit Tower, I ran downhill to my job at the City Regional Center. I kept looking behind me, perhaps hopeful that the Archangel was following me, but no such luck. What harm did it do to dwell in my fantasy for an hour? If nothing else, it made my glutes that much tighter.

I called my mom while I caught my breath. "Hey, Mom, sorry," I said after she answered. "Can we do lunch another day?"

"Where did you go?"

"I didn't want to get served."

"For heaven's sake, Sophia. You scared the life out of Nonna running through the house like that."

"I'm sorry."

"Be home for dinner tonight. We have a lot to discuss."

We said our goodbyes, and I realized I didn't have anything I needed for work. I didn't have my badge, a wallet, nothing. It was all in Gia's car.

Working at the City Regional Center was a financial tread-mill. I worked, racked up countless unpaid hours with families—most of whom couldn't have a simple discussion without breaking into Maury Povich-quality theatrics—and then I went back home. This cycle allowed me to pay for the basic necessities of employment: Food, clothing and transportation, but nothing else. If it weren't for my Nonna and Papa's house, I would have to commute hours for the privilege of my job. No one got into social work for the pay. It was a calling.

Every day I saw parents struggle and fight with their exes, with drugs, with the courts—all to get their kids back. I now wondered why anyone got married. Why anyone had children. Of course, there were the parents who didn't show up to court-appointed visits, who were too busy or drugged-out to care that their child waited at the window with palms pressed to the glass in hope. I knew exactly how they felt, too.

I hung up the phone at the Regional Center and was met by my boss, Bobbi Mack. She stood behind the waist-high counter that separated the preschool room from the entry way and crossed her arms at the sight of me. "What have you gotten yourself up to?"

"It's a long story. I don't have my badge, can you let me in?"

Bobbi was a larger-than-life black woman who used to be a police officer. Originally, she'd been hired to oversee supervised visitations that were considered dangerous. Then they expanded her duties so she taught mandatory anger management courses to abusive men. She worked her way up to director. Needless to say, she didn't take any foolishness from our clients and no one dared to give it to her. Least of all, the wife beaters. She'd toss them in jail so quickly, they wouldn't have time to whimper an apology.

"Well?" Bobbi asked me. "Have you won the inheritance lottery? Because I can't replace you, you know. You're my best intern."

I shrugged. "Nothing worth discussing. Any money requires Gia to compromise and that isn't happening."

"You need to let me talk to that sister of yours. Sometimes she has no sense at all."

"No offense, Bobbi, but I don't think even you're a match for her kind of stubbornness."

"I suppose the hope was nice while it lasted." Bobbi pressed her badge against the counter and lifted it to let me in. "I thought maybe you'd buy us a few new tricycles for in here. Maybe get your master's degree finished off and work on that doctorate. I hope they at least paid for your parking this morning."

"You know Gia, she found street parking. I would have been buying us tricycles for days if I had gotten any money."

"You all right?" Bobbi sighed.

"It was hard," I said honestly. "I've never seen my half-sisters in person. They both wore these slick, white pantsuits and a full face of makeup. They're not as pretty in person as they are in the newspaper."

"No?" Bobbi said.

"For real," I told her. "It was an eye-opener, but I don't believe money improves people. The two of them are likely plastic dolls—so basic."

"Money just highlights what's inside," she said. "Ain't good nor bad. What about the youngest? Does she exist?"

"She's real. Her name is Alisa. Blonde dancer-type who thinks her Instagram feed is a career, but she's young. She has time to figure things out."

"I'd really hoped I'd see you get some money. It would have been nice to see someone deserving get it for a change. It's probably for the best. I can't imagine designer togs would do much around here." Bobbi's gaze darkened. "I never thought about your leaving. I suppose you wouldn't have to work with that kind of money so I'm grateful the stingy old curmudgeon didn't leave you anything."

It felt dishonest to not tell Bobbi the whole tale but who could understand what Gia and I felt about our father's family? How it would be the ultimate betrayal to our steadfast mother to go and live with them for a year as though Mom never existed. I knew what Bobbi really wanted. She wanted me to admit the rage I had for my father's abandonment, and I wasn't ready to talk about the two girls who had a father in him. My emotions were still too fragile and raw.

"What's on my agenda today?"

Bobbi gave me her best mom stare-down. "You have two supervised visitations this afternoon. A new kid. His mom is fresh out of rehab, and I'm sorry to tell you that it will be a rough parting at the end of it. This morning you just have Oliver and his dad."

It was a comfort to know nothing had changed at the center. I craved the regularity of it all. I had a bigger calling in life than to sit on my duff and collect money. I had reached for the swinging double doors to the back preschool room, with its colorful carpet and brightly painted walls when I heard my name.

"Sophia?"

I turned. The lawsuit server with his angelic good looks and the quiet magnetism greeted me with a winner's grin. He'd tracked me down. I would have run again, but there was nowhere to hide for a person over three feet tall. It crossed my mind that I could camouflage myself like some of the smaller children and simply stand there believing myself invisible. He stepped toward the counter, and my heart rose in my throat as I spotted the nefarious envelope in his hand. Briefly, I thought about siccing Bobbi on him, but I quickly weakened under the power of his Lake Tahoe blue eyes. I pondered the age-old trick of claiming that I was Gia. Although we are not hard to tell apart. I'm the bookworm who wears wide-rimmed glasses, my hair thrown in a sloppy ponytail and torn boyfriend jeans so that I can get on the floor with the kids. Gia's hair is always styled as if she stepped out of the salon. She wears stilettos, tailored linen jackets, and pegged pants because she works in a respectable museum. There was all of that, and of course, the simple fact that he'd just seen us side-by-side and knew what we were wearing.

The process server smiled at me, and my will evaporated. His grin was infectious. He was charming and he knew it. No doubt that smile had gotten him out of many a mess. I could tell by how professionally he wielded it.

"Sophia," he purred my name.

I wanted to run just so I might hear him say my name again, but I stood there blinking rapidly, mesmerized by his boyish good looks. He looked like a surfer. A short buzz cut with longer blond locks on top brushed to the side. His fingers were long and lean like the rest of him and they were freckled from the sun.

"I thought I'd have more trouble with your sister, but I have to admit, you surprised me. Where'd you learn to run like that?"

"I chase toddlers for a living. You don't have to make polite conversation," I told him. "Do your dirty work and be on your way."

"Between your sister's driving and your track and field event, it seems I underestimated my price on serving the Campelli sisters."

"Give it here and go," I stretched out my arm across the counter.

He placed the envelope in my hand and my eyes were locked on his while sparks rushed up the length of my arm, which annoyed me to no end. He may have been cut like a Greek statue, but that wasn't his attraction. He held a firmness about him, an impenetrable armor to his personality that made me feel safe in his presence. Perhaps that's why I ran. He wasn't the kind of man who would give me a second glance, and the fact that he did put him in the category of my father's type—a player with the inability to commit to anything that didn't serve him.

"Do you always pursue your targets so relentlessly? Do you like playing Dog the Bounty Hunter?"

His fingers wrapped around my hand, and he didn't release the envelope. "I'll admit, I may have been slightly more motivated after seeing the two of you. You can't blame a guy for trying."

"Seriously?" I rolled my eyes. "Does that line ever work for you?"

"I meant that." He seemed offended.

"Does whomever is suing me know that I have no money?" I pulled my hand from his and swept the envelope across the preschool room with its tattered carpet and worn toys. "I mean, I don't even own all of this. What do they want, my mother's scrunchie collection from 1984?"

"Normally, a server doesn't know what he's serving."

"But you do." I raised a brow.

He nodded slightly. "My boss asked me to personally serve you and your sister." He pulled out a hundred-dollar bill from his chest pocket. "Gave me a Benjamin for my troubles. Little did I know that you two would make me earn it. I thought two young professionals living in San Francisco, how difficult could it be to hand you an envelope?"

"He didn't mention that we're Italian, I take it."

"He neglected to mention that. He also failed to mention that one of you drives like a bat out of hell and the other has been practicing for some kind of hilltop marathon." He held a hand to his chest. "This has been like grade school, chasing the pretty girls across the blacktop and they never let me catch them."

I felt the slightest satisfaction that we required chasing. "Is this your full-time career then? Pursuing innocent lawsuit victims?" I kept going when I realized I'd hit a nerve. "Does the work ever get to you?"

"I do have a career besides serving fair maidens across the land, but then I remember that I'm a lawyer at Sloan and Weiler, so I have no heart."

"That explains your suit. I thought it was a bit dressy for a process server."

"It's new." He traced the lapel.

"Do you have a name Mr. Lawyer at Sloan and Weiler? Or shall you forever be known as the man with the stone heart who served me up my first lawsuit?"

"Joel Edgerton at your service."

"Well Joel, I can't say it's a pleasure to meet you, but I do wish you'd followed me up to Coit Tower this morning. Lovely day, and you could have broken a sweat in that perfectly pressed suit of yours. You still look too unflappable."

"Coit Tower." He nodded. "You go up there often?"

I ignored his question. "The view was magnificent this morning. Sparkling blue, the entirety of the Golden Gate Bridge, absolutely no fog. It was lovely. Thanks for helping me to forget that idyllic image so quickly."

He waved his Benjamin again and handed it to me. "I think you should buy yourself dinner on me. You gave me a good run for my money, even without the stairs to Coit. I can respect that."

I ignored the bill. "Why don't you just tell me who is suing me instead? I have a child coming in who I will have to rip away from his father later, so you'll understand if I'm less than enthused about reading a bunch of legal gobbledygook."

Bobbi whistled from behind me. "Look at you," she said to Joel. "All flirtatious while you serve a lawsuit. You wouldn't get me to open my door no matter how good you look, young man."

Joel cocked his brow. "This is my first and last day as a process server, but I have to admit I didn't do half-bad when it came to picking my processee, did I? She's quite beautiful."

"That's probably for the best that it's your last day." Bobbi grimaced at him. "Don't go flirting with my social workers, you hear me? She has work to do." Bobbi raised her chin toward the door. "I assume you'll see yourself out."

He heaved a computer backpack over his shoulder and leaned in close to me, "You have nothing to worry about. I guarantee you that any will of Wyatt Wentworth's is rock solid and without loopholes. We were served with this lawsuit before the will was read this morning. As a courtesy, Mr. Trunkett wanted you to have it before the real processor delivered it."

"But you're not my lawyer. Why would he serve you?"

"Do you have a lawyer, Sophia?"

"Well, no, but—"

"Until you do, Mr. Trunkett will be representing your interests as the executor of the estate you've inherited. I'm certain you'll be getting an official service later from your father's attorney regarding this."

"Yes, you said that already. My father?" I was breathless at the mention of my father. "I've never met my father. How is it he could be suing me?" I couldn't fathom that the man I'd never met, the one I'd studied and scrutinized for more information to decipher his secrets, knew who I was. He'd finally acknowledged my existence—with a lawsuit. "The father I've never met is suing me?"

"I'm just the messenger," Joel Edgerton said. "Your father was told earlier the outcome of this morning's meeting, out of respect."

"I thought everything from this morning was a secret."

"For the most part. You might have warned your little sister if you were hoping for privacy. Alisa posted a picture on Instagram with the words, 'Billionaire. Yo!' written across her post. You might want to tell her—"

"I don't even know her. How would I tell her anything?" My eyes sprang open with a new thought. "Have you met him? My father."

He nodded slowly. "I've met him."

"What's he like?"

"Depends on who you are to him, I suppose." He gave me a pitying smile and turned to leave.

I didn't want him to go without playing my hand. "Joel, I do hope there are loopholes for my stepsisters' sake. Gia and I know how to live without money, but they don't." I had his full attention. "We're not interested in handing over our souls nor our lives for a year for thirty pieces of silver."

"A year?" He came closer to me and his blue eyes bore through me like one of my Papa's electric drills. "You're saying the will states you must give up your freedom for a year?"

Suddenly, it occurred to me not all of the will's details were public, and I'd just opened my big mouth—to a lawyer of all people, the most depraved of all creatures. No matter how good he looked or safe he felt, underneath he was able to shed that lizard skin and reemerge brighter and fresher than before.

"You're serious?" He placed his backpack on the counter and

stood over me in a protective stance. "There's a stipulation that lasts for a mere year, and you're unwilling to adhere to it?"

"Do I need to call the police?" Bobbi threatened.

"No ma'am." He saluted my boss. "I'm leaving." He lifted my hand and pressed a kiss on it. "Sophia Campelli, it's been a pleasure, and I hope to see you again someday under much better circumstances."

Joel strode from the building in two long steps. Behind the backpack, I noticed again how his muscular arms strained against his suit coat. "Remind me again, Bobbi, lawyers are the scourge of the earth, right?"

She scrunched up her nose. "Lower than low. Belly crawlers. Lawyers look up to snakes." We both laughed. "He's a fine specimen though," Bobbi admitted. "Too bad he knows it."

"I need to get out more. When I'm tempted by a guy who's here to sue me—and who now knows I've inherited a fortune— I've lost the plot."

"I can't believe you weren't going to tell me." Bobbi shook her head. She was like a second mother to me, so my silence was truly a betrayal.

"If I took that money, I could have plenty of men who look like him." I leaned over the counter on my elbows. "I wonder if I could get Chris Evans' number. Do you think? My people could call his people. Maybe I could produce his next movie in exchange for a walk down the aisle."

"I think you need to get back to work." Bobbi's detour into small talk was officially over.

I ripped open the envelope and yanked out the wad of papers when the high-pitched squeal of brakes stopped me from reading a word. I looked up, horrified to see something lumped in the street with a smart car stalled beside it. Before I could process the scene, Bobbi leaped over the counter and yelled back at me.

"Someone's been hit! Call 911, Sophia!"

Chapter Five

I was so grateful for her definitive instructions. I lifted my cell phone from my back pocket, and I dialed. Immediately, I realized I should have called from the Center's phone so they had an address, but it was too late now and they probably had technology regardless.

"911, what's your emergency?"

"Someone's been hit by a car in front of the Regional Care Center on Market! I'm inside. People are all around the victim."

The operator fired questions at me. Questions I didn't have the answers for. She wanted me to stay on the line until help had arrived, and I paced the center nervously, thankful there were no kids in the front of the center. I couldn't bear to see violence.

"I need you to step outside and tell me what's happening."

I didn't want to go, but I forced myself to put one foot in front of the other and step onto the sidewalk. "Okay, I'm outside."

"How many people are hurt? Can you tell?"

"I don't want to look!"

"Ma'am, help is on the way. I need you to tell me what's happening."

I braced myself because that's what decent people did. They

tried to help at the expense of their own comfort. I clenched my fist and my fingernails dug into my palm as I stepped to the edge of the sidewalk.

I forced myself to look in Bobbi's direction. She was standing over Joel, who was crumpled in the street like a wounded animal. I heard myself squeal his name. *Joel* was hurt? My Joel? That made it so much worse than a passerby I didn't know.

I noticed an elderly man in front of him on a walker. The man was unharmed, but frozen in the street.

"Sir?" I stepped off the curb. "Let me get you back to the sidewalk."

"The light was green," the old man said.

I looked up, and there was no traffic light. There was only the glow of a Boba tea shop's neon sign. I put my arms around the old man and helped him back onto the curb. "You're all right, but you've had a scare. Let me get you a chair." When I knew he was solid, I ran into the center, grabbed a desk chair and pulled it out onto the sidewalk. "Can I get you a glass of water?" I eased him into the chair. The old man shook his head.

Joel groaned in the street, which brought me solace because I knew he was alive. I saw no blood, but that didn't give me peace. Working with abused children, I knew enough about internal injuries to be terrified for him. I began to pray silently with the zeal of my Nonna. My mind scattered from one worry to the next and I found myself just saying the name *Jesus*, over and over again in my head. In times of crises I turned into both my scattered mother and my fervent Nonna.

Had the vehicle that stuck Joel been anything but a motorcycle with a roof (a smart car) he'd be gone already, so I thanked God for small favors and ridiculously tiny cars. The traffic on the street honked their annoyance at the stopped car in the Muni lane, oblivious to the fact that Joel laid crumpled in front of it, motionless.

His handsome face bore the pain he must have felt, and my body registered a visceral reaction to his agony. Joel's lower leg bent unnaturally, and it didn't take a medical degree to see it was broken, but his torso appeared fine. I knelt beside him and took hold of his hand while the operator still chattered on in my ear, but his hand was limp, and it scared me.

"Archangel Michael, defend us in battle. Be our protector against the wickedness and snares of the devil." I recited the prayer of St. Michael out loud as I'd heard my Nonna do so many times before. It was funny how things came back to you in moments of trauma.

Bobbi, ever more practical, checked his neck without touching him and spoke soothingly to him. For all her gruff exterior, she was a softie with a huge heart for people. I felt numb as I watched her, and I wondered if I'd ever be as calm in a crisis as she managed to be. The children would be arriving soon for their appointments, and I longed for the ambulance to arrive quickly and whisk Joel off to safety and away from their innocent eyes.

Even in the midst of a catastrophe, Joel had a regal appearance with prominent cheekbones and a wide, masculine jaw that I wanted to run my fingers along. Lying on the street, he still looked every bit as impressive as he had on the street in front of my mother's house. I half-expected him to rise and announce the great joke he'd played on us.

The curse of the Wentworth money has begun, I decided.

"I need to call the office," Joel slurred without opening his eyes.

"You need to relax." Bobbi said. "You couldn't call the office if you were dead now, could you? Sophia will take care of that for you as soon as she's off the phone with emergency services. She has your card."

Joel reached toward me and I moved closer toward him. I held his hand tighter and felt his close around mine. "You're going to be all right," I told him. "I prayed for Saint Michael to protect you."

"You did?" He slurred with a grin.

The strength in his hand failed and he let go. I placed the

phone beside me and picked up his hand again. "Joel, stay awake. Stay awake, please. You got through law school; this is a breeze."

He opened his eyes, and the brilliant blue appeared once again. My racing heartbeat eased at the sight. The ambulance arrived, and I hung up on the operator. The EMTs secured Joel's neck. A crowd had gathered, and I felt protective of Joel and tried to block people's view.

"Go away!" I shouted, but no one moved. It was as though this accident was a sideshow or tourist attraction. "What's wrong with you people? A man is hurt. Get out of here! Freaking vultures!"

Bobbi placed her hand on my shoulder. "It's all right, Sophia. Stay calm."

After what seemed an eternity, the paramedics transferred him into the ambulance, and it dawned on me as they started to shut the doors that I might never see him again.

"You're going with him?" the female EMT asked, and I looked at my boss.

Bobbi nodded toward me. "I'll cover you. You don't have your badge anyway."

"I am," I told the EMT as I climbed into the back of the ambulance. I took Joel's hand in my own again. He opened his eyes wearily and smiled the slightest smile with all the gallantry he might have mustered.

"You're so beautiful," he said.

"Save your strength, Romeo. You can flirt later." I had an urge to press a soft kiss to his forehead. I resisted. He was still the enemy.

He grinned and closed his eyes.

* * *

San Francisco General Hospital had received a huge overhaul, thanks to Zuckerberg's substantial financial donation. The trauma center appeared so high tech that it felt like I was on the

Starship Enterprise rather than in a hospital. Wide open and brimming with natural sunlight, the neon blue-lit glass of the desks and colorfully lighted wall art created a singles' bar environment, and I half-expected them to ask me for a cover charge. All that was missing was the pounding beat of dance music and a D.J.

The paramedics had whisked Joel away behind swinging doors and a nurse handed me paperwork. I literally only knew his name and where he worked, but I took his card out of my pocket and began to fill out what I could. Other than his name, title and place of employment? I only knew that his touch altered my world, and I didn't have the power to leave him there alone as if no one cared about his recovery. He wasn't a John Doe. He was Joel Edgerton, and he'd saved that old man's life.

The triage nurse took what little information I offered like it was dirty laundry. She said she'd get what she needed from "the victim's phone." I mean, I may not have been best friends with him, but *the victim* seemed unreasonably harsh.

"His name is Joel," I told her. "He'll be okay?" There was the hint of desperation in my voice.

The nurse pressed her glasses to her face. "I won't be able to offer you any information as you're not related to the victim."

"Stop calling him *that*! His name is Joel! I'm not related to Joel, I get it."

My anguish seemed to click in the nurse. "I'm sorry, Ms. I've been on duty for far too long today. I know you must be upset by what you've witnessed this afternoon. Would you like to speak to anyone?" She patted my hand. She was an older woman, and she wore a plum-colored uniform with a pink veil wrapped around her head. "We have excellent social workers on staff."

"I *am* a social worker!" I snapped my hand away.

"With all due respect, that doesn't mean you can process this kind of trauma alone. We see this kind of thing every day, but most people are not equipped to handle the harsh reality of such an accident."

As her voice softened, so did my anger. "No thank you. If I

need something, I'll let you know, but just find Joel's family for him. I'm sure he'll want them around when he's awake."

"You're going to wait? They're wheeling him into surgery."

I nodded. "My boss gave me the afternoon off, and it feels like the right thing to do. If he wakes up I don't want him to think he's alone."

"I can't really offer you more information on his condition, but if he wakes up I can tell him you're here."

"I wouldn't feel right about leaving. It just feels like someone should be here." I didn't know if it was my social worker compassion on overtime or my instant connection to the handsome lawyer. I told myself it was the former. It made me less pathetic somehow. "I'll call his office and they can notify—"

"We'll take care of that, Ms. Do you want some coffee?" the nurse asked.

"No. But thank you." I settled into straight-backed chair in the waiting room and stared ahead of me in some kind of trance. There were texts from my sister, but I didn't care to read them. The last thing I wanted to think about was our inheritance and the trouble it was already causing. My mother's terrible taste in the choice of Bradley Wentworth was legendary. I could only pray that it wasn't genetic, but considering where I was at the moment, it was highly likely.

In one day, my whole world had exploded. The father I'd dreamt about my entire life didn't come to meet me with arms outstretched, but rather served me with a lawsuit—and he'd used a stranger to do it. So much for my "Little Orphan Annie" dreams. I possessed what Bradley Wentworth wanted—at least for now—until Gia and I announced our forfeiture. Knowing my sister, I'm sure that we'd let "Daddy" sweat it out for as long as possible.

I'd waited hours and it was nearly dark outside when a blonde in jodhpurs and a riding jacket was denied entry until she handed over her weapon (a short riding crop.) Once she came closer, I realized it was one of my half-sisters. I didn't know if it was Tweedledee or Tweedledum, as Gia referred to them whenever they were in the news. To us, they were interchangeable. They were our Daddy's favorites—worthy of being parented and pranced about like San Francisco royalty. I sat up in my chair as she approached, unnerved by her getup. Her appearance confirmed what I'd always thought about her. That she dwelled in a very real fairy tale land where I imagined her mounting her horse any time she liked and riding off into the English countryside circa 1850 to engage in the annual fox hunt.

"What are you doing here?" she asked in an accusatory tone.

"It's none of your business." I crossed my arms. I wanted to tell her not everyone splashed the minutest details all over social media, but I refrained.

"Did your sister overdose upon hearing of her windfall?" she scoffed. "I suppose you have your Carnival cruise all booked. The whole fam going then?"

What's wrong with Carnival cruises?

I wanted to ring her stringy little neck. To reach my hands about her tiny throat and deny her the right to speak such vile venom ever again, but I composed myself quickly. "Gia is her name, and she's your sister, too. Or have you forgotten how prolific your father is? It's a wonder he had any time to buy you anything."

"He's your father, too. Or so you and your scheming mother say."

"So, our paternal *grandfather* and DNA says," I reminded her. Honestly, I've never spoken such critical words in all my life, but there was a resentment within me that exploded like a cat's hairball. "Don't ever speak of my mother. If she were scheming as you say, your father wouldn't be free to marry your useless debutante of a mother."

"How dare you!"

I realized I'd stepped over the line, though her mother made every Bravo housewife seem like a foreign diplomat when it came to etiquette.

My half-sister was like a pit bull and wouldn't let go. "Have you hired a moving van yet to come drop off your valuables at the mansion? Let me guess, a few pair of Skechers trainers and a knockoff purse from Chinatown?"

"You might want to back it up a little, Princess. We're not moving in, and without us, you don't inherit the money, so you may want to practice some humility because you may need our help on how to budget very soon." I allowed a slow smile to creep across my face. "Gia and I don't need your grandfather's money. We both have jobs and know how to budget. We'll be happy to offer assistance. Maybe there's an app that helps former heiresses. Might want to look into that."

Abject terror worthy of a horror movie showed on her face. "What do you mean you're not moving in? It's like two billion dollars for one year's work. And it's not even work. You do know you can never earn that money in a lifetime." She tried to sound confident, but her voice trembled.

"What makes you think I want to make that kind of money in this lifetime? It hasn't done much for the Wentworths for all I can see."

"I don't have time for this now, but please tell me that you cannot be that stupid." She swept past me toward the nurse's desk. "I'm here to see my fiancé."

"Name?"

"Quinn Wentworth."

Ah. So, she's Tweedledee. I should have known. She's the more stunning of the two.

"The patient's name," the nurse drawled.

"Sorry, it's been a trying day."

As riding a horse all day can be so stressful. The woes of being a casual equestrian.

She looked back at me quickly before continuing. "I'm terribly sorry. I'm nervous. His name is Joel Edgerton, and he was involved in an accident. His mother called me."

For a moment I forgot to breathe. The nurse stared at me, as if to ask if I knew Joel was engaged. *No, I did not.* Worse yet, I did not know he was engaged to my empty-headed half-sister. But it all made sense. Bradley Wentworth was using his future son-in-law's law firm to keep his underhanded deals in the family. I was more convinced than ever that Gia was correct. The quicker we escaped this toxic pseudo-family, the better off we'd fare. But my heart was a tiny bit broken.

While the nurse was preoccupied with Quinn, and since I knew Joel wouldn't be alone when he woke, I seized the opportunity to sneak out of the hospital and call an Uber from my phone. The car took me directly to North Beach and my Campelli family compound, a place I never should have left that morning.

Chapter Six

Nonna and Papa lived on the first floor of the North Beach Victorian, my mother lived on the second, and Gia and I shared the third floor. We both had a room with bay windows that looked out over the street. Between us, there was a single-windowed room that we used as a shared living space with a flat screen television on the exposed brick wall with an oversized sofa and two Ikea desks where we once did our homework—well, where I still did my homework as I worked to get my final license in social work.

If we were prone to smuggling guys upstairs, it wouldn't have been an ideal arrangement, but we were both desperately single and our old-school Italian Papa seemed determined to keep it that way. The three bedrooms on my mother's floor had all been adapted into one large room, while the first floor consisted of my grandparents' tiny bedroom, Nonna's dated kitchen and a dingy laundry room with ancient appliances. The full-sized water heater stood in the central hallway like a rusty sculpture, but Nonna paid no mind. She laced rope across it and used it as a clothesline to dry noodles. It was desperately shoddy, but I never noticed unless someone new came to visit.

Everyone was gathered around the kitchen table when I entered the house. "Where have you been?" Gia asked.

"It's a long story."

"Did you read the lawsuit?" she pressed, shaking the envelope in the air.

The lawsuit! "I started to skim it," I lied. "But I got interrupted and left it at the center. I got as far as Daddy Dearest is suing us."

"That's the least of it!" Gia slammed her palms on the table and Nonna jumped.

"Gia!" Mama chastised. "There's no need to get angry."

"No need? That man has some nerve. He should rot in—"

"Gia!" Nonna crossed herself. "Sophia, sit down and eat. *Mangia!* I made bucatini."

My stomach growled at the sight of the big bowl of pasta. Nonna made her own noodles from scratch. Bucatini was long straw-like spaghetti that had a hole through the noodle, which made it impossible to slurp. It wasn't for rank amateurs.

I sat in my normal place at the table and Papa scooped up enough pasta for three of me. "Careful, Papa, I want to have leftovers tomorrow for lunch."

He mumbled his disgust in Italian, and I fluffed my napkin.

Gia glowered at me. "Actually, I think now is precisely the time to get angry. This is a man who has used his money to get whatever he wanted in life. He uses lawyers like the mafia uses hitmen, and I'm done with it. Someone needs to stand up to his bullying and put an end to this tyranny. How dare he deny us and call our mother a liar! She's the Virgin Mary next to him! He's the trollop." *Only she said something much worse than trollop.*

Again, my Nonna crossed herself and closed her eyes in prayer.

"You're upsetting Nonna, Gia." Mama said. "She'll have her rosary beads out in a minute."

"We're fighting for that money, Sophia," Gia looked straight at me to let me know the decision had been made. A total about-face. "It's our money, and if I use the last penny of it to bankrupt him, it will be the best money I ever spent."

"No," Mama said. "Revenge is never the answer. People who waste their life on revenge are doomed to taste their own poison. Let him have the money. What has it ever done for him but make his bad character get worse?"

Gia and I both stared at her to question if we'd actually heard something negative about Bradley Wentworth escape our mother's mouth.

"I wish you'd known him when he was young." Mama stared off in the distance as if living in her fairy tale realm once again.

"I don't think that's how that saying goes about the poison," Gia finally said to snap our mother out of her false narrative.

"Don't be hasty, Gia. These people have a lifetime of using the law against others. Look at how angry you are right now. Life is too short to waste this energy on the likes of the Wentworths," I said.

"You haven't read the lawsuit yet, have you?" She stood with the paperwork, waved it in the air with gusto, then slammed it on Nonna's sideboard. "We can't afford to fight this lawsuit without the money. Do you not understand that? This makes it impossible to leave the money on the table. He'll take everything we have and then some."

"I haven't read it," I admitted. "I had a crisis at work today."

"You have a crisis at work every day."

I shrugged. "Pretty much. It sort of goes with the territory."

She sat back down at the old wooden kitchen table. Nonna was gumming a piece of bread and watching Gia closely for fear of another outburst.

"Our father's lawsuit demands that we get a paternity test to prove he is our father—even though the will says it doesn't matter. He's also protesting that our grandfather was not of sound mind when he made this will. We can't afford to get counsel if we don't take the money, so our ignorant dreams of walking away from this are over."

"Can't we just ignore it?" I asked her.

"Sure, Sophia." Gia rolled her eyes. "And let's ignore red bills from the IRS while we're at it. Seriously, sometimes you are so naive. We won't have the money for pasta wheat if we don't move into that blasted mausoleum."

I felt ill and stared at my mom. Mama always had a solution, but on this she simply shrugged.

"This creep wants to drag our mother's name through the mud. After all he's done to us, he still thinks that isn't enough. But here's the thing about this narcissistic, self-entitled jerk. His father knew exactly who he was and that's why he didn't inherit the money." Gia, normally so self-assured and confident, looked beat. "He knew who his son was."

I swirled my bucatini and waited for her point. "Nonna, this is really good tonight. I like it when you make it spicy."

She grumbled something in Italian. "Your sister, she giva mea heartburn, no?" She said in English.

"She gives us all heartburn, Nonna." I dropped my fork. "I know you're excited to play *Law and Order*, Gia, but you're overlooking a very important aspect that stands between us and that money. We'd still have to live with our half-sisters and possibly their parents for an entire year to get that money. Do you want to leave Nonna and Papa now?"

"You're not hearing me. This lawsuit gives us no choice."

I shook my head, determined not to believe her version of the lawsuit. I had no intention of living in that mansion after the awkward scenario created at the hospital. "Nope, I'm not living there. I ran into Quinn today at the hospital. I can't take five minutes in her presence." For once, I felt strongly enough to defy my sister's wishes.

"You always back down in confrontation, Sophia, and I'm not letting you do it this time. You have to stand up to bullies or they never relent."

If only she'd seen me at the hospital with Tweedledee.

"What changed since this morning?" Gia asked. "You were

adamant that taking their money was allowing them to win. You've done a complete one-eighty."

Today's accident was an omen. Gia had been right in the beginning. And she was forgetting I'd wanted to take it this morning. She was the one with the clearer head about it.

"All this screaming," Papa said. "I can't take it." He shuffled to the sink and put his plate on the counter.

I don't think in my lifetime I've ever seen my Papa move a dirty dish. Our world had been disrupted.

Gia didn't let anyone's actions dissuade her from her argument. "We wouldn't have to work. We could travel. Buy Mama's building, fix up Papa's house—"

Papa looked up from the sink. "What exactly is wrong with this house? It's been good enough for you until now!"

"Nothing's wrong with it, Papa," Gia said. "But we could get the house rewired so that it was brought up to code. We could buy Nonna a new stove!"

"I don't want a new stove!" Nonna shouted. "This generation thinks everything has to be brand new. Do you know how seasoned that stove is? What if the Italians threw out everything that was old? I suppose you think Michelangelo would come back and carve you a new David?" She raised her cupped hand in the air with her fingers pressed against her thumb. "*La gioventù è sprecata.*"

"Yes Nonna, youth is wasted on the young. Do you think we should take the money?" Gia asked.

"Take the money, no take the money, but leave my stove out of it."

We all laughed.

"If I were you two, I'd take that money." My mother smiled, a heart-filled, genuine grin that lit the entirety of her face.

Gia and I gasped collectively. "You would?"

"You'd both use the money better than those people. The Bible says that he who loves pleasure will become poor. I think it's about time for you two to take advantage of my mistake. You're generous, caring girls. You'll take the money, and you'll make San Francisco, maybe the world, a better place."

"I think we should talk to our own lawyer before we make any decisions," I said. "For all we know, there's a loophole that allows us to keep the money and stay here with our family where we belong."

"You heard Mr. Trunkett," my sister said.

"There's a lot we don't know about that old house and the family. We need to do whatever we can to keep our distance from that clan. Someone was hit by a car in front of the Regional Center today."

My mother gasped.

I nodded, encouraged by her reaction. "The curse has started. That family is cursed like the Kennedys and we need to stay away."

My sister scoffed. "Seriously? You're going to try that? Nonna, don't listen to Sophia, she's talking crazy."

I still needed to explain to my sister what happened with Joel. Maybe she'd see it for the harbinger it was. There was no further discussion in the kitchen as we cleared away the dishes. Our mother had given us her permission to move in with our father. A man who'd spent our entire existence telling us that we weren't worthy of him and didn't exist.

It was time to prove him wrong and redeem our mother's reputation.

Chapter Seven

I found it difficult to go back to work the following afternoon. The police tape had been removed from the street, and there was no sign there'd ever been an accident. No reminders, except for the sick feeling of dread in my stomach. I tossed and turned all night reliving what I'd seen and praying for Joel's full and complete recovery.

I wanted more than anything to check on him and see how he was doing this morning after his surgery, but I knew better. It wasn't appropriate and besides, Quinn made no bones about my presence not being welcome at the hospital. I had to assume that meant my short relationship with Joel wasn't welcome as well. If Quinn knew anything about Joel's health, I was the last person she'd share it with.

"You okay?" Bobbi asked when I walked into work. "You look pale."

"I've been better."

"In the midst of the crisis yesterday, you left your lawsuit here. I put it in your inbox."

I nodded. "Gia said what's in it makes our situation more difficult. Seems the Wentworth clan likes to stir up trouble."

Bobbi unlocked the cabinets and shoved paperwork into

them. "Speaking of the Wentworths, they were on the front of the local section of the newspaper today. I saved it for you in case you're interested." She jutted her round chin toward the waiting area with magazines from yesteryear. "The burial for your grandfather was yesterday afternoon. They wore Armani."

"Of course they did. No one invited us." I found it odd that though Gia and I were two of the five principals in our grandfather's will, we weren't welcome at the funeral. I took the manila envelope from my cubby. "My donor is apparently asking for a paternity test."

"I saw." Bobbi was stricken with a guilty look. She bobbed a shoulder. "It was opened, and I was curious. You know I'd never tell a soul."

I didn't care that boundaries were not our strong suit at the Regional Center. We saw too much pain to want to inflict any on each other. We were open books and knew every aspect of each other's personal lives. "And?" I asked her. "What did you think?"

Bobbi had seen more family dysfunction than a psychologists' convention. "I know your family—meaning, your mother and grandparents—have always been about forgiveness and moving forward despite life's unfairness." She shook her head, and her hair, which had the texture of a frayed cotton ball, lifted like butterfly in the wind before it settled back alongside her ear. "I have always admired that."

"But?"

"But," Bobbi said. "if I were you and Gia, I'd counter sue that man for anything left in his paltry pocketbook, and I'd use *his* father's money to do it. He's a despicable piece of greedy, selfish work, and that lawsuit lays it out remarkably." She patted her pointer finger on the envelope. "There's revenge and then there's doing what's right. This man needs a good dose of reality that only you can provide for him." She gripped my upper arms and looked me straight in the eye. "Sometimes you need to do the right thing. Even when it's hard." She shook her head. "No, especially when it's hard."

Bobbi's words sank in and settled like a knot in the middle of my stomach. This wasn't going away without a fight. "I have no choice, is what you're telling me?"

"You have no choice," she said plainly. "That handsome young delivery man was a sign for you. You may not be willing to fight for yourself, but you have to fight for what's right."

"Ugh. I hate conflict," I whined.

"People in your father's circle don't seem to get hurt, do they? He's like slow-seeping poison, and you have the power to stop him."

Did I?

"Speaking of your handsome messenger, how is the young buck after his accident? I should have asked after him first," Bobbi said. "But that lawsuit just made me so mad, and I couldn't bring myself to read the whole thing."

"I don't know how Joel is, actually."

"HIPAA," Bobbi stated. "They can't tell you a thing."

"Yeah, but I could have called his room once he got out of surgery, but it turns out that the dashing Joel Edgerton happens to be engaged to my half-sister Quinn."

Bobbi whistled. "No kidding. This new branch of your family has its claws everywhere."

"It makes me wish I could simply go back to yesterday before the will was read and pretend none of this ever happened."

"At this moment, so do I." Bobbi took a rag and wiped the front counter down. "Oliver is waiting for you in room two. His mom dropped him off early so Katie's in there with him now."

"Thanks."

Oliver Jessup was a quiet preschooler with a sullen personality and a permanent scowl. His father had been accused of child abuse, but in my job, one couldn't assume anything, and the files were sealed from me at my low level, so I couldn't discern if it was true except through my interactions. Custody battles were ugly, and couples often resorted to lies and distortions to gain the upper legal hand, but one thing was certain—Oliver loved his father and peered excitedly out the door's window as he waited for the man's arrival.

The main reason I believed Mr. Jessup was innocent of the charges was that he never addressed them. He never talked about how unfair the courts were nor his ex in a negative way. He usually spent his time loving on his son as if I wasn't even there. In fact, if all my clients were as easy as the Jessups, I'd probably be out of a job.

Often it was so awkward to be in the same room with parents and their children, but Charlie Jessup never made me feel that way. He sometimes engaged me in whatever game he and Oliver played. Whenever I'd start to imagine he was the perfect father, I'd remember my own. He was the perfect father to Quinn and Brinn for any and all who cared to read the society page. He was also the same man who pretended that three of his daughters didn't exist—except when it came time to sue them.

When I walked into the playroom, Mr. Jessup was already on the floor beside his son taking a game off the lower shelves. Katie, a fresh intern who usually only worked at night, was reading a book in the corner. She got up when I arrived.

"You're early today," I said to Mr. Jessup.

"Do you think we should ask Miss Sophia to play Chutes and Ladders with us?" Charlie asked his son.

Oliver tossed his head back and forth and stuck his lower lip out. "You and me, Daddy."

"All right." Mr. Jessup winked at me. "Just you and me." He began setting up the game. "You don't think she looks a little lonely sitting there all by herself? What if she wants to play the game?"

Oliver gave me a once-over and nodded to his father. Then, he came over to me and took my hand. "You sit here."

"Sophia?" Bobbi said from the doorway. "You have an urgent phone call."

It wasn't like Bobbi to let me have a phone call during work hours, especially with a client. Katie walked back in the room and smirked at me to let me know I'd owe her.

I rose from the floor. "You start without me, Oliver. I'll be back and maybe help your Daddy because you are really good at this game."

Oliver grinned. I had turned into a complete slacker in the last two days. Generally, parents stayed in the visiting rooms with their children and the supervisors sat outside the open door in a straight chair, but Mr. Jessup said it made him feel weird when I lurked in the doorway. He'd rather have me in the room with a book so that his son didn't question my presence as some kind of spy. The office hallway was filled now, as if clients had magically appeared in the last four minutes. More than likely I wasn't paying attention when I came in and had missed them entirely because my mind was so preoccupied with lawsuits and family drama of my own.

Benches of parents and siblings lined each side of the hallway and awaited their turn for a private space. The hallway took on a chaotic energy of its own. Stress dripped from those parents who argued their court cases in the hallway with their kids in listening distance. I made my way down the hallway to the office phone. Once there I tried to block the noise by pressing a forefinger firmly in my free ear.

"Hello?" I said into the phone.

"Sophia, it's Joel. Edgerton."

"Joel!" I said too excitedly. Bobbi winked at me from her desk chair and motioned for me to make it quick. I turned toward the wall and lowered my voice. "I'm so thrilled to hear your voice. How are you?" I could have smacked myself for such a stupid question. *How do you think he is? He just got hit by a car, dummy.*

"In pain," he said with a laugh. "Turns out, everything I needed to know I had learned in kindergarten. Starting with look both ways before crossing the street."

"At the very least, you should look the right way on a one-way street."

He groaned. "You mock my pain. I literally only had to look one way, and I failed. Thanks for reminding me of that."

"I would never mock your pain," I told him honestly. "One minute you're boldly walking away, the next, you're a pile in the street. It was so traumatizing."

"Oh, you were traumatized!" he laughed. "I'll admit that my life may have passed before my eyes. I suppose I'd be dead if it was a Mercedes that hit me, but there's something very torturous about being taken out by a smart car. I always assumed I could handle something that small. Stop the thing with an outstretched palm as it approached, you know?"

"You would have to see it coming, I imagine. I mean, a bike could do significant damage in that scenario."

"Right?" He laughed again, then moaned. "Don't make me laugh, it's so painful." He coughed. "I broke a few ribs."

"Your leg too, I imagine." I tried not to remember his leg bent unnaturally, but the image was something I'd never forget.

"I did break my leg, shattered it actually. It's now being held together by pins and other elaborate hardware. How'd you know?"

"It's not a visual I'll forget anytime soon."

"Ah, I see. I'm sorry about that." He coughed again. His voice was raspy. "That was what my surgery was for. The doctors worked hard to get that leg back together correctly so that I wouldn't be Humpty Dumpty."

"Joel, I know the real reason you were in that street. You saved that old man's life. He was so shaken. Bobbi called his daughter and she came to get him."

"I'm so glad to hear he's fine. Listen, I'm sorry to call you at work but I didn't have your cell phone number."

His voice sounded lighthearted, but I still saw him crumpled in the street and jolted my head to purge the image. "I'm not inclined to give my number out to people who sue me." *Nor those who happen to be engaged to my vapid sister.*

"Ouch."

"Joel, I—"

"Sophia," he interrupted me, and then he went silent.

In the meantime, I felt euphoric at the sound of my name on his lips like a schoolgirl who received her first text from a homeroom crush. It was wrong, I knew. Part of me wondered if his being engaged to Quinn didn't make him unattainable, and thus, due to my family tree, more desirable. I shook off the thought. I came back down to reality and made a conscious choice to speak in careful, controlled words. After all, romance in my family ended only slightly less tragically than *Romeo and Juliet*.

"I'm glad you're all right and I do appreciate your calling to let me know," I said. "Quinn was very concerned when she came to the hospital." *If by concerned I meant, unwilling to put down her horse crop, then yes, she was extremely concerned.*

"About Quinn, that's why I called."

I stopped him before I heard anything more. "I understand. It's good to keep lawsuits in the family. I'm sure you'll be my father's favorite son-in-law in no time flat."

"No, I just wanted to explain—"

"There's no explanation necessary. The less I know about my half-sisters going into this family farce, the better. Would you do me the favor of honoring that request?"

"I just need you to know I'm not representing her father." He cleared his throat. "Your father. I was doing my old boss a favor, that's all my serving you papers was about. There's no conflict of interest here. It was on my way and—"

"No, I get it. It was convenient. Got it," I snapped.

"That's not what I meant."

He hadn't said a word about his engagement. Only that there was no conflict of interest in his serving me a lawsuit. *He was definitely one of them.* "You needn't have worried, Joel. I genuinely cared if you were all right after your accident as I would care about anyone I watched get mangled in the street."

"I—It wasn't your imagination yesterday, all right? That's all I wanted to say. We—I—"

"Good luck with your marriage." I hung up the phone on its cradle. "You'll need it." The thought of someone actually joining that toxic waste dump of a family by choice confounded me. He must have been a lot dumber than he looked, but then money held no fascination for me.

I plastered a smile on my face and went to join the Jessups and their rousing game of Chutes and Ladders.

"No!" Little Oliver put up a palm. "Just my daddy."

"Okay, Oliver. I'll be right outside the door if you change your mind." I decided to leave Katie in there and retreated to the chair outside the door.

Bobbi lumbered down the hallway through the throngs of people, toward me. "He's okay?" she said, nodding toward the phone.

"Joel is all right. In a lot of pain but seems to be taking the bright side."

"You know that he was busy looking at you rather than watching where he was going. Those little electric cars sneak up on you—blasted things. They're too quiet."

"Trust me, he wasn't looking at me. He was saving that old man's life. Let's not forget Joel is engaged to my half-sister." I found myself saying his name more often than a pronoun. I had some weird need to make him more human. His name made me feel closer to him, which I knew would make my Nonna cross herself silly.

"He's engaged?" Bobbi looked down at her feet. "Well, does she know he looks at other women the way he looked at you? Because that is not a man who should be getting married—in my opinion."

"For all we know it's an arranged marriage. Who knows how rich people do things? It doesn't matter anyway. If Joel was looking at me, it was probably to assess if the lawsuit affected me and if my father had touched a nerve. Most likely, he had to report back."

"I doubt that. You'd have to be inhuman for that lawsuit to

not affect you and he knew that. You do remember I'm a former police officer, correct?"

Bobbi looked like a police officer through and through. A decade of retirement would never change that. She'd be an imposing figure until the day she died. "Hard thing to forget, Bobbi."

"We *read* people. I read Joel. He wasn't interested in the lawsuit like you say. In fact, I'd say serving it made him sick. If I had to guess, I'd peg him as a guy who doesn't have the stomach for dirty work." Bobbi turned on her utilitarian heel and went back down the hallway with her version of a mic drop.

"You're right, Bobbi," I called after her. "Maybe Joel plans to drop my faux sister and fall in love with *my* billions instead of hers." My heart still fluttered over being told it wasn't all my imagination.

Bobbi looked over her shoulder and smiled. "Maybe. Or maybe it's love at first sight." She cackled as she disappeared down the hallway.

I rolled my eyes. The world had truly turned upside down when Bobbi Mack was the office romantic. *Men didn't abandon women like Quinn Wentworth.* My father certainly hadn't when it came to her mother.

As I stepped back into the visitation room a few minutes later, my eyes scanned for life but the only thing in the room was an abandoned game of Chutes and Ladders and an open window, with the alphabet curtains fluttering in the wind. The traffic roared outside and the bars that normally protected the window were shoved open to the street.

"Bobbi!" I called with a blood-curdling scream. My heart hammered against my chest walls. I checked behind the bookshelves hoping for a rousing game of Hide and Seek but there was no one. I ran toward the window and looked out onto the grey dank street and saw nothing, not even a homeless person as a witness. By the time Bobbi got to the room I was in full panic mode. Katie came behind her, smirking as she always seemed to do.

"Where were you?" I screamed at the new intern.

"I had to go to the bathroom," Katie said innocently, though she'd broken the cardinal rule of the center. "They seemed fine."

How had I missed her slipping out of the room? Bobbi dialed 911 and calmly told them we needed an Amber alert. She gave her credentials, our address, descriptions of Charlie and Oliver and the state of his custody battle. "I'll fax over a photo immediately."

I leaned against the wall like a dirty, wet rag—for all intents and purposes, useless. I hyper-ventilated at the thought a child had been kidnapped by his father on my watch. And somehow, I blamed Joel. If he hadn't diverted my attention with this dead-end flirtation that would go nowhere, I'd have been where I belonged.

"Sophia, I need you to pull it together," Bobbi said.

But I couldn't. I'd let my guard down and trusted—that was my first mistake. Parents didn't go on supervised visitation for no reason. CPS was far too busy for that. I felt crushed by Charlie's betrayal and my own lack of conviction. I pulled the bars shut and grabbed them as I stared out the open window. Then, I prayed desperately that Oliver was safe with his father. *Charlie Jessup saw an opportunity and panicked. That had to be it. He'd come back with Oliver. He had to.*

Chapter Eight

The police brought me to the station. The back of the patrol car was the vehicle equivalent to the padded, locked cell with a city view. A younger cop who looked like Taye Diggs interrogated me as if I were a common criminal who'd actually helped Charlie Jessup escape with his son. I cried a lot, went through an inordinate amount of Kleenex, then they hooked me up to a polygraph and asked me the same questions all over again.

The lie detector test, which I volunteered for, consisted of probing questions like, "Have you had contact with the gentleman, Mr. Jessup, outside of the Regional Center?"

"No." *And ew.*

"Have you ever been romantically involved with Mr. Jessup?

"Ew. No!"

"Just answer the question, Miss Campelli. No commentary is necessary."

Finally, the fat man in a beige suit—which is never a good look—stood up and said I was free to leave. Three hours had passed when they dumped me back at the Regional Center. The air still hung heavy in the silence.

I approached the thigh-high counter, and Bobbi came out

into the foyer. She put her arms around me while I shook and sobbed some more.

"Is there any news?" I looked up hopefully.

Bobbi dried my cheek with a napkin, "I'm sorry, Sophia. There's no sign of them yet."

"It's going to get dark soon," I said as I looked out the window over her shoulder.

She stepped back, nodded and handed me the tissue. "We'll find them. Mr. Jessup would never hurt his son. Of that I'm sure."

"I would have sworn on my life that he'd never kidnap his son either."

"I'm sure that you understand I need to let you go, Sophia."

"But I want to be here, in case—"

Bobbi's face softened into its rare motherly version. "I mean, forever. I'm thankful that it's not going to burden you financially, but you must understand that we need to tell the press we've taken definitive action against the guilty party. There's no other outcome that will satisfy—" Bobbi paused. "They'll probably ask for my resignation as well, since I'm your supervisor and you're not licensed yet."

I understood why she wasn't holding Katie responsible. I was the one overseeing the visit.

Reality settled in and I felt numb. "Bobbi, I'm not an heiress. That life isn't for me. I'm a social worker. This is my calling. I can go on leave until all this is sorted out. There should be an investigation, and I'll cooperate with everything." I said with more confidence than I felt. "I'm entitled to a thorough investigation." My voice cracked.

Bobbi had both my hands in hers, and she squeezed hard. "According to your contract, a lost or endangered child is cause for an immediate dismissal." She let go of my hands. "You're not full-time. You're not licensed yet. This is protocol. You understand."

I nodded slowly as I clutched my stomach. "Of course. I have to leave."

"I'm sorry, Sophia. You're like the daughter I never had. If there was any way—"

"I'll get my things." I walked zombie-like to my cubby, which had already been emptied.

"I put all of your things in the box there."

A ream of printer paper had been emptied, and all of my personal items were inside. It actually reminded me of my mother. *Just one mistake can change the whole course of your life.* What bothered me more than anything was the calculated and clinical coldness of Bobbi. She'd been like a second mother to me and suddenly, she felt like a complete stranger. I'd never get another job in social work and we both knew it.

"The police have asked that you not leave San Francisco. They may have more questions," Bobbi said.

"They told me." I pushed through the swinging doors and collected the few picture books I'd brought along with my planner. I took in the soured-milk smell of the Center one last time and wondered if I'd ever be back.

"I'm sorry," Bobbi repeated as I walked toward the exit.

"I just want Oliver found."

"We'll find him. They've sent out an Amber Alert."

"I can't bear the thought of him out all night alone with his father."

"He won't hurt him," Bobbi said confidently, and I hoped she knew something more about the custody case than I did.

"He lost custody—" I said.

"You know as well as I do there can be all sorts of reasons for that. Go home and get some rest."

"I won't be able to sleep a wink until he's found." I took one last look at Bobbi. I'd lost more than a job. I'd lost my mentor, and the worst of it was that I deserved everything I had coming and more.

I walked home slowly. I didn't even notice as I went past the lit-up strip clubs with their pounding beat and gorilla-like bouncers. Numbed by the day's occurrences, I had no recollection of how I got to Nonna and Papa's, but the sun was starting to set as I approached. When I entered through the back door, the early evening news was blaring in the living room, and a picture of Oliver and his father flashed across the screen.

Bobbi appeared on screen, a microphone shoved in her face. "At the Community Care Center in San Francisco, our first priority is the safety of children and the families we serve—"

"I'm going to my room," I said aloud.

Nonna and Papa nodded in understanding and then looked to one another. As I passed the Saint Michael picture in the kitchen, I lifted it from the wall. A pristine rectangle of wallpaper marked its dismissal. "I need this," I said as Nonna stared at me.

Upstairs, I flopped onto my bed and stared at the marred, peeling ceiling. Yellowish-brown water stains and strands of paint formed the shape of a bear's face, and I'd grown accustomed to the familiar damage. How much of my life was worn and haggard, and I just accepted it as part of life? Clearly, with Oliver's kidnapping, I needed to pay closer attention to what went on around me.

"You're home." Gia came into my room just as the sun descended, leaving an orange hue to the room. Her perfectly straight hair swung back and forth like Newton's Cradle, and even after a long day at work, her makeup appeared camera-ready. *How were we even sisters, much less twins?*

Without saying a word, she shimmied out of her slacks and threw her jacket on my bed where I sat. She wandered off to her room in her bra and panties and spoke as she left. "Don't go anywhere. We have to talk."

Where was I going to go?

She wandered back in wearing black yoga pants and a pink racer-back T-shirt. She held two hangers for her discarded suit. She picked up the jacket off of my bed and dropped the hanger. "This needs to go to the cleaners." She finally looked at me. "This suit jacket was exposed to the Wentworth family yesterday. I need to get all the sadness off of it."

"We *are* the Wentworth family," I reminded her.

"Hey, they found Oliver. He's yours, right?"

"When?" I squealed.

"Like two minutes ago. It was on the news when I came in the house. His stupid father stole a boat and tried to sail away in the San Francisco Bay, but they were on him like flies on, well, you know. He basically had a rowboat in the Bay, what an idiot!"

"Is Oliver okay?"

"The currents must have kept pushing him back right where they started from." She shook her head. "What an idiot," she said again.

"Is Oliver okay?" I repeated.

"He's fine, but the dad was fighting the police when they tried to cuff him. He was cussing up a storm, and since it was live, it was all caught on the news before they cut it off." Gia laughed. "I love when that happens. Little weasel of a guy, but he put up a good fight."

I clutched at the collar of my shirt. "I'm so relieved. I still can't believe Charlie would do that. I've never seen a father try harder to be with his son." I sat up in my bed. "How did you know Oliver was mine?" While I was grateful Oliver was safe, the reality was I'd lost everything I'd worked for in one distracted afternoon.

"I saw your boss on television, and Nonna said you didn't eat and came straight upstairs. People are insane. You're better off out of that job. You and mom and your sick need to rescue people. Sometimes, people get exactly what they deserve. What's up with Nonna's St. Michael picture?"

I looked at the picture on my bed. I'd propped it up against the wall. "I could use some protection about now, that's all."

"I don't think that's what Archangel Michael looked like, do you?"

"Why not?"

"I think it's Nonna's way of having a hot guy on her wall. Approved by the Vatican and all." She giggled.

"He's the warrior angel. Defends us in battle." I wanted to ask if she saw the resemblance to Joel, but that was probably a question best left alone.

"Are we really having this conversation?" Gia asked. "So, listen, I think we should move into the mansion sooner rather than later. Now that you're unemployed, I don't see what is holding you back. The sooner we are in, the sooner we are out."

It took me a minute to process. "We're really going without a fight?"

"I told you, we have no choice. We can't afford to fight the lawsuit otherwise."

"I have to tell you something before we pack up."

"Does it matter? This is the only way to protect our family, so what could you tell me that would change that?"

"Well, it matters to me. Remember yesterday—"

"We need that stipend to start as soon as possible."

"A stipend?" I asked her.

"You *still* haven't read the will?"

"I haven't had time!" I tell her. "I was busy losing my job and getting questioned by the police, remember? I actually had to take a lie detector test." I stabbed the pillow with my fist. "And maybe flirting with Quinn Wentworth's fiancé."

"Wait, back up. What?"

I held up the picture of Saint Michael. "Remember the lawsuit server? The cute one who got hit by the crap car in front of my office?"

"Karma boy? Yeah."

"I was waiting with him in the hospital because he was alone." I drew in a deep breath. "Quinn came in."

"Our Quinn?"

"I wouldn't call her that, but yes. Turns out, he's her fiancé. I was flirting with our half-sister's fiancé."

"Ugh! You weren't! You have our mother's taste in men!

Someone hands you a lawsuit that completely alters your future plans and you decide yeah, this is someone who seems like relationship material."

"Take that back!" I snapped.

"We're moving in on Friday. Get your stuff together. I've already explained to Mom and Nonna and Papa why we have to go, and they agree. Mom is the one who suggested it," Gia said as if she'd won.

"I thought yesterday was just a temporary moment of insanity on her part."

"Don't look at me like that, Sophia. What choice do we have? Can you afford to hire a lawyer?"

"I can't hire an Uber at this point." I couldn't believe my ears. I never thought I'd see Gia give into expectations like this. Generally, when you told her what to do, she did the exact opposite. "It's going to be so awkward moving in with people who are suing us."

"We don't know that *he'll* be there. Just the sisters. You don't have to be the social worker here, Sophia. You don't have to fix everything. Just move in like we're tenants and don't make a big deal out of who they are. We're tenants for a year." She sat alongside me on the bed. "Very well-paid tenants who will oversee giving money to the needy. You should like that bit."

"I wonder if I'll have to run into Joel there."

"The fiancé? I'm going to guess that's a yes. She probably has him on an Instagram leash so he can take her picture 24/7."

I groaned. "I made a fool out of myself, Gia."

"No one feels sorry for a billionaire. You'll get over it. And if you really think he looks like that picture of Saint Michael, one can hardly blame you."

Chapter Nine

Gia and I arrived with one suitcase each at the Pacific Heights mansion that would be our home for a year. Gia chose the left curved marble staircase to the front door, and I chose to the right. We met under the elegant portico in front of the massive wrought iron and glass double doors.

Gia grabbed my wrist. "Look at where we are. This is nuts that people live like this. That we are going to live like this!"

We stood silent on the porch and took in the sweeping views of the sparkling San Francisco Bay, Alcatraz, and the Golden Gate Bridge. It was a clear, crisp Fall day and not even the tips of the bridge were obscured by fog. It glowed in all its orange vermilion color. I tore my gaze away and looked up into the dome of the rotunda that covered us. Elaborately carved rosettes circled in a complex, geometric design caught my gaze. The flowers became tinier and more intricate at the center where gold leafing was painted onto the flashing.

"It feels like we're inside a Faberge egg," I told Gia.

The air smelled of gardenias and the salty sea air. "It's a classic revival mansion designed by the most prominent architect of the day," Gia told me in her curator voice.

"It's a palace . . . a museum," I stuttered. "It is most definitely not a home."

There was so much to look at and take in, I could barely focus on one thing before another lavish detail, some other grandiose pronouncement of nauseating wealth, garnered my attention. Though we were barely two miles from our grandparents' home, we were a world away. I noted that the mansion had ample parking and several garages on the level below us, behind the massive gates and privacy hedges, but we hadn't been told of this. We were merely given the address as if the country bumpkin cousins were coming to stay. All we were missing was a grandma in a rocking chair on top of Gia's Mini.

All of our arrangements were made with the staff of Wentworth Manor, the pretentious name given to the home. Something told me that would be how we were treated—like staff that the Wentworth family tolerated until they got what they wanted. Eventually, we'd no doubt be cast out like yesterday's trash.

"The mansion was originally known as the Bloom Estate, named after the eccentric lady of the house in 1894. She would eventually be most famous for surviving the maiden voyage of the *Titanic*."

"Gia, enough. I really don't care about the history of this place. Can we go inside now?"

"Our great grandfather bought it from her in 1909, after she married an Austrian prince and left the country."

"Fascinating," I lied. "I love how our family ancestry doesn't come to us sitting around a warm hearth at Christmastime, but courtesy of Google."

"Ring the doorbell," Gia said.

The doorbell was a resounding bell that I felt vibrate in the depths of my chest. An older Asian woman answered the door. She was about a third of the size of the front doors, and she took her time checking us out. We stood stick straight as she did so.

"Gia," she finally said to my sister. Then, she looked toward me, "Sophia. Welcome to you both. I have your rooms all ready, and we are delighted to have you. My name is Mrs. Chen." She opened the door widely. "Leave your bags there on the floor. I'll have Mel take them up to your rooms while I give you a tour."

As we stepped into the foyer, my breath caught. It was as though we'd stepped back in time. The house was unexpectedly bright inside considering all the dark, carved wood that was everywhere. The foyer at center of the home was a large square lit from the top by an elaborate stained-glass domed window that gave a pastel pink tint to the marble walls. The carved wooden staircase wound upward encircling the skylight.

However grand, it was impossible not to notice the shabbiness, as if the renovation it needed forty years prior had been halted in time. I half-expected to see Miss Havisham on the mahogany staircase.

"I've arranged for both of you to be on the third floor. You'll each have your own room, but there are two full-sized beds in Gia's room should you choose to stay together. The house can get lonely and cold at night, so there will be no judgment. Until you both get used to the noises an old house brings with it, I'd recommend it."

We both nodded and made eye contact. It had been simultaneously decided silently between us that we would room together.

"The family is out this morning, but I'd love to give you a tour of the home. I know that it can get confusing being as big as it is—"

"How big is it?" Gia interrupted.

"It's 16,000 square feet. If you ever get lost, walk toward the glass dome. It's the center of the home and you can always navigate your way down to the kitchen. My room is beside the kitchen, and I'll show you where that is."

Gia, usually so calm and collected, appeared shaky and unsure of her surroundings. She stared at me, like we should make a run for it.

"Most of the rooms are named," Mrs. Chen went on. "You'll be in the Daisy and Daffodil rooms because they offer the best views of all the guest rooms." Mrs. Chen stood at the base of the staircase and faced us. "If there's anything you need—furniture, such as a desk or a different dressing table for example—just let me know and I'll do my best to help you find what you need."

We nodded, like two small orphans left on a stranger's doorstep.

"The kitchen is on the south side of the first floor," she said.

Which would be great information if I had a compass.

As if she read my mind, Mrs. Chen said, "If you're in possession of a smartphone, there should be a compass there. North always takes you to the front of the house and south to the back. There are laundry chutes in your room, and any soiled clothing will be returned to you, washed, folded, and put away, by that afternoon. Anything that needs hand washing or dry-cleaning will add an extra day to the process unless you let me know.

"Your sisters are on the second floor. Your younger sister, Alisa, has already arrived, and she's on the third floor with you. She and her friend are outside in the observatory taking photos."

"The observatory? As in Miss Peacock did it with the pipe in the observatory?" Gia laughed.

"Or the conservatory. It's a beautiful sunroom with a glass ceiling and walls. It no longer has a view after the hedge grew, but it's lovely just the same. There's also an extensive lawn out back. Your sisters like to take tea there and practice yoga on the grass."

Suddenly, my Friday splurge at Starbucks felt amateurish. Clearly, I had a lot to learn about wasting time and resources. Without a job, I suppose I had time to learn lethargy with the best of them.

Mrs. Chen, with her no-nonsense manner, showed us count-less useless rooms—the sitting room, the ballroom, the grand dining room, the everyday dining room, the breakfast room. My first thought was of San Francisco's homeless and how wasted all this space was for a few rich folks. I wanted to get my sister alone so we could plot our exit and come up with an alternative idea.

"There was no way we would make it a year in this gothic nightmare," I whispered to Gia.

"This is your—," Mrs. Chen paused. "Mr. and Mrs. Wentworth's bedroom."

I peeked inside as we passed. There was a massive French stone fireplace on one wall, and over the mantel hung a painting of the perfect family. Our father, his petite blonde wife and their two pristine daughters, all in white. I felt sick to my stomach at how easily Bradley's sins were erased from the painting.

"I need a little air. Is there a place I might get outside?" I asked Mrs. Chen with a tinge of desperation in my voice. I felt as if I'd be sick if I spent one more minute in that morgue.

"Down the stairs, make a U-turn and you'll be able to exit through the conservatory."

I ran as fast as my legs would carry me so that I didn't vomit on some grand piece of art that dated back to before California was a state. I ran through the observatory—literally a room of glass as she'd said—until I reached the opened doors that led to a lap pool. I saw the expansive lawn in the distance with a gazing ball in the center. I ran to it and fell to my knees.

I don't belong here. I've betrayed my mother by being here regardless of what Gia says.

"I'm glad you decided to move in." A deep voice hit me then bounced off the stone walls that surrounded the yard. I lifted my eyes and saw Joel in a wheelchair with his leg propped up on a garden chair. Papers were strewn in front of him on the teak table.

I clutched my forehead in my hands. "Not you." *How much more could I take?* I needed his presence like I needed another half-sibling in my midst.

His gaze brushed across his leg which was in a cast held out straight in front of his wheelchair, then he looked back at me. "I'm convalescing." He lifted a book from his lap. "Well, reading, too."

"You live here?"

"No, I don't live here. I'm living here now because my place is two story and you know—"

"This place is three stories," I told him.

"Yeah, but there's an elevator."

"Seriously? There's an elevator?"

"You wouldn't expect the Wentworth family to walk up three flights of stairs," he said in a cheeky tone.

"I suppose I wouldn't." I stared at his busted-up body. Even in sweatpants and a UCSF sweatshirt he was uncommonly good looking. Blazing blue eyes and blonde hair. He'd definitely be the Ken to Quinn's Barbie atop some outrageous twelve-layer wedding cake. "It seems you and I have had a run of bad luck this week."

"Does it?" he asked. "I would think that inheriting a few billion dollars wouldn't equate to a bad week for you."

"I lost my job. Well, first I lost a child in my care, then I rightfully lost my job."

"They found him," Joel said. "I saw it on the news."

"They did." I shrugged. "But you know, the foster care system doesn't take kindly to losing children. It's kind of a big no-no in social work circles."

"You make light of it, but I imagine it wasn't your finest hour."

I stood up slowly and fought the lump in my throat. "It was utterly devastating. I never saw it coming."

"I'm sure they'll take you back when all this gets sorted. Not that you'll need to work from the sounds of it."

"Oh, I need to work. I love everything about my job and I also like routine. The slow plodding predictability of my mundane life is gone. Everything has changed." I snapped my fingers. "Just like that."

"That's how life is. The only thing you can count on is change."

"So much change and all in one week."

"Do you really want someone to feel sorry for you after inheriting some inordinate amount and having to move into a mansion?" He placed the back of his hand on his forehead as if he felt faint. "The struggle is so real," he said dramatically.

I laughed. At least he made me forget that I wanted to retch all over the fantastic lawn. I turned on my heel. "I see how it is."

"Don't go on my account," he called after me.

I turned right back around and marched over to him. "Would you like it if your entire life was turned around and changed by someone else's decision?"

He waved his hand over his leg. "Uh, exhibit A." He sat forward in his wheelchair. "I will never be able to walk freely through a TSA checkpoint again. I will now light up their equipment like a Christmas tree."

We looked at each other for a long time as if we could read each other's minds. He felt so familiar to me as if I'd known him my whole life.

Before it became too awkward, he spoke again, "You're an amazing person, Sophia. You put aside your fears and came beside me after the accident. Waking up from surgery and hearing you'd been at the hospital says so much about who you are inside. I know you heard about Quinn in—not the best way."

I shook my head. "That's what decent people do, Joel. It was nothing more. Nothing heroic."

"I disagree."

My breath caught at his tone.

He cleared his throat. "All I'm saying is I love how you take the time for what matters. So for one day, maybe you can simply enjoy this new life and see what it has to offer."

"You're suddenly Buddha spouting wisdom after your accident?" I tried to make light of the situation rather than address the deep bond I felt to him.

"You want to rub my belly?" He chuckled as he lifted his shirt to reveal a cast of bandages. "That was supposed to be my taut abs."

"Regardless, I do not."

"You just missed your little sister. She was out here taking pictures and hash-tagging her life away. Apparently, I was in the way of her best shot, but it was too much trouble to push me out of the way, so they skipped off."

I decided to take the bull by the horns. "Why would you marry Quinn?"

He laughed out loud, "And here they told me your sister Gia was the mouthy one."

I smirked at him. "Never mind. It's none of my business anyway. Marry whoever you like. I was just surprised, that's all. She doesn't seem like your type."

"I don't mind saying. She asked me and my automatic response was 'yes.'"

"She asked?" I shook my head. "I mean, what's your love story?"

"Do we need a love story?"

"If you're getting married, it's generally required. Marriage is hard enough without having a love story. How did you two meet?"

"You sure you're a social worker and not a journalist?"

"I'm just curious." They hardly seemed like a couple. I couldn't have been the first person to ask.

He drummed his fingers along the crutch in his hand, "We're not getting married yet. All weddings are off until your year of living Wentworth is over."

"I'm sure she's worth waiting for." I tried to keep the sarcasm from my voice, but I wasn't sure if I'd succeeded.

"You should get to know her before you judge her. She's quite accomplished, and she's a lot deeper than you give her credit for."

"Accomplished? What is this, Edwardian England? Does she speak French and dabble in the arts as well? Play the pianoforte?"

"Excuse me?"

"I'm only saying first, you didn't do the proposing. Then, you call her *accomplished*. I can only hope when my future fiancé describes why he's marrying me it doesn't sound like a resume bullet point."

"She *is* accomplished."

At what? I wanted to ask, but I didn't. Because it made me sound petty and bitter and I didn't want to be either of those things. *Even if I was I didn't want to announce it.* The stay at the black castle was going to be hard enough. There was no reason to make things more difficult in the first five minutes. I needed to pace myself.

"I should go find my sister. Do you need anything before I go? I know how to find the kitchen now."

"I'll be fine. Quinn's coming home for lunch."

I nodded.

He lifted his book and motioned with his forefinger to come closer. With trepidation, I went toward him and those incredible eyes of his, which drew me in like a beacon. My thoughts pummeled my skull as I went toward him. *Quinn had everything in her life while I scraped by with nothing. The money wouldn't change that. She'd walk into the sunset with our dad and this handsome lawyer to call her own.* The closer I got, my eyes betrayed my stoicism and filled with tears.

"I know it's hard being here." He reached out and took my hand. "It's a sterile place without your grandfather here, but don't be too harsh on Quinn. Things aren't always as they appear, and I want you to get along."

I tried to grasp what he was telling me. There seemed to be so much more he wanted to express in his eyes, but he was clearly a man who played things close to his heart. Everyone in this new life felt that way—as if they were playing a giant game of chess rather than simply living out their lives. What a terrible contrast to my Italian home where everything was said aloud, and no guess work was necessary.

"Joel? Joel, are you out here?" Quinn appeared from by the pool and I dropped Joel's hand like a hot coal.

"Over here!" he called without taking his eyes off of me.

Quinn stared at me with her icy blue eyes as she came toward us. "You're here already." She said this like she'd discovered something unfortunate in her handbag.

Her tone made me wonder if I would be able to endure this for an entire year. Something told me that warmth and hugs weren't served on the Wentworth life menu.

I composed myself and cleared my throat. "My sister and I arrived a few minutes ago," I answered in a clipped tone. Unlike Quinn, I felt bad about my reaction. I'd been raised better than that, but this was going to be a long year if we didn't take some kind of effort to get along.

"Okay," she said, as though waiting for me to leave. I happily took the hint and left to find my sister. I looked back at Joel and wondered what he left unsaid.

Things weren't always what they appeared. I could only hope so.

Chapter Ten

Wentworth Manor reminded me of the Winchester Mystery House in San Jose, a historical tourist trap with stairs that went nowhere and doors that opened to twenty-foot drops. That's how it felt, like a labyrinth of endless emotional dysfunction played out in a house. There was no cohesion to it, nothing that felt like you could sit down and watch some reality television or relax with a glass of wine. I only hoped I wouldn't be as bat crazy as Sara Winchester by the time I left.

When I reached the heavy mahogany staircase, I saw my father in person for the first time and my breath caught in my throat. The man, the myth, the legend—that I'd only known from the gossip pages—was really here. I reminded myself to breathe as I stared at him. I blinked rapidly, but the mirage of my father didn't disappear, and it sank in that he was real and right in front of me in the flesh.

Bradley Wentworth was so handsome. Age had only refined his features—which was such an unfair gift to the male species. I was star struck by his bright blue eyes and his sharp masculine jaw. He was still blonde, which seemed to be a requirement as a Wentworth, with a dusting of sophisticated gray at the temples. His flawless skin gave him an eerie, wax-like appearance. He wore a dark suit with a crisp white shirt and a yellow paisley tie. He looked like a movie star.

His eyes widened when he saw me. "Mary," he said breathily as his heavy glass tumbled to the floor with a thud and rolled around on the imported carpet.

"I'm Sophia." I said my name loudly, as though he were hard-of-hearing. "Mary is my mother."

Bradley Wentworth flinched at the sound of her name and it made me want to say it again and again until it haunted his dreams. *Mary. Mary. Mary.*

"Sophia? You okay?" My sister, having heard the commotion, peeked her head over the third-floor banister and called down to me so that it echoed through the chamber of the grand staircase. At the sight of our father, she gasped.

Bradley peered upwards and gulped at yet another doppel-gänger of my mother staring back at him, this one more refined, more like the early original. His ashen expression floated from me to my sister and then eerily back again.

The heavy leaded highball glass he'd dropped hadn't broken. Instead, it rolled around in the amber liquid at his feet. He made no move to clean it. *Exactly how he lived his life.* Bradley Went-worth made messes and others were expected to come behind him and clean them up.

I could hear Gia's heels clicking as she descended the wooden staircase.

Bradley Wentworth—the male fashion icon of San Francisco —the man I'd watched my whole life from afar, swayed slightly as though a feather could knock him over. I made a move towards him, and he drew back instantly as if my touch would sting him.

"I'm not going to hurt you," I told him. "Are you all right? You look pale."

"This is my home," he said as if to convince himself.

I didn't have the guts, nor the legal understanding, to tell him it wasn't. I stood there numbly, waiting for my braver sister to rescue me, but the silence drew on for what seemed like an eternity.

His expression changed into a scowl. "Your mother tried to trap me. Did she tell you that?" He searched the floor for his lost liquid courage.

I felt Gia's hand on my shoulder and breathed a sigh of relief at her presence. *We had nothing to fear*, I reminded myself. We didn't come here on our own, we were summoned.

"Whatever you have to tell yourself to sleep at night," Gia told him. "I'm Gia, by the way. This is Sophia. We're your daughters. Your firstborn, you might say."

"You're not." He shook his head. Looking at all the blondes and blue eyes in the family, it wasn't a big stretch that we weren't his. I could see how he could easily deny us.

"I know our mother, and she's never lied to us, not once. You are our father." Gia flipped her hair behind her shoulder as if she'd been practicing for this moment all of her life. I half-expected her to jump around ala Maury Povich and taunt him, but she stood perfectly still.

Bradley's cool, dapper appearance disappeared under his seething rage. It was clear Daddy didn't like being told what he didn't want to hear. Even if it was the truth. "You don't belong here," he spat. "Mrs. Chen! Mel!"

"We have a court document that states otherwise. Today is November 8th and we begin one year's residency at the request of your father's will and testament."

Gia had to have practiced this moment.

"No." Bradley tugged at his tie. "There's been a mistake."

"There's no mistake," Gia continued without flinching. "We're your daughters. As is Alisa, so I'd say your dance card is full and if our presence bothers you, it's you who will need to make alternative living arrangements."

His expression darkened, and his eyes seemed to go black from their sea blue. His jaw tightened and his left hand curled into a fist, but he said nothing. The hair on the back of my neck stood out.

"From the math, I have deduced that Alisa was born during your marriage to someone else, so spare us the innocent, I'm-not-your-father act, huh?" Gia said. "It will save us all time if you speak plainly. But feel free to provide a hair sample if you want to be sure."

The blue in his eyes returned, and he straightened. "I see you have your mother's Italian fire."

Our mother had fire? If she did, it had been burned out a long time ago.

He shook his head and laughed at us in a way that made me feel small. "That Italian temper of hers. No man would put up with that."

"Mom's fiancé thinks it's hot," Gia said while our father's eyebrows rose. "Says he loves all that passion and that you don't know what you've missed."

Our mother didn't have a fiancé, but it was hardly the time to quibble. Gia's arrow struck a bullseye, and Bradley's cool demeanor disappeared. Just when I thought Gia had the upper hand in the confrontation, a woman I recognized instantly as Bradley's socialite wife, Chelsea Whitman Wentworth, glided into the open hallway above us. Her billowy white slacks made it seem as if she hovered a foot above the ground until she halted beside the grand staircase where we stood and placed her manicured hands elegantly along the bannister.

Chelsea wore a skintight jacket in periwinkle blue lace over the white slacks. Her long blond hair fell in straight ribbons over her shoulder and her skin. Her skin was impeccably smooth, and her complexion seemed as if it had been airbrushed. It was like she had a Snapchat filter on at all times. She was utterly stunning.

Her chin came up and she glared down on us. "I wouldn't get too comfortable here, girls. None of this is yours. Do you understand that? There's been a mistake, but rest assured our lawyers will get things straightened out quickly. Your mother is confused about your father. Look at Bradley. You look nothing like him with your dark eyes. You're much more—shall we say—immigrant in appearance."

Gia's smile rose to one side. "Our eyes are dark hazel, and whether your family came on the Mayflower or the last truck from Canada, we're all immigrants. You included, Mrs. Wentworth."

Reality settled in that no matter how much money Gia and I inherited, we'd never be accepted. Our father's lawsuit wasn't an anomaly of his character, it was a symptom of his greedy, glacial, emotionless self. I didn't think I could do it. I couldn't wait to exit this monstrous house with its emotional vampires. They would suck the life out of us, I knew it as sure as I stood on the patterned carpet. *I wanted out.*

"Save your threats, we know how to read." Gia removed her sweatshirt and bent to the floor. She placed her navy blazer over the pooled liquid on the carpet. She started to pat it gently. "This is a Siegler Mahal Carpet." She looked up at my father. "Do you know what this rug is worth?"

He shrugged and it seemed as if Gia was more disgusted by his treatment of the carpet than our mother.

"It's one of the most expensive rugs in the world," she said. "From Central Persia."

No response.

"Is this insured? I never thought I'd see one in person." Gia lifted the edge of the carpet. "Look at this workmanship. The intricate flower borders. The royal colors. Do you people take care of anything? Or does destruction follow you everywhere?"

"Darling, get off the floor! Most of our decorating efforts have gone into the garden house in Napa," Mrs. Wentworth said in an affected voice. "Honestly, savages," she said under her breath.

The rug looked like any other patterned rug to me. "Gia's the textile curator at the De Young Museum. She knows her textiles."

"This shouldn't be walked on," Gia said. "This should be on

display." She ran her finger over the edge. "Look at these selvages. I'd say this rug is at least 200 years old. "

The svelte blonde rolled her eyes and placed a hand on Bradley's shoulder. "We really should ready for dinner. The Smileys are expecting us, and their personal jeweler will be there for a show this evening."

My sister looked up from the floor where she was on all fours, rather *savagely*, it seemed to me. "This is my rug now," she said crazily. She looked up at me. "I mean, it's our house. No one cares about this rug, right? Would you even notice if I replaced it with something from TJ Maxx?"

"What in heaven's name is TJ Maxx?" Mrs. Wentworth asked.

"Oh please. You're not that stupid," Gia said. "Do you really expect us to believe that you're so special you're not familiar with discounted retailers? Right." My sister stood up and brushed herself off. "Look, we're not taking your mean girls act, all right? This is our house now. I seem to remember you being an heiress of some sort, Mrs. Wentworth. If you can't behave yourself, go stay at your inheritance house or your gazebo house because this is ours now, and if you treat my sister or me with your uppity attitude, I'll make sure Mr. Trunkett has you and that God-awful painting of yours thrown in the street."

My eyes were wide. I hated confrontation and my stomach churned. I wanted to race home to Nonna and stuff myself with gnocchi and tiramisu.

Mrs. Wentworth clenched her fists. "I will not be talked to this way. You girls are beastly!"

"This is *our* house!" Gia shouted. "Before you treat us like chattel who has invaded your home, I would suggest you deal with the real issue." She held her hand open to Bradley. "Exhibit A."

We all collectively gasped.

Gia tugged at the lapels of her yellow shirt and turned to leave. "You have the option of trying to get along. We don't want to be here anymore than you want us here. We can work together and make this year go by as easily as possible, or I'm sorry to say, you two will have to leave. Bradley, you've treated us and our mother like we didn't exist, and for that reason, I feel sorry for you. You'll never know what you missed, but this—" Gia waved her hand around again. "This is not going to happen. You will not bully my sister or me, or you'll be out of this house. I don't care how long you've lived here. Do we understand each other?"

The vein in the older woman's neck twitched, "How dare you think—"

"Chelsea, shut up," Bradley said. "That's enough."

Gia's calm, professional demeanor returned. "I've said my piece. I won't put up with my sisters being bullied. Without us, Quinn and Brinn don't inherit either, so please spare us any misplaced condescension." She looked at me. "I'm going to work for a few hours. I'll see you for dinner at Nonna's, Sophia. This place makes me lose my appetite." Then, in her great mic drop moment, she swept out of the room on the monster wave she created leaving a tumultuous wake behind her.

Joel rolled up behind Bradley from the sunroom, and though the air was still thick with tension, he chose to ignore it. "Would you help me get to my room, Sophia? The elevator is back that way by the kitchen." He pointed. "I could use a push. My body has had it today."

"Sure," I said eagerly. I came behind him and noticed that his wheelchair was battery powered. I didn't ask questions but was grateful for the reprieve. I wheeled him around the aging Barbie and Ken. Once we were in the elevator I exhaled. Neither of us pushed a button.

"Your sister's right to take the upper hand with them. They take no prisoners," he said.

"That's a strange thing to say about your future in-laws."

Joel opened his mouth as if about to tell me something, but quickly closed it. "Take my advice. Don't show weakness."

I wanted to crumple into a ball, and I'd been in the house less than an hour. "No amount of money is worth living in a home full of this kind of tension. I can't stay here."

"It sounds as if your sister has taken care of that. Trust me, they heard the threat even if they didn't acknowledge it."

"You think they'll go?"

"I do. Eventually. When it's been long enough so that you know it was their idea. They've only been here since Wyatt got ill, so it won't be that difficult. They've got a penthouse apartment on Nob Hill." Joel's eyes met mine. "Quinn asked me to give you this." He reached into his shirt pocket and pulled out two envelopes. "One is for your sister. I assume you're trustworthy to pass this on to your sister, seeing as how you could easily pass for her."

"What is it?" I asked as I took them.

"Your stipend. Mr. Trunkett dropped them off this afternoon after he learned you'd moved in."

I ripped open the envelope and saw my name on a check. "This is a check for ten thousand dollars!"

"Quinn said it's your weekly stipend."

I tried to fathom the amount—the extensive zeroes. "Weekly? This is an obscene amount of money." Terror took hold of me at the massive responsibility with such a number. "To whom much is given, much will be expected," I added absently.

"I wondered what the amount was. Quinn wouldn't tell me. Not a bad start I'd say. And here, I'm living in this place for free."

I found it odd that Quinn wouldn't share financial details with her fiancé but didn't say anything. What did I know about old money? Maybe I announced how tacky and bougie I was, but I couldn't help but wonder if there was something Quinn didn't trust about Joel.

I dropped the check into my back pocket. "I hate the way it makes me feel. I didn't work for this, and it just seems wrong that I won the daddy lottery."

"You did *not* win the daddy lottery, I can assure you of that," he said without further explanation. "Your mother worked for that money. Didn't she raise you without any support?"

"She did."

"It's the universe paying her back."

"God," I said. "We don't believe in that "woo-woo" business. God's always behind it." I stared down at him with a wary expression. "You seem to know a lot about us. I don't care for being the subject of petty gossip."

"Welcome to the Wentworth family. Don't you read the Chronicle? Petty gossip is this family's life blood. You'd better get used to it and learn how to control the narrative."

"I'm just me. What's a narrative?"

"A narrative is you controlling what gets printed, so keep your amounts and your relationships to yourself. Keep what matters to you silent."

"I'm Italian. Silent isn't my strong suit."

Joel's taught muscle down his cheek flinched. "Bradley says the only thing worse than bad publicity is to be forgotten altogether, so there's that."

"He has to have some merit to his personality, doesn't he?" I asked. "I'm sure not seeing it, except I did appreciate him telling his wife to can it." Bradley Wentworth seemed without character or moral substance. How on earth could he be my sweet mother's *love of her life?* "One redeeming quality, that's all I'm looking for at this point."

"You'll find it," Joel said. "It's in there."

"I hate being in this house—and I use the term house loosely. It's like living in Steinhart Aquarium's African Hall. Only colder. And with more lions."

He laughed. "Shouldn't you be going shopping?" He nodded towards the check in my pocket.

"I'm going to see if I can get my job back. I wasn't made for the idle life. It's really too bad when you think about it."

"It is," he said. "I could get quite used to it."

I hated how comfortable I felt with Joel. *He was engaged to my half-sister.* Though I couldn't figure out the connection between them, wasn't that how love was? It never made any sense. My mother's choice in a guy certainly didn't makes any sense. Love continued to mystify me, which is why I clung to work.

"You never told me which floor you were on." My finger hovered over the elevator buttons.

Joel grasped the tips of my fingers and looked me straight in the eye. "Spend as much time at your Nonna's as you can."

"How did you—"

"Let things settle," he said cryptically. "You're protected, but there's a lot you don't know so make yourself scarce."

"I'm protected? What?" The elevator door opened, and we were still on the first floor. My father and his wife stared at us with their Botoxed, expressionless faces. I searched for an excuse as to why I was in the elevator with my sister's fiancé for so long.

"I forgot my papers out in the garden," Joel said as he wheeled out. "Nothing like a ride in the elevator to remind you of your childhood, huh Sophia?"

"Yeah," I said. "Just like staying in a hotel as a kid." I split from Joel and made my way outside to the front walk, desperate for an Uber to take me away from the drama. But the sparkle in Joel's eye as he gazed back at me was the one thing that made me want to stay.

Who was this guy? And were Campelli women cursed to fall for men who loved other women?

Chapter Eleven

I had nowhere to go. I stood under the elaborate portico and watched the sailboats that dotted the San Francisco Bay. Mrs. Chen opened the front door and startled me. Joel was behind her in his chair.

"Will you both be here for dinner?" Mrs. Chen asked.

I looked to Joel and pressed my fingertips to my chest, "Not me. I'll be going back to my grandparents to grab some more essentials. Gia is picking me up." *In two hours, but who was counting?*

"Joel?" she asked.

He shrugged in his wheelchair. "My options are limited, so I'll be here. Quinn is out with friends, so I'll take dinner in my room."

"I'll serve at six-thirty," Mrs. Chen said. "Mel will bring it up."

"Perfect," he answered. "Thank you for your care, Mrs. Chen. You've made me feel at home, and it means the world to me."

"You're always sneaking about here; it seems right you should have moved in." She smiled and headed back toward the kitchen as my cell phone trilled.

"What did that mean?" I asked him.

He rolled out onto the portico. "Don't mind her, she's my biggest fan really."

My cell phone trilled. "Excuse me," I said as I pulled the phone from my pocket. "Hello."

A robotic voice spoke, "This is a phone call from San Francisco's County Jail Number One."

"Hello?" I said again.

"Sophia, don't hang up, it's Charlie Jessup."

"Mr. Jessup!"

"You're my one and only phone call, so please just listen."

"Look, I can't talk to—I'm no longer employed with social services. I'm sure you understand why."

"I'm so sorry. I never meant for that to happen, but my son . . . I don't have much time but promise me you'll check on Oliver. He's at his mother's at 771B Hyde Street."

"I can't check on Oliver even if I wanted to. It's not legal."

"You're a mandated reporter. He's being hurt there. Now if you don't intervene, you're breaking the law. Please Sophia, you're my only hope."

I caught my breath. *Was Oliver being hurt?* Or was this some concocted story to excuse a father's desperate kidnapping attempt? "You're in a police station," I said. "You're surrounded by mandated reporters. Can't you ask one of them?"

"No one believes me. I'm worried he'll pay for what I did Monday. Please. For my son's sake—I have no one else to ask. I thought I'd be out by now." The desperation in his voice sounded authentic and inwardly, I struggled. This man put my whole career track in jeopardy. *I didn't owe him a thing.* I paused and tried to collect my thoughts. Confusion reigned and I didn't even know what my gut instinct was in that moment.

"I can't make any promises," I told him.

"Call your boss then. Tell Bobbi. Please. The address is 771B Hyde. I have reason to believe he's in danger tonight." An electronic voice came on again and ended the phone call as abruptly as it had come.

"Trouble?" Joel asked as I slid the phone back into my pocket.

"No. No trouble," I lied rather than break any further client confidentiality. As if that mattered when I wasn't employed, but if I hoped to get my job back when Charlie's motive came out. He had to have a good reason for what he did. But looking into Joel's concerned eyes, it all felt pointless. We knew none of the same people. "That was my former client. The one who kidnapped his son on Monday."

"Well, he's not getting out any time soon," Joel said casually.

"No, he's not. Kidnapping is a felony for sure, especially when you're under mandated supervised visitations. It's probably not going to go well for him."

"I meant that you must be his one phone call so Monday must have gone nowhere. He's not even making bail after three days. It must be set high."

My finger brushed against Joel's arm on the wheelchair's armrest as I pulled my hand from my pocket. The mere touch undid me, and I kept talking rather than deal with the secret thrill I felt inside.

"He says his son is in danger." I noticed the pen in Joel's shirt pocket, and I reached for it and wrote the address Charlie had given me on my palm.

Joel reached for my hand and turned it over to see the address. "You're certainly not going there by yourself. It's almost dark and that's in the Tenderloin District."

"I should call my boss," I said under my breath. "Bobbi would know what I should do."

"You should go home and pack like you planned. This isn't your problem. He's caused enough trouble this week. If he's still in jail this many days later, well—"

"What if someone hurts Oliver? What if Charlie is right? He's worried for a reason that Oliver might pay for his sin. Why now? Three days later?"

So much for client confidentiality, but I imagined his name

was in the newspaper. I hadn't read anything because I couldn't face my part in the whole fiasco.

"Charlie is a kidnapper," Joel reminded me.

"I know, but he's not like that. He's—I think he's telling me the truth."

"Well, if you're doing this fool's errand, I'm definitely going with you."

I looked down at him in his wheelchair with his leg outstretched straight in its cast. "No offense, Joel, but what are you going to do? Bite someone for me?"

His expression turned grave. "I'm not kidding. You're not going there alone. I insist."

"You should worry about Quinn. I've been walking the City alone since I was ten."

"I worry about all of you. As soon as the press knows who you are and what you're worth, you're not going to be able to live incognito. That's a sketchy part of town. I know you're a city girl, but then you should know that going to the Tenderloin alone isn't a bright idea. Even in the middle of the day!" He wheeled himself closer. "Don't you read the paper?"

"No, it's filled with my father's eccentric fashion choices and horrible human choices. That depresses me."

Joel reached for my wrist and aimed his billion-dollar gaze at me. It felt so intimate, shame immediately flooded my soul. "You're not going to do this alone," he said in an accusatory tone. "It's illegal. It's dangerous."

"There's no one else. If Oliver gets hurt, I'll never forgive myself. Besides, what else can they do? I'm fired. Oliver's dad gave me the address. It's not like I stole it from the files. I was asked by a client to check in on his child. Perfectly reasonable."

"Then I'm coming with you."

"I'll be fine."

"I have a couple of cop buddies. At least let me call one of them," Joel said.

"For someone who is reading me the riot act on being overly

responsible for something that isn't my problem, you sure are doing the same thing," I told him with more venom than I felt.

"Guilty."

He let my wrist drop, and I felt the cold absence. His touch unnerved me in a way that made the simplest of common gestures feel cozy and conspiratorial, as if it should be kept secret.

"You feel responsible for Oliver's safety." Joel lowered his gaze. "I feel responsible for yours —for all of the sisters."

"It's a credit to your character. Quinn's a lucky lady." I left him on the porch at the top of the steps he couldn't navigate. As I turned around, he seemed so small under the massive portico. He wasn't a small man, but the house seemed alive — as if it swallowed up anyone who dared to compete with the status quo.

* * *

Uber dropped me squarely in front of Oliver's mother's house. I checked the address on my hand, and I was in the right place. *Or the wrong place as the case may be.* As dusk approached, I knew I shouldn't be there. Not without telling someone where I was going with the exact address, but I had to trust my instinct. Briefly, I wished I'd swallowed my pride and let Joel come along, but I was letting fear get the best of me. This was a normal home visit, nothing more.

I stood on the slanted sidewalk and thought about calling him, but I knew calling Joel would only feed my romantic notions, and I had to face reality. Joel Edgerton was engaged to one of the pony set and my own sister. I would face this like I'd faced every other crisis in my lifetime. Alone. He'd been kind because he loved Quinn, and any flirtations that I'd imagined between us needed to be forgotten.

The single garage door at street level wasn't wide enough for any modern car to enter. It was locked with a U-shaped iron latch and a padlock. I overheard screaming, but I couldn't make out any words. It was muffled by the glass window and the traffic behind me. Garbage swirled around in the wind, and I pulled at the ornamental iron gate in front of the interior staircase. It opened and before I ascended the stairs, I texted my sister.

"Gia, at 771B Hyde Street, checking on Oliver. FYI. I'll meet you at Nonna's."

I'd watched too much *Dateline* with my Nonna.

The cave-like, concrete staircase echoed the shouts from within the apartment. As I approached the door, I could finally discern the shouts.

A man's voice boomed, "Now he's not working. Now he's in jail! You happy? How do you expect to make rent this month? You don't think!" Something hit the wall where I was standing, and I jumped at the thump.

"Mommy?" It was Oliver's whimper.

"Get in your room!" a woman shouted.

"Mommy, I'm scared."

"I said get in your room!"

At this point I had no choice. The words were as clear as if I were inside. Credentials or not, I banged on the door. Hushed whispers replaced the screaming. The door opened, and Oliver's mother stood in front of me. Her long blond hair was disheveled, and her running mascara made it look as though she had two black eyes. Her appearance implied that she'd never seen a tattoo parlor she didn't visit. Her arms were covered by a tattooed sleeve with skulls, deep red roses and a vicious-looking cobra. She and Oliver's father went together like a Komodo dragon and puppies.

I can't even get a boyfriend and this chick has two men. Life is not fair.

I regained my composure at the sight of her. "Sophia Campelli, Child Protective Services," I lied. *So easily, too. But I had a mission. I needed to get Oliver out of that house.*

"Really?" she asked. "They didn't fire you after you lost my son? This damn state has no standards. Once you get a government job, you're set for life, huh? Well, I hope you're here to apologize for giving me the fright of my life."

"Actually, I do apologize. I'm not sure how your husband—"

"Ex-husband," she corrected.

"I'm not sure how he escaped the barred windows in the visitation room."

"Does it matter?" She crossed her arms. "Besides, I'm sure he had help." She didn't open the screen door, nor did she invite me in. "I get it. You're like the rest of them, huh? You fall for his choir boy looks and false charms, too. Let me tell you something about Charlie. He'll do whatever he has to."

"Our department has had a complaint, and I'm simply following up."

"I imagine they have. That's what happens when you lose children. People complain. Listen lady, my son is safe and warm tonight, no thanks to you. I suggest you go on your merry way before I call the cops."

"I need to see Oliver, please." I prayed she wouldn't ask me for my license, and I wondered if citizen arrest was really a thing. I didn't want to end up in a cell beside Charlie Jessup for impersonating a CPS social worker.

"Oliver!" She shouted without opening the door. "Get out here!"

Soon she slid Oliver in front of her between the crack in the door, "Here he is. Happy?"

"Oliver, are you okay?"

"He's fine," his mother said. "Don't he look fine?"

Oliver looked terrified. "Where's Daddy?"

"Your daddy is fine, Oliver. I promise."

"You promise? That man stole my kid and now, how am I supposed to get child support from a man in jail? Did you ever think about that?" She scoffed. "How Oliver might eat tomorrow? The only thing that man was ever good for was working."

"The report states—"

She interrupted again. "We should all be so lucky to have a government job and keep it while we are complete crap at it." She kept mentioning how it was impossible to lose my job and oh, the irony of that statement. It was salt in an open wound.

"Unless you have a warrant," the man shouted, "you need to leave now. You've seen the kid, he's fine. On your way now."

The door flew open all the way, and a man shaped like a gorilla stood behind Oliver and his mother. The hair on the back of my neck stood straight on end. It dawned on me again how stupid it was to come to this neighborhood alone. I didn't owe a thing to Charlie Jessup. He kidnapped his son. *What the heck was I doing standing on a stoop in the Tenderloin facing a man who looked like a wrestling star?*

But then I looked into Oliver's tormented eyes, and I stood taller. "No warrant necessary. I'm doing a well-check on Oliver, that's all. He's had a traumatic week, and we just wanted to follow up."

"He has had a week, no thanks to you. It's time for him to go to bed," his mother said.

"Mommy, I hungry."

"Mrs. Jessup," I said, ignoring the fact that she'd clearly moved on even though her divorce wasn't final. "Is there food in the house for Oliver?"

"Yes, there's food in the house!" she answered.

"Do you mind if I check it out?"

"I do!" Gorilla boy snapped. "Look, Miss Busybody, it's always you types who can't get a man or kid of your own that stick your nose into everyone else's business. Forty-year old virgins who want to tell the rest of us how to live our lives. Oliver's safe here. Now get lost."

He'd pushed my last button. I stepped past the three of them. The house was a disaster. The floor was littered with fast food garbage and the sink was piled with dirty dishes. I stared back at them and wondered how these two ever made the rent in San Francisco, where anything beneath $100k a year was poverty-level. The answer was, I probably didn't want to know.

Skin tingling at the risk I was taking; I opened the fridge and a stagnant smell hit me like a wave of nastiness. I covered my nose and checked the milk, which was past its due date. An open can of beans seemed to explain the stench, and I pulled it from the fridge. "It's dangerous to store food in an open can." I chucked it into the garbage can along with a bag of spinach that had turned into green, watery mush.

"Missy, you'd best get out of my fridge before I give your department something to come looking for, you got it?"

"Are you threatening me, Mr.—"

"Mr. None-of-your-business and yes, I am. You get out of my house now or—"

"Or what?" I trembled, but I couldn't back down. I needed to know Oliver had nourishment. "What is Oliver having for dinner?"

"He's having SpaghettiOs, okay? It's not like I had a lot of time to shop. I was searching for my son."

"That was four days ago, Mrs. Jessup."

"She told you to stop calling her that!" I felt a meaty grip on my shoulder and turned to see the look of the devil in the boyfriend's eyes. His clutch on my shoulders grew tighter while his pupils grew darker. My heart pounded as Mrs. Jessup stepped between us.

"Aw Beef, get outta here. You's only making things worse for me. Oliver's fine, lady. He's having SpaghettiOs for dinner, okay?"

Beef's grip on my shoulder tightened, and he lifted me from my crouched position in front of the refrigerator as if I was no more than a Barbie Doll. "Get out," he growled.

When I tried to make a break for it, he grabbed the back of my shirt and yanked me down to the filthy linoleum.

"Beef, don't!" Mrs. Jessup cried.

Oliver clasped his eyes shut and covered them with his fingertips. It was clear this wasn't the first act of violence he'd seen. I tried to reach for my phone, but Beef kicked it against the wall with a thunderous crash. He began kicking me like a soccer ball.

Instinctively, I covered my head with my arms when I heard a violent pounding on the door,

"San Francisco Police, open up!"

"What the hell?" Beef growled at me. "You came out here with cops?" He kicked me so hard in the ribs that I thought I heard one crack. The door slammed opened, and two police officers with guns drawn aimed their weapons at the monstrous man while I writhed on the floor. I couldn't catch my breath. The pain paralyzed me, and my surroundings were starting to go dark.

"Is that your son, ma'am?" The policeman's voice sounded far away, like he was in a cave.

"Yes," Mrs. Jessup said while I watched Oliver reach for the police officer.

"Please take him in the back room." The police officers turned their attention to Mrs. Jessup's meaty boyfriend. "Down on your knees, now!"

Beef hit the floor, and I tried not to move, but still on the floor, rested against the wall to brace myself. Then, the huge hunk of idiocy stood and lunged at one of the officers. The cop tazed Beef, and he hit the floor like a steak slapped on the grill. The other officer handcuffed the now complicit lump of a bully.

"You all right, Miss Campelli?"

"I'm fine." I said, shocked by the sound of my name. In truth, I was only partially present. I felt almost zombie-like as I stood slowly and groaned with each tiny movement. "CPS needs to come get the boy. He's not safe here."

One of the police officers came to me and helped me to the door, "We'll take care of him. Do you need medical attention?"

I shook my head, "I'm fine. I just want to go home." The last thing I needed was to answer more questions about why I was there. I held my side with little doubt that at least one my ribs was broken. My whole body felt fragile and splintered like shattered glass. More than the pain I felt, the realization stirred in me that I'd never get my job back. I'd probably never work with children again.

"I think we should take you to SF General and get that checked out," the cop said.

I shook my head vehemently. "I'll be fine."

"You're denying care?"

I nodded. The less obvious I made this disastrous and illegal visit, the better. The short trip home in a police car was a blur. When one of the officers dropped me at my grandparents' house, I pressed the doorbell rather than fumble for my keys.

Once inside, I wilted into my sister's arms. "Thank you, Gia. I don't know what would have happened if you hadn't sent the police." I sniffled on her shoulder, but pushed her back. "No, don't get too close. I'm in agony." I inhaled the scent of fresh basil and looked at my sister. "How did you know I'd be in over my head?"

"You're usually in over your head, so it would be a normal assumption, but what do you mean?" Then she looked at my face. "Soph, what's wrong with you?"

"Shh. I don't want Nonna and Papa to know."

"Know what?" She looked into my eyes. "Are you hurt?"

"Can you sneak me some ice out of the fridge? I just want to lay down. I'll be fine if I can just lay down."

"Sophia Bella, is that you?" I heard Papa call from the kitchen.

"It's me, Papa."

He came to me and kissed my forehead. "*Sophia Bella, you're home.*" I winced and pulled away before he grabbed me in an Italian bear hug.

"I hurt myself running, Papa, no hugs."

"*Vieni a mangiare un po 'di pasta!*"

Pasta was truly the answer to everything in my grandparents' house. "Thank you, I'll eat. Pasta will help, you're right. I'm starving." I shuffled to the table where my Nonna had prepared enough food for a small army, but on sight of the food, I knew I'd never be able to swallow a bite. "How will you ever get used to us not living here, Nonna?" I forced the question out so nothing seemed amiss.

Nonna came toward me and put her hands on my cheeks. She kissed me hard on each cheek and mumbled at me to clean up when I was done. She moved into the living room to watch her nightly game shows. She and Papa ate biscotti dipped in Vin Santo while they watched *Jeopardy*. After their nightcap of sugar and booze, there was *Wheel of Fortune*, and it was off to bed.

Gia brought me a bag of frozen peas, and I placed them on my side. "Are you going back to the mansion tonight?"

"I just want to huddle in my bed and forget any of this happened. I don't want that money, Gia. It's poison. Look at what's happened since we got it. Joel got hit by that car. I lost my job. You saw a priceless rug ruined. I think my rib is broken. This isn't our life to live. God is sending us a sign."

"Now you sound like Nonna with all her perilous warnings."

"What if you hadn't sent help tonight?"

"I told you, I have no idea what you're talking about. Send help where?"

"The text I sent with the address of Oliver's. How did you know to send the police?"

"I didn't send the police anywhere." She went to her bag and rummaged out her phone. "You sent me a text?" She opened her phone. "Did something happen?" She showed me the text that she had yet to read.

"If you didn't send the police, who did?" My body was in so much agony. I started to tremble.

"Maybe a neighbor. Soph, are you all right? I think we should really get you to the hospital." She whispered it so my grandparents wouldn't hear.

"No, they knew who I was." I tried to eat, but my mind stirred. "Someone must be following me."

"Sophia, come on. Eat something. It's been a creepy day meeting that donor we call a father. You just need to calm down. You sound like you might be losing it."

"I am losing it, but I need you to believe me." I knew I wasn't loud enough for the neighbors to call the police. They were literally there the minute I needed them. "When was the last time you needed a police officer and he knocked on your door at precisely the right moment? In the Tenderloin?"

"You're going to upset Papa with talk of the police. Shh."

"I'm not going back to that house," I told her. "I'm done. Those fake heiress sisters of ours can find a way to get that will overturned because I'm done."

"And what happens to mom? She has no retirement, and this house will cost her too much in taxes to sell. She'll have nothing more than a trailer on some freeway in a flyover state. What about Alisa? She's too young to be there on her own."

"Alisa's too clueless to notice we're missing. The idea of going back to that house makes me want to crumple into a fetal position and never leave here."

"That's exactly why we need to go back. That, and the lawsuit isn't going away." Gia put together an easier plate for me. She lifted a few pieces of bruschetta with fresh tomatoes, a slice of beef roll and a spoonful of pasta. "Here, try some of this. You can eat it with your fingers."

I couldn't touch it. "I think I'm going to be sick." I rose. My Nonna and Papa turned to face me, and I smiled. "Amazing as usual, Nonna!"

"I know," she said in Italian. She put her biscotti down and shuffled over to me at the table. She kissed me on the temple. "I'll wash the dishes. Gia, take your sister to the hospital."

I had to give her credit. Nonna didn't miss a trick.

Chapter Twelve

My grandfather took into account every scenario. The world really was infinitely unfair and tipped to favor the wealthy. One broken rib gave me a few days' reprieve from the mausoleum and healing time in my Nonna's home. My current plan was to binge on bad television, *pasta e fagioli* soup, pizelle cookies, and old-school Italian smothering. The reprieve would do nothing for my girlish figure and everything for my peace of mind. Four days away from the mansion— and Joel Edgerton—was exactly what was needed.

The morning after the attack and my hospital visit, Gia showed up at breakfast from the mansion. I smiled at the sight of her because it felt like all was right with the world again. We were home. Mom served fresh mozzarella and thin, crisped slices of sourdough left over from the restaurant. The family all settled around the kitchen table, and I vowed I never take such simple moments for granted again. I teared up at the warmth and comfort I felt with us all around the table. Maybe it was the pain in my rib or even the side effects from the meds. But as I sniffled, I knew I'd give up any amount of money for my old job and my old life.

I had a good life. Why didn't I recognize it until it was too late?

"I have a surprise for you girls on this beautiful Saturday morning!" Mom stood up from the table abruptly and ran upstairs. She returned with a pillowcase filled with something. "What do you think it could be?"

"I hope it's a puppy." Gia laughed.

Mom flipped the pillowcase over and emptied wads of cash. Genuine stacks of cash cinched together by paper bands! We all watched in amazement while she dropped them onto the kitchen table. We expelled a collective gasp.

"You didn't take my money," Gia said without inflection.

"You gave her money too?" I asked, then I looked at my mother. "Mom!" I stood and tried to feign surprise, but I sat back down when my rib protested. "You were supposed to use that to prepay the rent at the restaurant."

"Listen," Mom said with one fist on her hip and the other in the air. "I tell that greedy landlord that my daughters have money and he'll hike the rent. You're Wentworths now. No relation to the poor Campellis of North Beach. I tell the landlord, then what happens? He hikes my rent, we can't afford to stay, and I fire all my employees. They're out of a job. You give that man nothing until it's required, *capiche*?" She pressed her fingers together.

Mama had the ability to go from zero to catastrophe in seconds flat.

"Our status isn't going to stay quiet forever, Mom." I hoped it stayed quiet long enough so Oliver's mother didn't sue me for unlawful entry. Tell the former Mrs. Jessup I'm attached to the Wentworths and the sharks would surely start circling if they smelled that blue blood.

"Mom, why on earth did you get all this cash?" Gia asked.

She shrugged her bony shoulders. "I wanted to see what it looked like to make it real, you know?"

"Not really," Gia said. "Didn't you see the zeroes in your bank account?"

"Did you know you have to make arrangements to get this kind of cash? It's like calling ahead for a pizza. You have to tell the bank you're coming and how much you'll be withdrawing." She giggled. "It's so exciting. I felt like I was in a movie and Brad Pitt was going to help me pull off a great heist."

"Bank robbers don't look like Brad Pitt, Mom." Gia shook her head. "You really have to call ahead? That's good information, I suppose."

Nonna put a frittata down on the table. I should have known bread and cheese wasn't considered a meal on her part.

I couldn't take my eyes off that pile of bills. "What are we supposed to do with all this cash? It looks like we've made a drug deal."

"Duh." My mom lifted a few bound stacks of money and threw them in the air. "We're going shopping!"

"Do you need something, Mom?" Gia asked. "What exactly are we shopping for?"

"Yes, I need my daughters to dress like heiresses before Sophia goes back to the house."

"She means me. Gia dresses fine," I said.

Mom lifted a single stack of bills, "Papa, let's rewire the house, huh?"

"No," he said sternly. "Dirty money. Keep it away far from me. Nothing will make up for the shame that man brought on my daughter. In Italy, we would have taken care of him. He would have married you proper or paid the price."

"Papa, it was thirty years ago," Mom said. "You have to let it go. And in Italy, it sounds like my punishment would have been a life sentence being married to that guy. We should be grateful he became Chelsea Whitman's problem instead of ours."

I stared at my mother, anxious to see if she really believed that. Her expression gave nothing away.

"Ahh!" Papa swatted his hand in the air. "I never forget." He tapped his temple. "You wrong my family, you're my enemy for life. Maybe the next life too, huh?"

Gia laughed. "You're such a gangster, Papa."

"Mom, you need to use this money for the restaurant," I told her. "Gia and I will shop when we need to. I can't even get a shirt on with my rib, so the last thing I want to do is try on clothes."

"The restaurant is fine. Someday, Giovanna will take over for me," Mom said about one of her strays—this one from Italy. "But until then, that's not my money, and it's important that you girls dress the part of proper heiresses. Brad needs to know the only difference between those awful blondes and my daughters is the price of their clothes."

"Lord, I hope that isn't the only difference," Gia said. "When my days are spent attending fundraisers for the likes of 'save the unicorns' please just take me out." She stood and twisted and turned. "Look at this suit. It's cut to perfection. What do I need to slap a label on my butt for?"

It was true, Gia had a good tailor. Her ninety-five-dollar suit looked like a million bucks, but my mom was right in that if we wanted to look like we belonged, we probably had to do something about our wardrobes—at least mine. Mostly because mine consisted of stained sweatshirts and yoga pants designed to look like work slacks.

Papa was bored with the conversation and he left for the living room and clicked on the television for the morning news.

Mom sighed. "I put the money you gave me aside, and I made an appointment with a stylist today. She works in all the stores in Union Square, so we won't be limited to one store. She says she can get you both an entirely new wardrobe with just a few questions and one fitting. Wouldn't that be nice?"

"Union Square," Gia said. "Mom, just because we're rich doesn't mean we're wasteful."

"Mom, how do you even know what a stylist is?" I asked her.

"I know things," she said in an offended tone. "Plus, she comes to the restaurant all the time. She always wears this impeccable black suit because she says she doesn't want her customers to get sidetracked by her look so they can focus on their own."

"Fascinating," I said as I dipped a biscotti in my latte.

"Mom, we gave you a lot of money. Did you pay the restaurant bills with any of it?" Gia asked.

"I love that my girls are so generous." She kissed each one of us on the cheek with a loud *mwah*! "But your job now is to prove to Bradley Wentworth that you turned out better because of his absence. You can't do that dressed in rags. Do it for me. To tell him that I was better off without him, no?"

I looked down at my oversized sweatshirt and jeans. She had a point. "So, this is an Italian vengeance thing?"

"Not vengeance," Mom said. "Vindication."

My Nonna rattled off in Italian that Bradley was the devil and God didn't forget men who abandoned their children. At this point, my Papa rose from the sofa and walked into the kitchen to kiss Nonna on her cheek. "*Tu sei l'unico per me.* You're the only one for me, heh?"

Nonna nodded and they stared deeply into each other's eyes.

"Seriously, Nonna gets more action than me. I need a date," Gia said. "Will new clothes help me get a date?"

"You're worth a couple billion dollars. That will get you a date," I quipped.

"You need a more upscale look; both of you," Mom continued. "After we shop, you're finally going to buy me that crab lunch you promised me." She looked down at the money on the table. "What did you think of your father when you met him?"

Gia and I froze. There it was. The question we'd been waiting for.

"Well," I stalled. "He's not what I imagined you would pick."

"What do you mean?"

"I thought he'd be . . . I don't know . . . more manly. More solid." Which made no sense. I saw his pictures in the paper, his Chiclet teeth, his wild fashion choices. I shouldn't have expected John Cena or anything. "He was slighter than I imagined. Effeminate maybe?" I was walking a thin line. I didn't want to offend my mother, but I also didn't want her to think she'd missed out on anything by Bradley's coldhearted rejection. "He reminds me of Anderson Cooper—only crueler."

"Cruel?" Mom's interest was piqued. "Really?"

"He's a very selfish man, Mom." Gia added. "That can't surprise you. And I never trust a man with manicured fingers. It's creepy."

"What's she like?"

"She's awful," Gia said. "Last night, they got kicked out of whatever dinner party they were invited to, so she came home and barked at Mrs. Chen, that's the maid, to get them something to eat." Gia brightened at a memory. "No one eats their meals together at the house. They all split off into their rooms apparently."

"That's strange."

"It's a strange house, Mom. The family is . . . I don't know. Disjointed somehow. Brinn avoids her mother like a virus. If Chelsea enters a room, Brinn leaves it. Quinn tries to get everyone to get along from what I can see, but something happened that broke them apart and healthy conversation doesn't appear to happen."

"I suppose we shouldn't be gossiping," Mom said. "I wouldn't like it if people came into my home and judged how we live."

"Because we have a water heater in the kitchen with pasta hanging off it? Or for other reasons?" I asked.

Papa yelled at me in Italian and we all broke into laugher.

* * *

I hated shopping with my mom and sister. Hate is a strong word —abhorred shopping with them. In theory, it sounded so idyllic: *Girl time. Unlimited money to shop for clothes. Lunch on the wharf.* In reality, it was a waking nightmare. Mom still thought polyester was the height of fashion and she never met a poly-blend she didn't love. "Spaghetti sauce wipes right off," she'd say as a selling point. As if your clothing was supposed to double as a plastic tablecloth.

Gia, on the other hand, felt she missed her calling as a fashion designer and never missed an opportunity to tell us she had a degree in fabrics so we should bow down and listen to her expertise. Which, I suppose, if we were wearing a carpet or drapery from the eighteenth century, might mean something. Gia always went overboard on accessories, and I'd end up looking like a mannequin with one too many pashminas tossed casually around my neck. It made movement impractical, like wearing a snowsuit in the dead of summer. The idea of shopping with either of them, regardless of the poor, overwrought stylist, did not sound worth taking another pain pill for.

If I'm honest, working with kids, my mom's polyester styles made more sense, except that they didn't breathe and I'd end up sweating like a worked-up sumo wrestler in a sauna, so I planned to fight for natural, breathable fabrics.

I made one last attempt to get out of it as Mom opened the front door. "My ribs are really sore. You two should go without me," I ventured.

"Nonsense, it's a family day," my mom said.

Gia scowled. "You dress like a hobo. You're not staying home. It's not an option."

As we started to exit, Papa made unusual grunting noises. When we looked at the television Papa watched, Bradley Wentworth was on the local morning news while my Papa swore at the screen—in English for a nice change of pace. The room became silent.

"We're joined by Bradley Wentworth, heir to the shipping fortune of his late father, Wyatt Wentworth." The older female morning host of the local news leaned in and touched Wyatt in a way that would be considered inappropriate by anyone's standards.

"Actually," Bradley lifted a forefinger. "I am not, in fact, the heir to the shipping fortune. I will still be on the company's board, naturally, but the bulk of the money and stock options have bypassed me and gone directly to my girls." He paused and looked straight into the camera with his searing blue eyes. As if passing off the inheritance was his idea.

No wonder my mother had been so enamored of him. He had a magnetic pull to him and even though I knew he'd abandoned my family, I *wanted* to know him. Like a pathetic lump, I wanted him to love me. *Imagine how much more powerful he'd been when he was young and handsome.*

"Your girls have turned into such incredible, accomplished young ladies. I can vouch for so many of us here at *Wake-Up San Francisco!* that we have enjoyed watching them come into their own."

My father looked down in false contrition. "I'm here to announce that I actually have five daughters, not two as the press has reported, and I wanted you to hear it from me first."

"Five!" The aging blonde couldn't hide her shock. She pulled away slightly.

"It's true. I've been blessed with five beautiful daughters. God has been so gracious." He pointed at the ceiling.

"God has been so gracious?" Gia stuck her finger in her throat. "Interesting way of saying he rejects monogamy in marriage. God made him do it. Gosh, he's vile."

"Shh!" Mom snapped.

"My wife and I have not had the easiest road in our marriage." Bradley wiped an imaginary tear from the corner of his eye. "But we have persevered, and our family will overcome this monkey wrench my father has thrown as well. I couldn't be happier for my girls. I know they will use their time and money in the service of others, as they always have."

My sister had all she could take and threw a coaster at the TV. "What a crock of—"

"Gia!" Mom chastised.

"Wh-what's the name of your other girls? Naturally, we all know Quinn and Brinn, but the others?"

Bradley cleared his throat, and I watched my mom as she willed him not to announce our names to the world. "I'm very proud to announce that I've recently discovered I had twins before my marriage to my wife, Chelsea." He looked down as if shamed and continued not looking at the camera. "I was young and wealthy. A young woman took advantage and saw her way out of poverty. I was too naive to know the difference, but I can't blame the twins. They are innocent in this."

My papa's fists tightened. "I'll kill him."

"He doesn't know our names," Gia snickered. "All this crap because he can't answer the question. Taken advantage of—do people believe this crap?"

It was my mom's reaction that worried me. While the family was aghast and vocal about it, she stayed silent. Her olive complexion paled. She stared at the television without blinking and lowered herself slowly to the sofa, as if the pain and hurt came to her in a fresh wave. The veil had been torn, and she now understood who Bradley Wentworth was—who he'd always been. She could no longer ignore reality and live in the fairy tale past she'd created.

Mom grabbed the remote and clicked the television off. "I think it's high time the world met the woman who took advantage of poor Bradley Wentworth, don't you?"

"No," Papa said. "Leave him be. He's beyond help. There's not an ounce of humility in that man to change anything. Stay out of it."

"No one is beyond help, Papa," Mom said. "But no one talks about my daughters like that and gets away with it. He can say what he likes about me, but those girls never got a cent from that cheapskate bastard. I'll be darned if I'm going to let him paint them like the children of a failed gold digger."

"Mom," Gia said, "we'll handle this. Let us handle it. We're inside the house. We'll figure out the best way to handle this."

"Why would any television station give him an outlet to spout his ugly lies?"

"What else do you expect from a station that thinks interviewing a bathtub retrofitter is legitimate content? It's dirty laundry," Gia said. "People love it and Bradley Wentworth is supplying it, but we will have the last laugh, Mama. He will reap what he's sown."

"Girls." My mother looked at us. "I've done you a terrible disservice. I've set a terrible precedent."

"What are you talking about?" I asked.

"Bradley never loved me." She settled deeper into the couch as if this information was new to her. "All my life I've made up this story in my head. He loved me, but we couldn't be together. It was all so romantic—the unrequited love that could never be— and I've wasted so much time."

"He's not capable of loving anyone but himself, Mom." Gia sat next to our mom and rubbed her back gently. "It has nothing to do with you."

"Mama, he's very persuasive," I told her. "Very charming. You couldn't have known. If he can fool the entire city of San Francisco, what hope did you have? A young high school girl with stars in her eyes."

She looked numb, as if not a word had infiltrated. "Life is not a fairy tale." She looked both of us in the eyes. "I taught you to wait for Prince Charming and believe if your fantasies didn't come true, it was better to be alone. You girls have to get out there and live. For me, you have to live your lives."

We both nodded violently. "We will, Mom. You taught us to make our own way in the world. Neither of us is sitting around waiting for Prince Charming. But life's not over for you. You're young. You're beautiful. Every day is a new opportunity now that you know you made a mistake."

She shook her head. "It's more than that. I clung to a lie for nearly thirty years."

"It's better to cling to a lie of false hope than to be a dirt person," I told her. "Bradley Wentworth is a dirt person and that has eternal consequences."

Mom smiled. She took one of Gia's hands and one of my own in hers. "Just don't make the same mistake. A godly man would never lead you on. Nor would he abandon his own children."

I felt like that was obvious, but I nodded in support anyway. It dawned on me how easy it was to believe in the fantasy. Joel Edgerton was the fantasy. In stark contrast, his fiancée Quinn was the harsh reality. We weren't being kept apart in some romantic plot. We were never meant to be, and if I learned anything from my mother, let it be that.

I didn't really believe that Bradley never loved my mother. The emotion on his face when he saw us was proof that he'd never forgotten her, and she'd penetrated his hardened heart at some point. Mama meant everything to him at one time, of that I was sure. He simply wasn't man enough to claim it.

Sparks were sure to fly if they ever saw each other again, so it was up to Gia and me to make sure that never happened. For both their sakes.

Chapter Thirteen

Mom didn't want to deal with parking the car in Union Square, so regardless of my aching body, we walked. We lived in North Beach which was directly down Nob Hill from Union Square. The operative word being *hill*. Technically, it was little more than a mile, but it was straight uphill. In fact, that particular day the sun was out and bright in North Beach, but Nob Hill was covered under a blanket of blinding fog.

"Parking is so expensive, and we're so close," she said on the way. "Isn't it lovely out here, girls? I love San Francisco in the Fall. I love the little droplets of fog when I'm walking. Breathe it all in—"

I groaned to show my protest. Breathing deeply in San Francisco could often be met with the stench of urine and the like. "Hard pass, Mama."

By the time we reached the boutique, we were a bedraggled threesome. To say I was sweating is to put it mildly. My makeup was sliding off my face, and I felt like I glistened like a Christmas tree. The crisp fall air did nothing to spare us from a sweaty "glow" as we took to those hills. We stood outside the address for a moment while Mom checked the address once again to stall so we could all catch our breath. It was moments like these when I was reminded how I'd never be blonde and elegant like my half-sisters.

"Maybe we should have taken an Uber," Mom said.

"We look awful," Gia said.

She looked the best of the three of us because she dressed decently, but she wasn't looking at a mirror. She was looking at Mom and me. I'd worn my best jeans—they were designer, albeit from some discount shop and probably three seasons past their prime. I wore my expensive Disneyland sweatshirt with a sequined outline of Mickey Mouse that I'd thrifted. This was as good as it got from my wardrobe, and I wasn't motivated to change it.

"I don't want to go in there. It's just going to be lipstick on a pig. I've got an Italian afro and no patience to straighten it or try and be acceptable to society."

My mother had also done her best to look upscale. She had a pair of jeans on that were too short for her, so she'd rolled them up to look like some kind of 1950's teenager with her slide-on Kids. But as a whole? We all looked like something the cat dragged in from the dumpster in Chinatown, and no matter how much cash my mother had on her, we weren't Union Square material.

"Well, are we going in, or aren't we?" Gia focused on my mom's printed cloth purse. "Did you have to bring that?"

"I thought it looked like one of those Vera Bradley purses," my mom said. "I needed something to carry—well you know, the money," she whispered.

"My ribs ache from walking," I whined. "Can I just take a cab home, and you pick out some things for me? You know I don't care what I wear." But that wasn't quite true. I'd seen Quinn and the way she wore riding crops and still looked like she could enter this boutique without looking back. I hated to admit it, but she owned the hospital that day she walked in, and I felt completely invisible beside her. Clothes wouldn't change the chasm between us. Quinn was who Joel loved, who Joel accepted, and while he may have been off-limits, most men of San Francisco probably didn't want a ragamuffin social worker without a job. I needed to make an effort or I'd be running the hills of San Francisco alone forever.

"You're not leaving. We have an appointment," my mom hissed. Like we could never back out of an appointment. It was written in the book of life or something.

The office had modern gray hardwood floors and white sofas. Accessories, such as high-end handbags and jewelry, filled the mirrored-back shelves. (Incidentally, there were no Vera Bradley handbags to be seen—just Prada, Burberry and Gucci as Gia pointed out.)

In back of the office there was a pedestal stage up two stairs and encased in a three-point mirror. White drapes elegantly covered the rest of the back wall, and I assumed that's where the magic clothes were kept. At least that's what I hoped, because I wasn't capable of traipsing all over Union Square into different stores.

Man, how I hope that isn't the case. My body already felt like the beating I'd taken was fresh, and I wanted to splay out on one of those pristine white couches and take a nap. *Wake me up when this is over.*

"Ladies!" A spritely redhead in five-inch stilettos came to greet us. She walked as if the shoes were a part of her person. She had no trouble in them, and that's what I respected about my sister Brinn. She moved easily in any kind of heel, like a swan gliding across a pond. Brinn had an elegance to her that Quinn didn't. Even though I would say Quinn was much prettier, Brinn held a room captive when she entered a room because of her quiet confidence.

"Sophia." My mother nudged me, and I noticed the redhead had her hand extended. "Hello, I'm Sophia."

"Elaine," the redhead said as she lightly shook my hand. "Ladies, I'm so glad you're here today. Now that we're all acquainted, is there anything I can get you? Tea? Water? Cappuccino?"

Tomorrow was Sunday. The first night of our weekly family

meeting, and we agreed we'd focus on outfits for the dinners. Elaine didn't judge us, which made me feel slightly better about the trip. I mean, why would she? My mother had a stack of cash in her faux Vera Bradley, and Elaine stood to make a lot of bank on the Wentworth's indigent relations.

"I've taken the liberty of selecting many outfits for you young ladies for several occasions. I have business, business casual, cocktail hour, and even a few soiree gowns. If you see anything you like, you can either come with me to pick out more items or send me to get you more variety."

"Sophia, let's start with you. Your mother tells me you work with children and dress to get messy. Is that true?"

"This is my fancy sweatshirt," I told her honestly.

Elaine smiled. "One suggestion I would make is your shoes—"

I looked down at my feet. I had my good running shoes on—Sauconys. *Those babies weren't cheap.* "I walk to work. Sometimes run and I chase children all day long, so—"

"One can be comfortable," Elaine said. "And still not appear as if they came from the gym. May I suggest something like this?" She held up a ballet flat with a Chanel logo on top.

"If I wore that to work, that shoe is probably more than my families make in a week. I think I'd feel guilty."

"Okay, not for work. But right now, you're in Union Square. You could wear a Chanel flat and be perfectly comfortable while still looking like a Wentworth. I want to elevate your style. You're going to be under much more scrutiny now."

"I'm a Campelli," I said angrily.

"Sophia, Elaine is only trying to help. Those would be nice for the dinner tonight, don't you think? Your sisters would probably recognize the logo. Is that Coach?" My mom asked.

"Chanel," Elaine said with the slightest haughtiness in her voice. My mom may not have caught it, but Gia and I did. "They're made from lambskin, Sophia, and they will mold to your foot as if you're wearing nothing."

My mom took the shoe and made the mistake of turning it

over. Her eyes went round. "Elaine, would you excuse us for a moment?"

"Absolutely, but before I go," Elaine pointed to the hanging racks on the back wall. "Sophia, this rack is for you to look through and Gia, this one is for you. All of the clothes should be in your size and ready to wear. We'll still want to tailor everything for the perfect fit so Olga is in back and ready to oblige. The dressing rooms are there." She pointed to the corner near the entrance. "Let me know if I can help you get into anything."

"Can we have a moment?" my mom asked.

Elaine disappeared like a ghost, and the three of us stood in front of the racks. My mother still had the taupe Chanel ballet flats in her hand.

Gia leaned into our group. "Do you think they keep Olga in the closet chained to a sewing machine?"

"These shoes are nearly $1,000." Mom whispered.

"They're Chanel," Gia rolled her eyes. "Oh, and lambskin."

I shrugged. "If I wore them to work everyone would think they were fake anyway."

"Not now they wouldn't. Now that your father has gone on television whining about how you got his inheritance."

Ugh. I'd forgotten about that. This whole nightmare wasn't going away. It wasn't something I'd wake up from any time soon. I thumbed through my curated rack. "Let's just get this done, can't we? I want to get some of Nonna's pasta before we have to go back to the mansion and have that meeting. I don't think I'll feel like eating tomorrow." I lifted out a black dress that was shaped like an ice-skating costume with a cinched waist and a shorter skirt. It had sprinkles of sparkles on the shoulders but was understated. "I could wear this to dinner."

"At the mansion?" Mom asked.

"It's simple. Practical," I said.

"Practical for who, Taylor Swift?" Mom wasn't buying it. "I would think that would be more for a date."

"It's not for her sisters, Mom. I'd venture to guess it's for Quinn's fiancé," Gia said.

"What?" I feigned ignorance. "What on earth are you talking about, Gia? Joel is engaged to my sister."

"His name is Joel then?" Gia asked.

"You know his name!"

"Actually, I didn't remember it," Gia said coolly. "I distinctly remember you telling me that he looked like the Archangel Michael from Nonna's painting though. And then, that weird running thing you did when he tried to serve you with the court documents. He makes you act completely stupid. That's all the proof I need. Regardless of Quinn, he's not for you."

"Is that where that painting went?" my mom asked. "Sophia!" She said my name with as much disgust in her voice as if I'd made a pass at a Catholic saint.

"Can we get back to shopping? Fine, you both think the dress is too much for dinner. What would you suggest? These linen pants?" I held up a pair of winter white slacks. "They'd look good with a little of Nonna's gravy on them."

But Gia wouldn't shut up. "She was locked in the elevator with Joel for quite a while."

"How would you know that?" I slammed the pants back on the rack.

"The house isn't *that* big, and the help talks. Your sisters talk. Alisa noticed and she told me when I got back from work."

"Alisa is like ten, what does she know? She's still mourning the breakup of One Direction, so she's obviously not thinking clearly."

"She saw you go into the elevator pushing Joel's wheelchair and said the elevator didn't go anywhere, and you were in there a while."

"That's ridiculous. I was helping him to his room, then we discussed my job and his accident. Remember, he was coming to serve me when he was hit by that car. It was my fault."

My mother held up her hand. "Sophia, have you learned

nothing from me? He belongs to someone else. I raised you better than this. You've seen the results of this. A man who looks elsewhere when he's engaged is not a good catch."

"Mom, nothing happened. Nothing is happening."

"And nothing ever will," Gia said. "He's in love with Quinn."

"He's not!" I couldn't help myself. "I mean, they don't seem right together. They don't connect. I've never even seen them kiss."

My mom looked at me as if I'd gone to the fantasy suite on the Bachelor and come out bragging about it. "The smartest thing you can do in life is learn from me. I held a torch for a man who was incapable of loving me. I wasted decades of my life. You're an heiress soon and the entire world is at your fingertips. Don't they have some kind of upscale dating app for women like you?"

"Mom, I'm not meeting someone on a dating app."

"What's wrong with a dating app?" Gia asked. "It's better than hitting up your half-sister's invalid beau. He can't even roll away from you."

"Gia, shut it. I just wanted to look nice for our first family business dinner. Joel won't even be there!"

"Maybe you should spend a few more days at home," Mom said.

As usual, shopping with my mom and Gia was a bust. But not for the typical reasons this time.

"These clothes are fine," I said to my mom. "I'm going home."

"You're not going anywhere until you have a week of outfits picked out."

"Mom, do the math. Two of these outfits cost what we brought. Besides, I can't waste money like this."

"Sophia, it's important to me that you go to this dinner in one of these outfits, okay? It's important to me," Mom said.

"Why does it matter to you, Mom?"

"Because I won't have my girls seen as less than those vapid socialites we've watched grow up on the society page. My girls are as good—no, they're better than anyone that man raised, and I intend to prove it. If it takes ridiculously expensive clothes for a seat at the table, so be it."

I wished she didn't care. I wished she would take us to TJ Maxx and let us shop until our hearts' content and feel good about it. That's who our mother was, and I didn't like this change in her—this competitive streak I didn't know existed. I'd never seen her care what anyone thought, much less these interlopers who had taken me away from my family and placed me in what seemed to be a very fancy lunatic asylum.

I tried clothes on until my body should have been in traction. I got a few Brandon Maxwell dresses, designer blouses, some Chloe pegged slacks, which were seven hundred and fifty dollars and would have been seventeen bucks at Marshall's. But I didn't argue.

Mom handed Elaine the cash and put the rest on her credit card. I would hate to see that bill. And who knew Mom had that much credit? But I left my good sweatshirt in the pile that Elaine promised to have delivered to the mansion with all of the rest of the wardrobes we purchased.

"Now that I know your style, I'll keep an eye out for new outfits," Elaine said as she opened the door for us.

"Please do that," Mom told her.

When we left, Gia wore a black pair of vegan leather pants by a designer I'd never heard of, a Stella McCartney blouse, and these to-die-for ankle wrap heels by Fendi. She looked as if she'd just stepped off the runway, and I wondered how someone who looked exactly like me could sport that kind of style while I'd just look like I was playing dress-up.

I fell in love with a pair of Frame skinny jeans that hugged every curve like a Porsche hugs the road. Elaine paired it with a bulky sweater with oversized buttons from Top Shop, and to finish off the look, I slipped into the taupe Chanel ballet flats and made them my own.

For as much as I protested, I felt like a million bucks when we entered the limo provided for us to get home. My mood quickly dropped. Mom still wore the same old worn black jeans and fake Vera Bradley purse, now empty of its ill-gotten gain.

"Mom, we didn't get you anything," I said. "And if anyone is going on a dating app, it's you. It's time."

"It's past time," Gia agreed.

Chapter Fourteen

My life goal was to restore families, but my own seemed like a disjointed and lost cause. Some puzzle pieces didn't belong together, and no matter how I jammed them to fit, little slivers of light showed through the cracks. Once back in the mansion, I knew I'd left traditional Sunday dinner behind in lieu of the formal charade where five strangers masqueraded as family.

For my first family meeting playing the role of heiress, the stylist chose a black pencil skirt, above-the-knee boots, and a Chanel belt that cinched me tightly in the waist. I felt quite scandalous in it, but it seemed the perfect ensemble with my treacherous new responsibilities.

"You look amazing," Alisa said from her bed. She was on her stomach with her chin on her fists. "My mom took my check and put it in some college fund," she scoffed. "As if I'm going to college."

"You should go to college," I told her. "Having money is no substitute for ignorance."

"Sophia!" Gia hissed.

"What?" I asked Gia. "College grows you as a human. I want her to have everything life can offer her. She can go to some Ivy League school and—"

"I'm not really college material." Alisa sat up and swung her legs around to the front of her bed. "I wasn't really high school material either, but Mom said I had to finish that."

Since I'd been gone for two days, Alisa had someone drag her bed into our room and now we were three. Gia, Alisa and me. Alisa's wall made the entire suite feel like an expansive dorm room. She'd tacked up Shawn Mendes and Post Malone posters and pressed little clear clips that held twinkle lights across the entire wall.

"So now we live in a giant Instagram backdrop?"

"Yeah," Alisa said. "Isn't it cool? I went viral this week. Changed my name and I tagged Quinn and Brinn. Picked up 50,000 followers—in one week!"

Alisa may have sounded like a ditz, but I'd checked her Instagram, and she was no rookie. She was wildly creative and her feed was a work of art. She knew how to connect to her followers and she genuinely had the opportunity to be a social media influencer at her age.

Gia obviously enjoyed being a mother figure to Alisa, and I felt like a third wheel, so I made the immediate decision to have my things transferred to my own room. The noises in the mansion no longer scared me—not as much as running into my birth father and his wife did. I wouldn't have the same stellar view, but I could still see the Golden Gate and I imagined myself reading *Jane Eyre* in the chaise by the bank of bay windows.

I had to romanticize unemployment until I found a way for Bobbi to take me back. My ribs burned with pain at the thought. Bobbi wasn't going to ever let me near that place.

"I think I should have my own room so you two have more space. I'll have my things moved."

"No!" Alisa wailed. "We have plenty of space. This room is bigger than my apartment with my mom. I want my sissies here," she said in a baby voice. "Come on, Sophia, this is going to be fun, like a giant slumber party. We're getting to know each other."

I hardened my heart against her obvious manipulation. "I'll spend plenty of time here, Alisa, I promise. But I want to be able to flick the light on at night and read. I haven't been sleeping since my rib got cracked." I unzipped my skirt again, utterly enthralled by the quality of the zipper. "Who knew they made zippers that slide like this? Check it out!" I thrust my hip toward Gia and zipped up and down again. "This thing is on rails."

"What about that material?" Gia asked. "The construction on that garment is ah-mazing. I was born for good clothes—I have no idea why God had me born poor." Gia laughed. "What was I thinking, that tailoring could take the place of these epic raw materials?"

"You were thinking we were lower middle class in San Francisco?"

Gia shrugged. "There's that."

"What if we don't make the year and get the inheritance?" I panicked briefly. "A Ross zipper is never going to feel right again."

"Relax," Alisa said. "We're going to get the money. It's a year of dinners together and remodeling this old haunted castle. How hard could it be?"

Out of the mouths of babes, I thought, and not for the first time. The Wentworth family dysfunction was about to show Alisa how difficult it could be. Airtight wills did not stop greedy relatives from securing dirty lawyers and allowing settlements to drag on for decades. Alisa might be collecting social security before the big money came in, but for Gia and me, the stipend alone was enough. More than enough.

* * *

The formal dining room seated twenty, but Mrs. Chen had set the heavy wood table at one end. Five places were set with heirloom china on top of elaborately beaded gold chargers. The tablecloth was a salmon color. Gold linen napkins were rolled in the center of the plates and secured with sapphire rings. Candles glowed against the honey-colored wood walls and multi-colored floral settings picked up all of the hues of the china.

"This is lovely, Mrs. Chen," I told her.

She shrugged. "Mr. Wentworth used to eat this way every night. He preferred a formal dinner. He said it made people aspire to act better." Mrs. Chen gave my dress the once-over. "Did you borrow something from Gia?"

"No." I touched the Chanel belt. "It's mine. My mother took us shopping yesterday."

"Hmm," Mrs. Chen sniffed. She was not impressed by the label, nor the outfit.

Brinn came into the grand dining room after me. Lately, she always looked as if she needed a good scrubbing. She was blonde like her sister, but the color had grown out. It had a brassy brown tone to it and always looked disheveled like she was in an eighties cover band. This look was new, and I wondered what contributed to it. Of all the sisters, I felt sorriest for Brinn.

She'd been in graduate school for finance before her grandfather passed. Graduation would have to wait. It shocked me that her grandfather would put her education on hold for this ridiculous farce of a family coming together. Finance was already her second choice after she'd shattered an ankle and lost her ballet career. Today, the setbacks looked as if they were taking a toll on her person. She'd gained weight and didn't seem to put in any effort to her appearance. Tonight, she wore black jeans with a black stretchy top and a long strand of pearls thrown on haphazardly as if to cover a multitude of fashion sins.

Quinn, on the other hand, took to money naturally. She had her mother's movie star good looks and hung with the polo set. Brinn was too serious for that life to satisfy her and currently, depression seemed to follow her like the San Francisco fog.

"Hey," Brinn said as she came in.

"Hey," I answered.

"Just us so far, huh?"

"Alisa and Gia are almost ready."

"You three are having a slumber party up there, huh?"

"That's what Alisa suggested." I smiled. "But I'm moving into my own room tomorrow. It's a bit crowded in there, and Alisa seems to really love Gia."

"Cool," Brinn said without inflection. "So that means you're the other one—"

"Sophia," I reminded her. "I wear the glasses." *And dress like a bum usually.* "Gia has them, but she generally wears contacts all day. They annoy me."

"Oh right."

Quinn swept in without a word. She wore flowing white slacks with a white silk shirt boasting huge, black polka dots. She carried a large manila envelope and set it at the head of the table. I resented her power move.

Gia and Alisa came in and sat beside me. Clearly, lines were drawn. Now all five of us were at the table. No one said a thing to each other. Watching Quinn ignore us all and play on her phone filled me with rage for some reason. She was so arrogant and sure of herself. Why? Because she was born with a silver spoon? She'd be in spork territory soon enough if not for the rest of us.

I stood up with a clatter. "We're in this together as equal partners. Why is Quinn in charge of everything?" I stared at the envelope. "Maybe the agenda should go to the woman with a job. Or design experience. Either way, both of those people are Gia. What has Quinn done to warrant being in charge of this fiasco?"

Gia's eyes were enormous when I looked at her.

"Gia, do you want to run the meeting?" Quinn asked. "By all means, run the meeting. Do you know what you're supposed to do? Because have at it. I certainly have better things to do than redecorate this house."

Gia stood, and her chair scraped along the wood floor. "Sophia, can I talk to you outside for a minute please?" Gia said in her soft, wait-for-it-I'm-going-to-kill-you voice.

I followed her out of the oversized dining room, and she slid the pocket door closed behind us. She turned on her heels and hissed at me like a snake. "What the heck are you doing?"

"I think it's just stupid that—"

"No, I'm not really asking what you think. I'm asking you why you are making that excruciating situation last any longer than it has to. Do you give a rat's behind how this museum house is decorated?"

"No, but I just don't see—"

"I don't need one more thing on my plate, do you see that? Miss pony-slash-sweater-set can take a day off from riding her fifty-thousand-dollar horse to go over some plumbing designs, no?"

"No?" I said meekly.

"Yes. Yes, she can. Then neither you nor I will be bothered with it. We just sign off on whatever she says at the family dinners and we're done. The year goes by. You get your own center to help underprivileged children, and I get more rich friends to lend quality textiles to the museum. Capiche?" Gia straightened her jacket at her hips with a sharp, angry move. "Now, get in there and shut up so we can get this dinner over with."

"Joel said—"

"Ahh," Gia nodded her head, leaned back on her heel and crossed her arms. "That's what this is about. Joel the Archangel. I should've known that you couldn't possibly get that excited over house plans."

"No."

"Sophia, he's engaged to your sister. Would you steal my fiancé?"

I thought about it for too long.

"You wouldn't!" Gia exclaimed. "This is just a crush. I'll grant you there's a visceral connection between the two of you, but it will pass. You'll look back and wonder how you were ever attracted to him at all. He's just your latest broken bird, and you want to fix him. When he's all mended and better, you won't look twice at him."

Somehow, I doubt that.

"She doesn't deserve Joel, Gia. She didn't even stay at the hospital when he got hit by a car. Who does that?"

"It's none of your business. Do you understand that?"

I thrust my fist to my hips. I understand it. But I don't like it.

"You're right. You're totally right. I'm not thinking straight."

"None of us are. How could we? But Quinn is the oldest—"

I opened my mouth to remind her we were the oldest, but she stopped me with her hand.

"The oldest that our grandfather knew and trusted. Since when do you want to be in charge anyway?"

I didn't want to be in charge. I wanted Gia to be in charge. *Like she always is.*

"Is something the matter?" Bradley Wentworth, a.k.a. our donor, approached us under the rotunda at the base of the stairs. Gia and I both became silent. Even after everything I knew about him, I couldn't deny he had a regal presence about him. Not just the fact that he was excruciatingly handsome for his age, but he had an ability to change the energy of a room when he walked into it. I wondered if there was a painting hidden somewhere in the basement that showed his true age. I wanted to chalk it up to plastic surgery, but it wasn't that. Bradley showed his age, but in that way that gave him more power and sophistication. His height only deepened his hypnotic influence, and I could see what Mama saw in him.

"Everything is fine," Gia said, unmoved by his magnetism.

"You're not really planning to stay here for an entire year," he said as if he'd already packed our bags for us. "I haven't seen the will, but I'm certain alterations could be made. The law is a living, breathing entity. It's meant to change with circumstances."

"Unlike one's moral standards," Gia answered. "The will requires us to stay."

"Your presence makes my wife uncomfortable," Bradley said.

"Does it?" Gia asked. "I suppose that's an added bonus."

"Girls, I'm going to explain something to you. This isn't easy for me to say, but I genuinely care about you and I don't want to see you get hurt. You're not getting this money. Living here won't make you a Wentworth, no more than standing in the garage makes you a car. Breeding trumps legal red tape."

"Does it?" Gia asked. "Then, we'll win there too because we were raised by decent people. Upstanding people."

Bradley pursed his lips. He'd clearly lost patience because Gia hadn't given in to him. He honestly thought he could simply speak the words and make us go away as if the will never existed. "We can fix this with the lawyers. You both know what the right thing to do is. You'll sign over that money to my family and this travesty of justice can end. Why in heaven's name would you two think you had any right to this money? From a man you never even met."

"I believe it's because your father wanted to do right by us before he met his maker. Why would you take his dying wish from him?"

"Girls—"He gave a slight smile.

"Your soft, calm demeanor may affect the other women in your life, but you're going to have to work harder with Sophia, Alisa and me. We've lived in the real world." Gia gripped my wrist. "The will states that the daughters can vote and have you removed from Wentworth Manor, so I'd ask that in the future, you'd stop harassing my sister and me."

"Harassed? You come in my house—"

"You're skating on thin ice, Bradley. Or should I say Breedly? You're very good at that aspect of life, but we won't be turned away as easily as our mother. We see who you are."

I gasped. *I can't believe she said it out loud. That's our private name for him.*

He leaned in and whispered something to Gia. I could tell by her lack of expression it scared her, but he'd never know it. No one had a poker face like Gia.

"Is everything all right here?" Joel rolled up in his wheelchair.

It was obvious he and Bradley didn't think much of one another. Joel seemed to have the same vaccine that Gia did. He was untouched by Bradley's hypnotic presence. I could only dream of being freed of it—and Joel's too.

"Are you ever going home?" Bradley asked Joel. "It's as if my house has been invaded."

"I'm engaged to your daughter. So probably not. From what I understand, your daughters are the rightful owners of this home now. If their presence bothers you, perhaps it's time for you and your wife to go back to the penthouse on Nob Hill."

"My daughter isn't marrying you, Joel. No matter how you've managed to pull the wool over her eyes. She's just lost her grandfather. You took advantage of her grief."

"Do you really want to go there, Brad? I was invited here."

Bradley reached out to grab Joel's shoulders, and I shot between them, hovering over Joel's body cast. "Get out of here, or I swear the first thing on tonight's agenda will be getting you out of this mansion. Do you understand me?"

Both Gia and Bradley stared at me with their mouths gaping wide. I felt Joel's hand lightly brush against mine, and it filled me with even more fire. One just didn't pick on someone in a wheelchair who couldn't defend himself.

Mrs. Chen emerged from the dining room and stared at the men. "Dinner is on the table. You two get out of here!"

It was then I noticed the grand rug from the foyer was gone. In its place the wood was darkened. I imagined my sister had a new display item at the museum.

As we walked back to the dining room, Gia shoved me into a small portico with a house phone in it. "Enough with Joel, Sophia. I mean it. You get yourself fixated on saving people and you throw yourself to the wolves. First that kid Oliver becomes an obsession to the point where you got yourself beat up and lost your job. And now this whole thing with Joel. It's not your job to save the world. Stand up for yourself, not these random strays! If

Joel is vapid enough to fall for Quinn, he deserves her. Let's go get this dinner over with."

As we walked out of the portico, my eyes caught Joel's. I couldn't explain it, but something didn't add up, and I was determined to get to the bottom of it.

Chapter Fifteen

We entered the candle-lit dining room as coolly as possible. I was beyond annoyed with Gia. She was everyone's hero but mine. She assumed the worst with Joel, and it didn't sit well with me. She should have known nothing would happen with Joel. Even if Quinn didn't want him, I knew my place. It was obvious to anyone with eyeballs, yet Gia was determined to make me the scandalous other woman just because we had a perfectly innocent conversation in the elevator. Just like all of my other crushes in recent history, my obsession with Joel would go nowhere.

But I still didn't want him to marry Quinn. He deserved better.

"Excuse us," Gia said as she sat next to Quinn. *Her new favorite?*

I could play her game, so I sat at the other end of the table. "Did we miss anything?"

Quinn inclined her head. "Now that we're all here, Mrs. Chen will begin serving. She's going to bring everything family-style so we are not interrupted."

Mrs. Chen and someone I'd never seen before brought in a mix of salads, crab cakes, and a charcuterie board that made it seem as if we all belonged to the cheese-of-the-month club.

"We won't be working on the house remodel tonight, nor the gala I've planned to introduce ourselves to San Francisco society," Quinn said. "Mr. Trunkett has called an emergency meeting to tell us something urgent."

I had to admit, Gia and I knew nothing about house remodels, galas or Mr. Trunkett, so maybe she was in charge for a reason. I didn't have to like it though. I crossed my arms in front of me like a toddler.

Mr. Trunkett shuffled into the room from a side door I hadn't noticed before. He always appeared like he was at death's door and had once again risen from his crypt for one last meeting before his official retirement. His pallor had a blueish hue that made him more ghostly than ever, especially in the creepy old house.

"Ladies," he said as he sat with his ratty, leather briefcase before him.

"Hello, Mr. Trunkett." We all greeted him in unison like a bad remake of that movie, *Charlie's Angels*.

"I know you girls haven't had a chance to get to know one another well yet. Sophia, I was very sorry to hear of your misfortune."

I wished I could disappear into the woodwork. "Thank you."

He unwrapped his leather satchel and placed a single sheet of paper on the table. "Before you plan the events necessary, I have the results of the DNA tests that were court-ordered by your father."

The room became eerily quiet.

"The results are quite astonishing," he said.

"He's our father?" Quinn looked to Brinn. "He's surely our father."

"I am happy to report that he is the father of each and every of you. Paternity has been established with ninety-nine point nine percent accuracy for all five of you young ladies. Bradley is indeed your father."

We all breathed a sigh of relief and for some reason I

wondered why any of us were happy to claim this creep as our dad, but I suppose the devil you know is better than the devil you don't.

"I haven't shared the results with Bradley yet, as I wanted to speak to all of you about the surprising results that we received during the testing. It will be up to you to decide how to proceed, and I have no plans to make the results public. I cannot promise what your dad or Chelsea might do when they learn these results."

"What surprising results?" I asked. "It seems it's turned out exactly as we expected it to. Exactly how our grandfather, Wyatt Wentworth, expected it to turn out."

"Not quite," Mr. Trunkett paused and looked at each and every one of us in the eye before he went on. "It seems that Bradley Wentworth is not, in fact, the biological son of Wyatt Wentworth, Senior. Therefore, that means none of you are Wentworths by birth or ancestry."

It was as if he'd dropped a bomb. We all gasped, but no one had the breath to question anything at first. Not Wentworths. It didn't seem possible.

Gia recovered first. "Well, Amelie Wentworth, sweet Christian woman," she said. "You little minx."

"Quiet," Quinn said. "There must be some mistake. My grandparents were so in love. I never saw such love."

"That's how you should remember them," Mr. Trunkett said. "We know that Wyatt, Jr. was in fact Wyatt's natural-born son because of his blood type and the rare condition he inherited, but we are not sure who fathered Bradley at this time. Your true ancestry remains a mystery."

The saintly Amelie—the reason Wyatt wanted to do the right thing by his granddaughters, legitimate or not—wasn't the religious heroine her legacy made her out to be.

"Did Grandfather know this?" Quinn asked.

Mr. Trunkett shrugged his shrunken shoulders. "I don't know the answer to that question. I can only tell you that I'm reasonably sure that Bradley didn't know this, and it's going to be difficult for him to process. Before I go ahead and give Bradley the results, I wanted to get your feedback on the way you'd like me to proceed."

"Hah, can we do it on national television?" Gia whispered to me.

"Since you were all named in the will, whether related by blood or not, nothing has changed from your standpoint. However, things may change significantly for Bradley's claim on the estate, and I'd like to give my advice on how to proceed. He would legally be considered the son as Amelie was married to Wyatt Senior at the time of his birth, but—"

Alisa whistled. "Yeah, I mean, what's the best way to tell someone their life is a total lie? Quick like ripping off the Band-Aid or slow and painfully learning your mom wasn't the angel you thought she was? Not a lot of choices there. I mean, both totally suck."

Mr. Trunkett tried to hide his lack of patience for the young Alisa. "If this proceeds to court as your father wants it to, this will all come out and it could open the door for any number of shysters. The will is iron-clad, but that doesn't mean people can't bring frivolous lawsuits against the estate which will cost you both time and money."

"That's why we're here." Gia heaved a huge sigh. "The only reason Sophia and I came to Wentworth Manor was because we couldn't afford to fight Bradley's lawsuits. You're saying there could be more?" She dropped her forehead in her hands and spoke to the table. "Greed is sickening. Going to work has already been a problem for me with the photographers trying to take pictures of me as the supposed heiress." She lifted her head. "They've been snapping pictures of our mom at the restaurant as the wanton woman who failed to get her man."

"They've been calling my mom 'the side piece' and shouting rude questions at her," Alisa said. "Any way you look at it, this isn't good."

"This scandal might make our lives unbearable. We never asked for this life, Mr. Trunkett." Gia slammed her hand to the table, and the silverware rattled. "What good is all this money if I can't live the life I want to live? How can we get off this crazy ride?"

"Everything in the dark comes to light," I said. "The truth will come out eventually about Bradley's paternity. I see no reason to lie about it now."

"I don't want any of you to lie." Mr. Trunkett cleared his throat in that way he had that made him sound as if the cough would kill him. "However, I think it may be best if your father's paternity does not come out for public consumption right away. I would offer him and his lawyers the same advice, but I cannot promise they will take it. I wanted you all to be prepared."

How ironic that the father who ignored Gia and me for being "illegitimate" would have to wear the title himself. A slow Grinch smile took hold at the thought, which probably made me a terrible person, but it was the truth regardless. How I'd love to be a fly on the wall when Bradley learned his "old money" image was as bogus as his plastic smile. I secretly hoped they found out his father was the stable boy—which again, probably made me a terrible person, but there it was.

"It's going to be very difficult on Bradley," Mr. Trunkett said.

"Cry me a river," Gia said.

I also refused to feel sorry for Bradley. "I vote for the Band-Aid," I said. "The sooner he knows, the sooner he can drop this ridiculous lawsuit, and we can get on with improving this house. Our grandfather gave us a task, and the sooner it's done, the sooner we can all go back to our own lives." I looked at Quinn and felt my heart squeeze. "Quinn can marry Joel. Brinn can do whatever it is Brinn does, and Alisa can grow her followers with fabulous new clothes and vacations."

"Oh my gosh, I so can't wait!" Alisa puckered her lips. "I'm going to create my own makeup line. Kylie Jenner look out! I'm going to have Lips by Alisa kiosks in every airport across the country."

What a goal.

Quinn scowled at me. "For your information, Brinn is a prima ballerina and she's a graduate student in finance at UC San Diego. Well, she was until Grandfather passed, but she'll go back as soon as all this is over."

"I'm sorry, Brinn." I said honestly. "I knew that. You're very accomplished, and I'm just angry that this money and lawsuits have taken over our lives. It's not your fault."

Brinn ignored my apology. "Wyatt is the only father Daddy has ever known. He'll be crushed. All he ever wanted was to impress Grandfather. He's already been blindsided by being left out of the will in this way. How much more can he take?"

I wanted to be decent and care about poor Bradley Wentworth and the lies he'd been told, but then I thought about the times we couldn't afford new shoes and how he never cared.

"I'm sure he will be crushed, but it doesn't make it less true." I pressed my glasses to my face forcefully. "Get it over with quickly and he can start the healing process. It's not like he ever thought about how tough he made life for us, did he? Maybe this is payback. You reap what you sow and all that."

"He's already been made to feel awkward in the house," Brinn said angrily. "Does he really need to know that he's not really a Wentworth?"

"I'm afraid he does have to know," Mr. Trunkett said. "He's the one who got the court order and he's entitled to the results. I'd like your permission to tell him before we are in front of a judge and it becomes a public spectacle."

"Who knows about this?" Gia asked.

"Only the lab and the people in this room. Bradley wasn't given the results because they didn't want him to have a chance to doctor them."

"My dad would not do that!" Brinn said. "You're all awful

people if you think my dad would do that. He's been the most amazing father, and you're all just jealous!"

"He would totally do that," Gia said. "He only ordered these paternity tests to try and destroy the will's contents, even though it says paternity didn't matter. Wake up!" She shouted at Brinn. "I know he's your father and all, but we are all proof positive that he is far from perfect. Bradley does what he wants, and you come second, whether you believe it or not. He'd take this money from you as easily as he'd take it from us."

"That's what makes me wonder if Grandfather knew," Quinn said. "Why else would he say paternity didn't matter when he gave away his billions?"

"Bradley has got to be told as soon as possible," Gia said in her matter-of-fact tone. "I think Mr. Trunkett should tell him privately and give him a chance to drop this ridiculous lawsuit."

"He won't drop it." Brinn looked down at her clutched hands.

"Why not?" I asked her.

She looked at me and sighed. "Because he's got nothing else to do, and he thinks the money is his."

It was clear that she loved her father, but she knew exactly who he was. That had to be hard. At least Gia and I could loathe him from afar.

"I'll tell him," Quinn said.

"I'd like to be with you," Mr. Trunkett said. "I want to answer any legal questions that may arise. And also let him know it's best for him to drop his lawsuit, and we will keep the information about his paternity in the family."

I hadn't known my father long, but he didn't seem to have any shame. I wasn't hopeful this nightmare would end with him knowing the truth.

"For now, this information stays within this room. No one tells a soul, is that clear?" Mr. Trunkett wheezed the words. "I'll set up a meeting and get back with you, Quinn."

We all nodded. The love of money truly was the root of all

evil. Mr. Trunkett left the single sheet of paper on the table and stood to go, but Quinn stopped him.

"Before you go, Mr. Trunkett, the girls and I have been discussing our first appearance together as a unified group. We'd like to have our first soiree and announce our plans for the house remodel and our future."

I looked at Gia, and she smiled as if to say, yes, this was decided without you.

"I meant to comment how much restraint you young ladies had shown in keeping all this out of the public eye for this long. Especially you, Miss Alisa, with all of your followers. My office tells me you've been quite reserved in your feed, as it were."

"It's time," Quinn gave a nod of her chin for emphasis. "People are asking at the club, and I can only ride off on my horse so many times before people catch on. Certainly, there are rumors about the inheritance, but we will have a unified story by the time the party is given."

Quinn mystified me. She was naturally "old money," and she wore her wealth with ease. I had to wonder if she was our grandfather's favorite and if he hadn't wanted to leave it all to her at one point.

"Once we discuss this with your father, I see no trouble with the sisters presenting a united front. I think it's a wonderful idea." He smiled as if it was the first good news he'd had all day.

"We are planning it for the end of January, after the ballet's opening night gala."

"Wonderful. I'll be in touch." Mr. Trunkett had never removed his jacket during our meeting. It made me wonder if he slept and showered in his suit.

"Do you think we could speak privately for a moment?" Quinn asked me.

I looked to Gia, but she was taking pictures of Alisa, who was posed against the exposed brick of the dining room wall. "Sure," I finally answered.

The food, including the charcuterie plate, went mostly

uneaten. None of us had any appetite. We were forced together as surely as if we shared a jail cell.

I looked to Gia. What could Quinn possibly have to tell me? I silently prayed that it was Joel had broken off the engagement. Then, I sank deeper into my chair. It was as if I'd already been poisoned by the Wentworth curse—what I wanted seemed to matter more than the feelings of others.

Chapter Sixteen

I followed Quinn into a floral sitting room that I'd never noticed before. "This house is unreal. It goes on forever. It's like someone is creating rooms and adding them overnight."

"It's not that big," Quinn said. "When the remodel starts it won't seem big enough."

The mahogany ceiling and walls in the room had already been painted over with a soft white and creamy yellow. Floral accents gave the room an updated, spring-like flair. Elongated sofas were set into an L-pattern and were decorated in large periwinkle and cream stripes. I sat on one edge and she sat on the other so that we faced each other in the corners where the sofas met.

Up close, Quinn wasn't as stunning as her mother. She had a slightly crooked nose and a fuller face void of the high cheekbones her mother and sister possessed. She had the body of a horse-woman. She was lithe with muscular quads and a rounded derriere.

"I owe you an apology," Quinn said abruptly while I still scrutinized her up close.

"For what?" I asked her.

"I judged you and your sister harshly when you came to the

house originally. I don't like change, and everything in my world changed in one day."

"Mine too," I reminded her.

"I understand, but I thought yours changed for the better and mine changed for the worse and now I know that isn't true."

I shook my head. "No, it's not."

"Joel told me you lost your job."

"I deserved to," I admitted. "I didn't follow protocol."

"He also told me how kind you were to him after he'd been hit by the car outside your office."

It suddenly felt hot in the room, and I felt my face flush from guilt. "It was traumatizing. I don't think I was myself, but I couldn't leave his side. Thanks for saying all this. It's really big of you." I stood to leave when Quinn grabbed my wrist.

"Sit down, please. There's more."

Here it comes. Stay away from my fiancé. I see your pathetic attempt at flirtation. I'd better stop before I ended up in a chokehold.

She drew in a deep breath. "I haven't known him that long, but Joel means the world to me."

I laughed uncomfortably. "I'm sure he does. He's your fiancé."

"Joel saved my life once, Sophia. And you saved his—"

"I really didn't," I held her hand as she held mine. It was awkward as anything, but I couldn't let go. "Joel was hit by that car, and my boss called the police. I stood and did nothing really."

"He said you were very comforting to him and that you kept him awake when all he wanted to do was sleep."

"I tried to keep him talking." I shrugged. "Anyone would have tried."

"Anyone would not have stood in a filthy San Francisco street and kept him talking. I don't believe that for an instant."

I felt sick to my stomach pining over Joel. Quinn wasn't the ice princess I imagined to her to be, and I was starting to see why

Joel loved her. It took a big person to apologize to me. Especially when it wasn't deserved.

"I hope that you're not angry that I showed up in the hospital. It had to be unnerving to find me there," I told her. "I hope we can move on from that. I was trying to make sure he wasn't alone."

Her breathing became labored, and she closed her eyes and focused on it for a moment. "What I'm about to tell you can't leave this room, Sophia. You can't tell Gia. You can't tell your mom. You can't tell anyone. Do you understand?" She gripped my wrist tighter.

I was so hungry for information in that moment that I would have agreed to anything, but she didn't ask for my firstborn, so the answer was easy. "I promise." I pressed my forefinger in front of my closed lips. "I won't breathe a word. Unless it's a danger to you or others, then I'm legally a mandated reporter."

She drew in a jagged breath. "I can't tell you why Joel is here, but it's pertinent that he remains here in the house with us. Do you understand?"

"I think so."

"I've been keeping this to myself since Grandpa died, and I hadn't realized the toll it was taking on me."

"Quinn?"

"Joel isn't really my fiancé."

"Did you break up?" The lump in my throat rose like a buoy. "I didn't—"

"It's not like that. It was never what you'd call a love match. We're together for a reason."

"Is it ever in this realm? I assumed that's how rich people did it. They made alliances."

"It's not 1740s France, Sophia. We are allowed to marry who we fall in love with," Quinn said, offended. "If I can't come to conclusions about your lifestyle, I hope you'll try and do the same for us."

"I will," I promised. After flirting with her man, it was the least I could do. "You're in love with Joel. As is should be. I didn't mean to—"

"That's why Grandpa wrote the will the way he did. We can't get married until the year is up so Joel had time."

"Time?"

She shook her head and lowered her voice. "Just a minute. I'm going to check the doors." She rose and walked around the room checking the latches on all of the doors. "I picked this room because there are no cameras in here." She sat back down and grabbed for my hands again. "I promised Joel that I'd tell you that he's an amazing man. He's a one-woman guy, and he's very loyal. He's put himself in harm's way for me many times, and I know he'd do the same for any of us."

"You want me to stay away from him," I told her. "It looks bad. Listen, I completely understand, and I'm so sorry if I overstepped my boundaries. It can't be easy to wait to marry the man you love." Even as I said the words, my soul ached at the idea of her marry him.

"He's not in love with me, silly. He's doing a job." Quinn looked around and then came closer to me with her hands still clutched around mine. "He says you have him turned inside out, and he worried that it would show, so he told me. He said he's never felt this way before, and if he had to go on pretending with you, he'd have to give up the assignment."

"What?" I exhaled a choking sob that I immediately regretted. My heart began to race.

"You can't tell anyone. Least of all, our father and my mother."

"Why are you telling me this? Who is Joel? Why would you lie about this?" The questions came tumbling out of me in rapid succession like a faucet I couldn't shut off.

"I'm telling you because I can actually feel the chemistry between you two, and I find it humiliating as the woman he's supposed to love. But what's worse is we will have to start all over again if Joel has to leave. I can't have that happen."

"Now it's me who is sorry. I never meant—"

She brushed her hand in the air. "It's not your fault. He's here to protect us. That's all I can say for now. No one but you knows that he's not really my fiancé. Not even Brinn—though she'll be the first to tell you he's completely wrong for me." She laughed, and it was the first true sign I'd seen of her young age. Now that she was closer, I saw that she carried the weight of the world on her shoulders.

I couldn't even fully comprehend what she was telling me. Was anyone what they seemed in this strange new world? I'd go to my own room tonight and digest it piece by piece. But for now, it meant our chemistry wasn't forbidden. Our connection was genuine. Even if I had to hide my feelings, the fact that they were permitted made everything feel brighter as if rays of sunshine laid a path before me. Briefly, I wondered if this was all some elaborate test of my character. Maybe Quinn had hatched some dark revenge plot.

"Joel trusts you, and he asked me to tell you the truth. He said he didn't want you thinking he was a player or that he was haphazard with his emotions."

"I didn't do anything to be ashamed—"

Quinn's grip on my hand tightened. "Relax. I'm not accusing you of anything. I'm just asking that you both tone it down. I know that kind of chemistry is hard to deny or fake, but for our safety, I ask that you keep it behind closed doors."

"I promise!" But my heart felt so light and alive inside that I wondered if I could contain the secret.

Joel worried that I'd think he was just a flirt. Everything around me took on a brilliant hue as if the stars themselves were shining in the sitting room. *I didn't imagine what's between us.*

"The night you went to that crazy woman's house, and he sent the police after you—"

"Joel sent the police after me that night!" *How had I not figured that out?*

"He called right after you left," she said. "He memorized the address from your phone call. He would have gone himself naturally, but the wheelchair—"

I didn't know what to do with the excess energy this news gave me. I supposed I'd have to find a treadmill somewhere in the mansion, but I felt as if I was walking on air. I'd been looking after myself since I was a small child. I'd never known what it felt like to have someone worry for me like this, and it felt like heaven.

"He sent the police," I said again. "I needed the police! He's so amazing." In my mind, I wondered how could Quinn not see this? How could she not want him for herself?

"Gross," Quinn said. "He's like a brother to me. Look, you'll need a date for the party in January. It can't be Joel for obvious reasons. Do you need me to find you someone?"

"I'll figure it out. I'm an heiress. How hard can it be to find a date?"

Quinn lifted a brow. "You'd be surprised."

My phone rang, and when I looked at the screen, it was Bobbi. "I need to take this. I promise, your secret is safe with me."

"Not even Gia or Brinn," Quinn reminded me.

I nodded, and she skirted out of the room. "Hello, Bobbi?"

"Thank God you haven't changed your number. I worried after all the press."

"Bobbi, I would give you my new number. Are you calling with news? Any word on my job?"

"It's Sunday night, Sophia. You're still fired. For your information, you can't lose a child from your care, get fired, then illegally enter that child's home as a civilian, cause a police incident and get your job back working with children." She sighed in annoyance. "Did you learn nothing working for me?"

"Your former cop self is showing," I told her.

"Sophia, you know I'd do anything for you, but this is not a quick fix. You nearly got yourself killed, and Oliver is now in protective custody."

"What?" I leaned against the dark wood wall.

"His father is still in custody. He's got a twenty-thousand-dollar bail to raise, and his mother and that man with the meat name are currently waiting to be arraigned for the drugs found in their apartment after your attack."

I slid down the wall. "And I went shopping yesterday." I yanked off the ridiculous belt. "I failed Oliver. I failed Mr. Jessup, and now everything is more broken than when I started."

"You haven't been in the business long enough to trust your intuition. Most of the time it is not as simple as bad parent, good parent. Most of the time they are both jerks in their own way. Your job is to determine where the child is safest even if it's not with a parent."

"I trusted my instinct the other day when I learned Oliver was in an unsafe environment."

"And you broke protocol, and now Oliver is in foster care with no family member to take him. Listen, you'll be a good social worker one day, but the rules exist for a reason. It's not going to be easy to get your job back in the system, but I imagine your recent windfall might help with that."

"Is that why you're calling me? To tell me how I screwed up again?"

"No, I'm calling you because I want you to bail out Mr. Jessup. It's only two thousand dollars, and he's a good man. You'll get it back. Oliver needs his father at home."

"But that's not protocol." I didn't understand what she was trying to tell me. "You just told me not to break protocol."

"It's not protocol, but I've been doing this job for thirty years, and you need to trust *my* instincts even when you can't trust yours."

"This conversation never happened," I told her.

"Precisely." Then, she hung up on me.

I didn't know if I trusted Bobbi's instinct at this point. If life as a Wentworth had taught me anything, it was that everyone seemed to hide a dark side.

Chapter Seventeen

I took the stairs two at a time. I couldn't wait to see Joel and see if anything changed between us now that I was equipped with this amazing new knowledge. I wanted to ask him a million questions before I left the house to bail out Mr. Jessup. I wanted to thank him for saving my hide.

I knew I wasn't the man-stealing sort. It pained me that even Gia didn't believe that, but I was too excited to care.

My things had been moved back to my own room while I was at dinner. *Wealthy people want for nothing.* Other people did life's annoyances. That couldn't be good for human growth or potential.

The view from my room was straight off of a postcard or a famous Instagram post. I couldn't decide whether I enjoyed the fiery red tips of the Golden Gate as it reached for a cloudless, blue sky—or if I preferred the cloaked image at night when the bridge was obscured by the surrounding city lights. At night, the Bay Bridge sparkled like it was the galaxy of stars.

My room was on the northwest corner of the house, and my bed faced the bridge. One of the changes I wanted to make to the mansion was to add automated shades so I could press a button and be greeted by the stunning views. It struck me how easy it was to get spoiled by this lifestyle. Just a few days in the mansion and already I had become too lazy to get up and open my own curtains.

I dug into my purse to check how much cash I had left. Forty-two dollars and some change. Not enough to make bail for Oliver's dad. I couldn't ask Gia; she'd tell me to stay out of it. She would say I'd already caused enough trouble. She'd probably be right.

My cell phone dinged with a text message. From Joel. *You there?*

I'm here. Could I be any more pathetic?

I fell. Can you help me get up?

I paused. It sounded like a ruse, albeit one I was happy to give into. *B right there.*

I snuck down the stairs like I was on a spy mission and stopped when I saw Bradley at Joel's door. The sight unnerved me, and I tip-toed back up the stairs and waited. The knocking stopped, and from my vantage point, I saw Bradley enter his own quarters and shut the door.

I went down the stairs again and quietly knocked at Joel's door. "Joel, it's me," I whispered.

"Come in," he said.

As I opened the door, he was sprawled on the floor partially under the grand mahogany four-poster bed in his room with his casted leg sticking out.

I rushed over to his side. "You really did fall."

"Of course I did. What do you take me for?"

"I just thought—well, I thought maybe you wanted to see me after I heard the truth."

"Shh," he said as if we were being spied upon.

"What was Bradley doing here?"

He shrugged as if he didn't know what I was talking about.

"Bradley was here."

He ignored me again. "I can get up, but I can't reach the brake on my chair, and I can't get to the bed from this position. The chair keeps rolling away."

"I doubt I could either from that position. I haven't run in a week." I tried to make him feel better about himself, but I still questioned what was going on with my father. "Going from athletic to couch potato is not an easy transition."

"That's nice of you to say so, but I'm a slug."

"You're not a slug."

"I'm becoming a slug. You pointed it out yourself when you said I could bite someone for you and that was about it."

"I didn't mean it that way." I looked down at his position and thought about how to get him up to the massive bed. Why hadn't he asked my father for help?

Joel's wheelchair had rolled toward the bathroom, which was all white and gray marble with an original clawfoot tub. I retrieved the chair and parked it alongside him. "This house has a lot of bathrooms for when it was built," I said since we weren't discussing the real reason I was there.

"It does." He grimaced in pain. "Quinn said this was the original master bedroom, so it makes sense. The other side of the house has a better view, though, as you well know. It makes sense Wyatt moved over to that side."

"Is that true?" Our conversation was not only stilted, it was painful. I wanted to come out and ask him what he, Bradley and Quinn were up to, but I knew I'd never get a straight answer.

I should have just stayed in my lane. Just like Gia said. Put your head down and power through the year.

Joel reached for the wheelchair's lower bar. "This sucks," he said as he assessed his situation. "Who knew you relied so heavily on a femur?"

"God, maybe—He made it the biggest bone in the human body so it insinuates that it's going to be an important one."

"*Touché.*"

"We should get a hospital bed in here. This one is much too high for you."

"Do you think?" he asked with a laugh. "By the time I get one delivered, I'll be out of it. This is short-term."

"You do realize that's the position I've seen you in the most? You're so tall, but you are literally always on the ground or down in that chair."

"Does that make you feel superior? Man, talk about hitting a guy when he's down."

Gia would have had the perfect snappy comeback, but I was hurt. "I didn't mean it that way. I don't feel superior to anyone." I propped the pillows against the massive headboard to ready it for him. "Maybe we could get one of those hospital slings to help move you in the future."

He slapped his hand on his chest. "Ouch. You really know how to hurt a guy. No one is transferring me to a bed like a slab of beef. Haven't I endured enough humiliation?"

"I really wouldn't know about the humiliation." I locked his chair and held it in place while I watched him struggle into it. It was one of those swift, athletic looking wheelchairs made of nylon and it didn't seem big enough for him. With a heaving grunt, he lifted himself into the chair and groaned in pain once he was in it. "I'm over this."

"I bet. I only have a cracked rib, and I'm over it. I can't run or laugh without excruciating pain. Your situation is so much worse. You'll be in that cast for a long time yet."

"Some days I wonder if I'll ever be back to rights." He slapped the bed. "One more move. I can ask Mel to come up if it's too weird. I need momentum from behind."

I didn't want him to think I was nervous around him. I wanted to trust him, but Bradley's presence and Quinn's strange confession had done nothing to ease my questions. "No, don't call Mel." I stood at the side of his chair. "It would be weird if he found me here, don't you think?"

He grinned. "I'm not exactly in a position to try anything."

"But maybe I am," I quipped.

He laughed, and the icy chill between us melted slightly. "I can't believe you said that. Hashtag 'me too!'"

That made me laugh. "You're safe," I reassured him.

Joel could flirt all he liked. In fact, he could do a full court press for romance, but I wouldn't fall for his lines any longer. Until I figured out what he and Quinn really wanted from me, I was determined to keep my walls firmly in place. No more shameless jokes.

"This bed though." I stood with my hands on my hips. "It's like straight out of a 17th century castle." I clucked my tongue. "Do you ever wonder how many people have died in it?"

"Really? It's not creepy enough in here with the red damask and frigid air out of that fireplace? You have to bring dead souls walking the night into the equation?"

"I didn't say there were ghosts. Only that there's been a lot of history here." I looked at the bed again. "Where did my grandfather die?"

"In the hospital, Sophia." Joel looked me up and down, then to the height of the mattress. "Maybe this isn't a good idea. You're not exactly hardy, and then you've got that rib. Let's call Mel."

"I'm stronger than I look," I said. I didn't want him thinking I was some wilting daisy just because that was the name of my bedroom. "Let's just do it quickly. You lift off the chair and I'll hoist you from behind. On the count of three."

He raised his arm. "Wait. Give me a minute. I gotta psych myself up for this." He repositioned himself in his chair. "Any word on your job?" he asked while we waited.

We were apparently doing small talk now. "Yes, I'm still fired. Speaking of which, do you happen to have any cash I can borrow?"

"For what? I'm not that kind of lawyer. Not yet."

"I'm going to bail out Oliver's dad. He's been stuck in jail for over five days now."

"Definitely not," he snapped. "You're not going anywhere near that family if I have anything to say about it."

"Well, you don't," I told him. "It's my fault he's in jail."

"Did you kidnap his son?" Joel asked. "You did not. That's why you're here, and he's in jail. Save your money."

"But now the mom is in custody. She must have lied to get full custody in the first place, don't you think? My boss says . . . well, I need to make things right, that's all. I can't stand to think about Oliver in foster care after all he's been through."

"Then don't think about it. Look at what that family has already done to you. You have two cracked ribs, bruised arms and no job. What part of you says, 'Hey, let's go back for more?'"

I grimaced at him. "The part that thinks of what that boy has endured at the hands of his mother and her wicked boyfriend. SpaghettiOs for dinner being the least of their crimes."

"You have no assurance that the dad is any different. Birds of a feather and all that."

"He is different. My boss Bobbi said so, and she's a former cop. She has a sixth sense, I'd swear it."

Joel hoisted himself onto his bed while I held his wheelchair. He breathed a sigh of relief.

I wandered around his grand room. "This room is really dark."

"It's original to the house—'more wood, more better' back then." He smiled that magnetic grin of his. "It showed you had money, I suppose."

"I would think building a mansion in Pacific Heights showed that. This fireplace is fantastic." I ran my fingertips along the carved wood mantel. I answered his question about work without facing him. *No need to taunt myself with those eyes of his.* "Child Protective Services took the little boy from his dad under false pretenses."

"Even if this guy gets out on bail, he's not getting his kid anytime soon, Sophia." Joel punched the pillow behind him. "This guy kidnapped the boy. Then, the mother allows her boyfriend to beat up a state representative? He should have waited for his court date. Like a normal person."

What he said made sense, but I still felt responsible. "Oliver is in foster care because his mother made false allegations against the father of her kid because he was bothersome to her new life. As a man, doesn't that bother you?"

"Not as much as you getting beat on by a man twice your size. That's what bothers me."

"I hate injustice," I said. "But I didn't have a court order to enter Oliver's house so I would have been fired for that—if I hadn't already been fired for his dad kidnapping him."

"That's something, I guess. You killed two birds with one stone. If you're going to leave, go out with a bang I always say."

"I should go."

"Do you know where bail bondman's offices are?"

"No, but I know the city well enough. I'll find it."

"This is not your circus, not your monkeys," Joel shook his head and it was clear I exasperated him. "It's rare that people find themselves as victims in these cases. Maybe the kid's dad is better than the mom, but that's not saying much. I can say without a doubt that this dad isn't worth it."

I felt his eyes following me as I touched everything and scrutinized every painting along the dark paneled walls. "I think I may have prejudged her. The mom. Her boyfriend was bad news, but she doesn't go with her ex." I lifted a framed picture off of a small table. "You know, he's very normal and dresses conservatively and she's all tatted up. That always makes me wonder what happened. He married her for a reason, you know? Was she strait-laced when they met and became wild or did opposites attract? Or was it something more sinister that brought them together?"

"You'd make a good detective," he said. "You do seem to notice everything. But I stand behind my first assessment that they're both bad news, and you'd best stay out of it."

I put the picture down and turned to face him. Joel was so dreamy. I kept thinking I was making too much of him in my overly romantic brain, but every time I looked at him, he epitomized my type of sexy. He possessed a captivating smile that started in his eyes and had the power to light me up from within.

When our eyes met, it felt as if we'd known each other forever, and the slightest touch from him made me feel important—as though I finally mattered to someone.

His blue eyes blazed with a fire. Clearly, he hated being stuck in that bed when I was so headstrong and determined to finish this mission. People would have thought him out of my league, most likely. Now, with a few billion to my name, no one would question it—what a pathetic statement on society. Before the heiress situation, people might have wondered what that man with the perfect jawline and swoon-worthy baby blues was doing with ol' four eyes.

"That first day I saw you at the reading of the will," Joel said. "Everyone was laser focused on Mr. Trunkett, but not you. You took in the whole room, the architecture, the people in it, your sisters, me out in the lobby."

My face went hot. "You noticed that. I thought you looked like my Nonna's picture of Saint Michael. With a short haircut."

"You—I—what?"

I shrugged. "It was stupid. He's the warrior angel, not an innocuous Precious Moments figurine you'd find in a Hallmark store, but strong, mighty. He's the protector. The patron saint of people who do dangerous work like the military or police officers. He's been painted by the great masters, and I thought you looked like the painting my Nonna had on the wall. I thought maybe that's why it felt like I knew you. I've been seeing that painting day in and day out my whole life."

Naturally, I was immediately horrified by this admission, but it was too late.

His gaze warmed even more. "You know a lot about this saint. I should be honored for the comparison, I guess. That must be why Gia keeps calling me Michael."

"My Nonna is really Catholic. Like *really* Catholic. Gia can't hardly say anything in the house without Nonna crossing herself." I stepped toward him. "Do you need anything before I go?"

"Can you help me get these pillows behind me?" Joel motioned for me to come closer and as I did, he swung his arms around my neck. We were face to face now. I felt far too weak to help him at that point. The sharp blue of his eyes rendered me useless.

"I'm sorry. I wasn't ready," I told him.

He slid his arms down, and the electrical current between us followed his touch like a live wire after a storm. *Why not Gia?* I wanted to ask him. *Why did he pick me to flirt with? Am I easy prey?* The newest heiress without an extensive dating history? Men who looked like Joel had never looked at me before. Then there was the whole Quinn being his good friend and not his fiancé fiasco. My father at his door with no answer.

It was all a little too convenient. Life never worked out like that. When you felt someone was too good to be true? You usually ended up with a cast member from *90-Day Fiancé* who looked like Bigfoot and had the charm of Harvey Weinstein but offered the golden ticket—a green card. Was I Joel's symbolic green card? What did he want from me?

"You ready to try again?" I moved in closer. He smelled fresh. His scent was earthy and spicy—maybe sandalwood?

He put his beefy arms around my neck again, and on the count of three, we heaved him forward and I shoved the extra pillows behind him. There was a loud thump as we both overcompensated and the motion threw his head into the heavy headboard. I felt as if my rib cracked for a second time, and we both moaned in unison.

"Ouch." He rubbed the back of his head. His hair was so closely cropped that it provided no cushioning at all.

"Oh gosh, I'm so sorry! Joel, are you okay?" I touched the back of his head, and my hand rested on the back of his neck. He laughed at our clumsy attempt. I pulled my hand away slowly from my rib.

His tone changed. "I need a favor."

Here it is. The reason he really needed my help. The reason he'd been so nice to me and made me believe there could ever be something between us.

"Sure," I said to let him know I hadn't been fooled by his sales pitch. "I knew it was something."

He used his fists to push off from the bed and sit up straighter. "I need to talk to your mom, Mary."

"I know who my mom is, Joel. About what?" I pushed the chair next to the bed, locked it on both sides, and hiked across the room to the grand mahogany door. "Wait, let me guess. It's top secret. You work for the CIA, and you would tell me what you have to discuss with my mom, but you'd have to kill me. That about sum it up?"

He looked as if I'd slapped him. "CIA? What on earth? I wanted to ask your mom a favor before she comes to the gala at the house."

"My mom won't come to the gala. She won't set foot in this house. You seem to forget this inheritance has robbed her of what matters most in life."

"I haven't forgotten. That's why I need her help."

The door slammed open, and Gia stood in the doorframe. "Sophia." Her eyes darkened with disappointment.

"Gia, what are you doing crashing into a guy's bedroom without knocking?"

"Trying to keep my sister from making the biggest mistake of her life." She grabbed me by the wrist. "Stay away from my sister, Michael or Joel, whatever your name is. If you want to get all googly-eyed, find your fiancé. My sister may be naïve and not understand your type. But I do!"

I caught a glimpse of Joel's stricken expression before she dragged me out of the room.

She kept her hand on my arm and scowled at me. "You know what they think of us here. Do you have to prove it in the first week?"

All I could think was that my captivity had only just begun.

Chapter Eighteen

Gia dragged me back upstairs to my own room. The curtains were shut now, and it felt empty and void of personality without all the posters, twinkle lights and youthful energy Alisa brought into the room. Now it felt like some bed and breakfast up by the northern Oregon border, with its ancient heavy furniture and lifeless bedding.

I jumped up and plopped on the four-poster bed. "Gia, there's nothing you can say to me now that would make a difference or make me feel worse about myself than I already do. I thought I had something special with Joel and he was marrying the wrong sister. I was pathetically wrong and everyone knows it. Isn't it enough that I have to live in the house with everyone knowing what a fool I made of myself?"

I'd thought Quinn's confession meant something. I thought Joel might profess his love—or at least his extreme like — for me. *I live in a fantasy world of my own making.* Joel was flirting because it was allowed. He was safe with the false premise of a fiancé. I was too ignorant to realize it was just innocent flirting, but now I knew. A handsome bloke flirting with me shouldn't go directly to picking out a wedding gown—especially when I never planned to get married in the first place. Joel made me abandon all reason in less than a week.

"Come back and live with Alisa and me. This room is creepy, and I don't like you in here by yourself. Especially with that dangerous stepfather of Oliver's out there stewing over being thrown in jail because of you."

I looked around the room. "It is creepy, but I can focus on the view. Open the curtains."

Gia yanked opened the yellow drapes.

"The mom's boyfriend or whatever she'd call that slab of beef is locked away. I'm perfectly safe. Not to mention, he has no way of finding out where or who I am. Thank goodness the newspaper didn't name me in the kidnapping debacle with Mr. Jessup. Speaking of which, do you have any cash?"

"How much?"

"Two thousand dollars?"

"Sophia, what is going on with you? It's like I don't even know who you are anymore. First, I find you in your sister's fiancé's room." She thrust a fist to her hip. "Let that sink in a minute. Your sister's fiancé's room," she repeated. "A man I distinctly told you to stay away from not fifteen minutes ago."

"He needed help getting up. I—"

"Now, you're blowing through cash? We just spent a fortune on clothes. What could you possibly do with another two thousand dollars until your next check? You haven't spent that much money in one fell swoop since you helped me with my car."

I didn't feel like explaining. "You know my heart. If you want to assume the worst, I can't stop you. Only do you have the money on you?"

"I don't have the money. What do you need it for?"

"I need to go." I tried to walk past her, but she barricaded herself in front of the door.

"Where are you going? You can't just walk around like a normal person anymore. It's dark outside, and you don't have a car. Please Sophia, talk to me. You're worrying me. I can't have you losing your mind with everything else in turmoil."

"I have an Uber account, and I grew up in the City."

"Not as an heiress, you didn't. Just because we haven't been named as Wentworth heiresses yet doesn't mean the media isn't onto something. There's a reason they're following me and bothering mom at the restaurant."

"I don't have any big money yet. I just have a creepy bedroom in a mausoleum."

"People don't know that!"

I pressed on her shoulder, but she didn't move. "Gia, if I tell you where I'm going, you'll tell me not to go and I don't want to be told what to do. I'm tired of not having my own life. You'll tell me that this is none of my business. I'll disagree with you, and this argument will start all over again." I reached for the doorknob behind her. "I need to do something. I feel so useless holed up in this crazy house without my job. Please just let me go."

"That kid!" Gia said. "This is about that kid! Honestly, do you have some kind of death wish?" She stepped close, put her arms around me and pulled me towards her. "Sophia, think. We have to get through this for Nonna and Papa. Mom can pass the restaurant onto one of her strays, and we can go back to the old country if we want. We never have to see these people again after this year is over."

I stiffened. "We've never been to Italy. It's Nonna and Papa's old country, not ours. Our 'old country' is when North Beach was actually Italian. We'll finish this debacle so we don't get sued, but I'm going back to social work as soon as I can. It's who I am."

"We only have each other right now, Sophia. Please don't put yourself in danger. I can't do this alone and you don't know this kid's whole story. You're not thinking long-term. You're panicking."

Her plea tugged at my soul. How I wished I could just drop it, but I knew Oliver was out there alone without an advocate. Who knew what kind of foster situation while I languished away in this spider-webbed mansion?

"Bobbi asked me to do this. She's never asked for a thing from me, and she can get me my job back at some point. I wish I could just forget it, but it's not in me." I stared into my sister's eyes. "It's all I have right now. The only purpose I feel."

Gia shook her head, "I'm sorry. I don't get it. I don't get why you always put others ahead of yourself. It's like you have no survival instinct."

"I do have a survival instinct. You should have seen me take on that monster, Gia. I was no wilting violet, and he's in jail now instead of damaging Oliver any further." I let out a sob. "If I don't help that little boy, who will?"

"The people in charge of that sort of thing!"

"I *am* the people in charge of that sort of thing, and I was fired. If only the system worked like that, but it doesn't. They've taken Oliver away from immediate danger, yes, but I think the courts put him in danger by listening to his mother. His father may be his only hope, and he's in jail."

"So what? You're going to bail the kidnapper out?"

"I am."

Gia moved out of the way and let me through. "I'll never understand you."

"I'll never understand why one rug is worth a fortune and that thing from TJ Maxx is less than your weekly coffee. You have your purpose, I have mine."

I climbed down the massive mahogany stairwell. "There's no way to brighten this baby up without ruining it," I called out to her.

"You're right. Sometimes, we do more damage than good," she said in her double-meaning way. "Call me if you get into any trouble. Wait, no better yet, call the police!"

"I've got this! I'll be in a bail bondsman's office." I stared up at her. "It's like the safest place to be—next to a casino. You don't think they plan for security?"

I stepped onto the landing of the second floor and was met by my father.

For the first time since I'd met him, he wasn't in a suit. He wore a button-up aqua dress shirt that was pressed as if no one was in it and casual black slacks that were probably worth more than what most people made in a week. He didn't seem to wrinkle, not his face nor his clothes.

"You're going out now?" he asked me.

"I am." I looked toward his bedroom door which was open slightly.

"It's dark outside. Do you have a companion?"

"A companion?"

"A friend," he said as if I didn't know the meaning of companion. "It's not wise to go out at night alone. I don't allow the girls to go out at night without a proper escort."

"Well, I'm fresh out of proper escorts, but I'll be fine." I tried to imagine him as a doting father, but the image didn't compute for me. When I tried to walk around him, he stepped in front of me again. He stared down at me and in some small way, his gaze felt fatherly . . . concerned.

"Would you like me to go with you?" he asked. I stared at him so long the silence became unbearable. "Would you?" he asked again.

I glanced at the open door to his secretive room and wondered what his icy bride might think of such a scenario. "Are you asking me if I want you to go with me? You don't even know where I'm headed."

He chuckled. "I don't want my daughter out at night. Is that so hard to believe? We've had a terrible loss recently with my father, but also a huge gain with more family in Wentworth Manor. It feels alive again like when the girls were little. I—I welcome the liveliness."

I looked around me to see if there was another sister behind me. He never treated Alisa, Gia or me as any kind of gain to his life. "Do you know which sister I am?" I asked him.

"Yes, Sophia, I know who you are." His voice was deep and smooth as butter, but it was in direct opposition to the man I'd met before this evening's dinner. I questioned who the true person was, even though I knew deep in my heart. The man he was let my mom raise us alone without money for food or clothes. Worse yet, he denied us as his and left my mother devastated like there was something deeply wrong and unworthy about her. But there was a longing in me that wanted his love and protection, and I couldn't deny that either.

"I don't need an escort. Thanks just the same."

The man who stood in front of me looking suave and handsome was the same man who sued me to steal my inheritance. As curious as I was, I didn't want to go anywhere with Bradley Wentworth. The thought of running into my mother while beside the man who destroyed her made me sick to my stomach.

Did he do this to Mama? Did he confuse her and make her believe he was a deep and sensitive person when his actions showed otherwise?

"I know it's hard after all these years, but the truth is, we shouldn't waste more time. Your mother wouldn't let me see you two. Did she tell you that?"

"You're lying," I snapped.

"Why would I lie about such a thing? Why don't you ask her?"

I shook my head at him. He had the same glacial blue eyes as Quinn. I'd never seen eyes like that on anyone, and it made me annoyed that I'd inherited the brown cappuccino-in-the-saucer eyes with flecks of green from my Italian heritage.

"I don't need to ask her." I stood tall. "Please don't make this any harder than it has to be. We have to be here. Alisa, Gia, Quinn, Brinn, we're all stuck with each for a year, but you don't have to be here. It would be easier for Alisa's mother if you went elsewhere to live for the year. If you really cared about us, you'd leave."

His gaze went cold. "Possession is nine-tenths of the law, and this is my home, Sophia. I'm not leaving it. Chelsea will want to be involved in the remodel, naturally. This is her home, and she has such exquisite taste."

That's questionable. "It's not her house to redesign!" I surprised myself by the outburst.

"This is our home," he said coolly. "You know that, Sophia. That's why your conscience is getting the better of you. You know this money doesn't rightfully belong to you, nor your sisters. I married Chelsea because she was from the right stock."

My inner Gia flared, "Well, at least one of you is!" I willed myself to shut up about his illegitimacy. It would be better coming from Mr. Trunkett, and I didn't want to take pleasure in giving him bad news. It made me just like him.

"Pardon me?"

I changed the subject quickly. "If you did the right thing by our mother, none of this ever would have happened. This is your fault, so please don't point fingers."

He flinched at the words, and I knew I'd hit a tender spot. *God forgive me, I kept going.*

"You and your favorite daughters would have inherited it all. I'd be home with my grandparents and my mother having Sunday supper like we always do. We'd watch *90 Day Fiancé* and go to bed for the next day's work. All of that has changed because you lied. You'd have inherited all those billions on your own without this fiasco of a family bonding experiment. Yet here we are, Bradley. Here we are."

A slow smile crept across his face as if he felt sorry for me and my inferior intellect. "Sophia, the laws for possession and property are extremely complicated. I don't expect you to understand them, but this is not going to turn out as you're expecting. I'm only trying to spare your feelings before you get too wrapped up in this fantasy of yours."

I searched for breath while he kept talking.

"I would have been willing to share. God knows I would have. Can't you see how your mother has poisoned you against me? Can't you see how diabolical she is?" He looked at the floor where my sister had positioned a cheap carpet and I had to smile. "Your mother seems like a saint, I know that. She's always slaving away at that restaurant, exactly like she did in high school. Bringing over more Italians as labor to get their citizenship. She does all as a single mother who is selflessly caring for her aging parents. But why don't you ask her what she did with the money I asked her to set aside for you."

The ground felt unsteady. "You're a monster. You have no idea who my mother is. She's the most generous person on earth, and she'd never keep a cent from us."

He nodded. "I understand how you feel. It's natural to feel that way. But I had to separate from you and your sister. If I couldn't help in raising you, there was no point in taking the constant rejection. I needed a clean break. I don't expect you to understand. I was young and naïve. Your mother had to keep her image, and I understood. Her parents were not too understanding. Old school I guess you'd say. But now that you're here it's stupid to waste more time. We've all made mistakes, but I've forgiven your mother." He put his hand on my shoulder and I felt an icy chill. "This isn't your battle to wage, Sophia. You can love both your mother and your father."

I heard a door creak and turned to see Quinn peeking out of her door. "Sophia?" she called. "Will you help me curl the back of my hair? I cannot make it look right, and I'm practicing for the gala."

"I was just on my way out—"

"Please?" she asked.

My head was spinning. I knew my father was lying, but he said everything so convincingly. It was hard to believe there wasn't a shred of truth in his words.

"Sure," I said. "Will you excuse me?"

I nearly leaped into her room. She closed the door quickly

behind me, and I stopped to take in the magnificent surroundings. This room certainly didn't need to be redecorated.

"I thought you could use a rescue," she said. "My dad loves to hear himself talk sometimes."

"Thank you."

"Listen, I don't want you to be offended. He's been telling that story so long that he's the victim in it. Don't take too much to heart with Daddy. He means well, but he's utterly incapable of seeing anything he's done wrong. He rewrites history until he's the hero in every tale."

Where I'm from we call that a personality disorder. I just nodded and smiled.

Quinn's room was so elegant and girly. There was a mirrored four poster bed with a long, matching dresser under the bank of bay windows. Her view wasn't as grand as my own, but I supposed that extra set of stairs made the slightly inferior view worth it. Dusty pink linens covered the bed and matching curtains splashed luxuriously along the gray carpet. The room was sophisticated, feminine and well put together. Just like Quinn. The green-eyed monster started to roar from within once more.

One wall was dedicated to her horse with photos and trophies in glass cases. "This is your horse?"

Quinn softened immediately. "Avery Lane. In dressage, the horse is the sport. Without the right horse, nothing matters." She ran her hand along the picture of her horse. "This horse is a champion. Together, we're fire."

"It's a sport?" I asked. It looked like rich people parading around on expensive equines.

"It's in the Olympics," Quinn said. "It's a sport."

"Thanks for rescuing me, I do appreciate it, but I really need to get to the bank," I told her.

"Do you need some cash?" Quinn asked.

"Maybe."

Listening to Bradley confused me about Oliver's situation. Everything I'd been taught in school said not to get involved.

Never get personally involved in your clients' lives. They will suck you under with them. After all, I didn't really know if Mr. Jessup was any better than Mrs. Jessup regardless of what Bobbi thought. Birds of a feather and all that. I couldn't afford to make another mistake in the matter of that child's life, and I knew he was safe in foster care.

"Are you all right?" Quinn asked me.

"Actually, on second thought, I'm going to stay in tonight. I thought I needed the money, but I was wrong. It can wait until the morning."

"I was serious about needing help with my hair. Brinn is worthless with hair. All she knows how to do is pull it into a severe bun so I look like a nun or an austere maid in an old Nazi movie. That's the gift ballet gave to her."

"Well, that and a rocking body," I joked.

"True. She does yoga and Pilates now. That girl has more energy than she knows what to do with. It has to go somewhere."

"Mine would go to sitting at my Nonna's table for my tiramisu. That's why Brinn's body looks like hers and mine looks like mine."

"Don't be funny. You're a runner and it shows." Quinn sat at her mirrored vanity, and I started to brush her blonde locks. "Are you any good at up-do's?"

"I'm okay with them."

"My gown is strapless, and I have a great neck."

"You do," I agreed. *I mean, what else does someone say to that?*

"Did you and Joel have a discussion? Or should I say, *the talk*? Define the relationship and all that?"

I continued to brush her hair and focused on not yanking it out by the roots. "No, nothing like that. I may have misread his signals. Sorry if I made that more awkward than it needed to be. I'm around kids most of the time so I think I was confused."

Quinn pulled away turned around to look at me with her luminous skin and the icy blue eyes of our father. "He wimped out." She shook her head. "I don't know what to tell you, Sophia. We're living in a time when men can't man-up. I'm going to—"

"No, please don't say a thing. It's already mortifying enough. Let's just drop it and if you really want to help me, find me a date for the gala."

"Done. I have the perfect guy for you!"

Chapter Nineteen

The next morning as I opened the curtains, a shroud of fog lay heavy over San Francisco. It matched my mood, and I knew I'd have to force myself out of my room. I slipped into my yoga pants and running shoes and thought I'd hunt for the gym. This house had to have one somewhere.

It was only 7:43 a.m. When Bobbi called again. I didn't want to answer since I hadn't done as she'd asked, but what more could she do to me at this point?

"Good morning, Bobbi."

"Charlie Jessup is out of jail," she said abruptly.

"What? Who bailed him out?"

"I don't know who bailed him out, what am I the FBI now? My friend at the station let me know in case I considered him a threat."

"Do you?"

"Of course I don't, Sophia. I already told you that. Do you think I'd ask you to bail out someone I thought was a threat?"

I'm getting paranoid.

"Listen," Bobbi continued. "I'm having a meeting with Oliver and his foster mother. The situation is rapidly changing as Charlie has asked for an emergency court date. I thought you might join us—in an unofficial capacity of course. You might shed some light on the relationship between father and son. The foster parents are genuinely concerned about Oliver's behavior."

"I'll be there. When and where?" I sounded too eager.

"Tomorrow. The zoo. We're meeting by the merry-go-round at 10:30."

"I'll see you then. Bye. And thank you, Bobbi."

"It's unofficial!" Click.

Unofficial or not, I had a shot at my job, and I wasn't going to blow it. If Bobbi knew anything, it was how to break a rule to best serve the public, and I planned to take full advantage of that. I finished lacing up my running shoes and headed toward the elevator for the first-floor gym. It was next to the conservatory. Or as normal people would call it, the sunroom. The gym was better than anything I could afford to join. There were no sweeping bay views from the first floor, so the treadmill was in the corner by the bank of bay windows which faced the lawn.

I stepped gingerly onto the track and pressed the quick start button. Even with the padded track and my running shoes, I felt every step in my ribs. I struggled to breathe at the leisurely pace and quickly understood that I wouldn't be running anytime soon. I grabbed my side and forced myself to walk slowly through the pain.

"Are you going to be long?" Chelsea Whitman Wentworth, a.k.a my evil stepmother, stood at the entrance to the gym.

She wore skintight leggings that only accentuated the fact she'd probably never eaten pasta in her lifetime. As beautiful as she was with her luminous skin and the perfect figure that belonged on a twenty-year old and not a woman of her age with two kids, she was no match for my own mother's natural beauty.

"Maybe we should work out a schedule if you're planning to use the gym." She smoothed her flat stomach with one hand. "Generally, this is for my private use."

I looked around the gym which was filled with every piece of equipment imaginable. There was an elliptical, the treadmill, a recumbent bicycle, countless weight machines and free weights. I paused the treadmill. "Isn't there something else you could do until I'm finished with the treadmill?" I let my arm sweep around the room. "Full gym at your disposal."

"Well, darling, you see it's *my* gym. I had all these pieces brought in so I wouldn't have to leave the house. My trainer prefers that I warm up on the treadmill."

"It's quite a big enough gym for two people at once. Maybe even ten." Someone missed the cardinal lesson of kindergarten and sharing day.

She drew in a deep breath as she raised her chin. "You and your sister really do say anything that comes to your mind, don't you? You must tame that if you ever hope to land a husband."

With a few billion dollars, I could have a husband built—one who only says yes and looks like Ryan Gosling.

"My sister doesn't want to get married, but trust me, if she did, she'd have no trouble finding a man to love her for exactly the way she is. Even without the inheritance," I said, knowing where Mrs. Wentworth would go next. I tried to be angry with her, but she was too set in her ridiculous ways to do anything but feel sorry for her. *Oh my, someone is in my gym. My day is utterly in ruins!*

"Maybe that's the curse of the women in your family. Spinsters for life, perhaps?" She shrugged. "We all have our lot in life."

"Do we?" I asked her. My rib was killing me, but there was no way I was getting off that treadmill, no matter how much I ached. "Maybe we'd rather be single than married to a —" I stopped myself. I was better than that. My mother's words about money ruining a soul reverberated through my brain. "Never mind. My mother wouldn't approve."

Chelsea Whitman Wentworth walked toward me. Her skin, which appeared radiant and airbrushed from a distance took on a waxy, zombie-like appearance up close. I hadn't wanted to judge her harshly without knowing her, but sadly, she seemed to be every vapid thing I thought she was from our brief introduction in the society pages. If I had to guess, I would say she wasn't bothered that her husband cheated because she didn't appear to love our father. But mention my mother, and she became fired up. That's where she found her passion, in stealing him from people who might love him. Her jealousy seemed to take over whenever Mary Campelli was mentioned, and I had to admit to taking a secret pleasure in this fact.

"Your mother will never get this house," Chelsea said through her teeth.

I laughed. "Do you think my mother wants this mausoleum? You don't know her at all, and I'm sure anything Bradley told you about her is a complete lie."

"Bradley has never mentioned your mother as I'm sure he doesn't even remember her. In fact, I'd be willing to bet he's not even your father."

Oh yeah, I wanted to shout. *You're probably married to the stable boy's son, but I am indeed Bradley Wentworth's daughter, we all are! And who knows if there's more of us out there?* Again, I saw my Nonna crossing herself. Darn that Catholic guilt already!

I stepped off the treadmill. "I'll come back later. It's stuffy in here. I have no battle with you, Mrs. Wentworth. I'm only here because my grandfather asked me to be."

Mrs. Chen appeared at the entrance to the gym. "Sophia, you have a guest. Security let him in and is with him."

I held my ribs, as they felt like they'd fall out if I didn't. "It's only eight in the morning."

"Nonetheless, you have a guest."

"Sophia has a guest here?" Chelsea asked as if I wasn't entitled to have anyone in *her* home. "How delightful. Well, invite her guest into the floral room, she'll meet them there. Mrs. Chen, would you get Sophia a water? She's been working out and doesn't have one." Chelsea looked straight at me with her dead eyes and bogus manners. "We can't take the chance to get dehydrated while working out."

"No," I said.

"He's waiting for her in the floral room," Mrs. Chen said. "I'll bring water there and some coffee maybe?"

"He?" Chelsea raised her eyebrows as high as they'd go with all her Botox. "Well, isn't that interesting. Gentlemen callers already."

Gentlemen callers. Chelsea really did want it to be 1820. I grabbed the small towel I'd brought with me and fast-walked to the flower room, or whatever it was called. This house seemed entirely too small at the moment. When I got there, I nearly fainted.

"Mr. Jessup?"

"I think we're on first name basis by now don't you? Charlie."

"What are you doing here?"

"You mean what am I doing out of jail?"

"Well, yeah, that too. How did you find me here?"

"I've been reading a lot of newspapers lately. I've had extra time on my hands and it's big news that there is a new heiress in our fair city. Still just a rumor. They haven't put names to you yet, but I recognized your picture."

Was there the tinge of blame in his comment? I couldn't tell. "No, but they will out us soon enough. Why are you here?"

"Sophia, you know why I'm here. I need your help getting my son back."

I shook my head. "I don't know what I can do. I mean, you're out of jail now, that's a first step."

"We've requested an emergency court date. We need your help vouching for us as parents. We've made mistakes, but—"

"We?" I asked, wondering if he had a rodent in his pocket.

"Tanya and I are making another go of it. I bailed her out of jail as soon as my father bailed me out last night." He massaged his golf cap in his hands. "He came down from Oregon to do it. Took a few days for him to get here, but when Tanya and I saw each other . . ." his voice dropped. "I remembered everything I ever loved about her."

"You loved about—" I stopped myself. "You should call

Bobbi. She's in the business and she can help you, but I have no power in the system anymore. Trust me, I've thought long and hard about how I might help you and all I've done is make things worse."

"You!" Joel wheeled into the room and pointed at Mr. Jessup. He managed to appear foreboding even from his wheelchair. "You need to stay away from her, understand?"

Charlie held his hand to his chest. "Me?"

"Do you have any idea what your kidnapping fiasco cost this woman? I could wring your neck. How dare you show up here!"

"I'm working with the authorities, I'll do whatever I can to get her job back for her, but you have to understand, my wife wasn't well. She has—"

"No, you have to understand, Mr. Kidnapper. You almost had this woman killed. She has two cracked ribs to show for the favor she did for you. She checked on Oliver like you asked and your wife's boyfriend kicked her in the ribs."

Mr. Jessup looked genuinely ill at the knowledge. "Beef hurt you?" He came toward me with his mild-mannered nature, and I flinched. Instinctively, I moved behind Joel's wheelchair.

"I think you should go, Mr. Jessup."

"Sophia, I'm so sorry I brought you into this. I was blinded by my fear for Oliver's safety. Please try to understand. I need your help to get an emergency court date. I need you to testify that—"

"That you kidnapped your son from your court-ordered visitations? Because she can testify to that, but as far as getting Oliver back in your custody, you're on your own for that. You need to leave right now before I call the cops. You'd be surprised how quickly they get to this neighborhood."

"Joel," I tried to stop him. He seemed so angry, and I'd never seen him that way. It unnerved me. But bless his heart, he still managed to be protective and threatening from his wheelchair wearing a cast the size of a small child.

"You cost Sophia everything she cared about. Her job, the safety of a child in her care and her body. Look at the size of her,

Mr. Jessup. Do you think she was any match for this monster your wife is dating?"

"I never—she's not dating Beef. That's her brother."

Mr. Jessup appeared broken, and I couldn't fix it. I couldn't put this mess back together and I wondered why I'd ever bothered. It felt as if the entire world was against me. Except for Joel and for the moment, that was enough.

Chapter Twenty

Joel insisted on going to the San Francisco Zoo with me. I drove his Prius, which was surprisingly roomy and incredibly luxurious inside. I felt bad I'd given him such a hard time over it. The irony was not lost on me that he was hit by the even more economical smart car.

"Charlie said he's getting back together with his wife." I shook my head as I pulled into the parking space. "How could that be possible?"

"Do you think that will help them get custody?" Joel asked.

"I don't know. I'm only here because I want to see how Oliver is doing after all this strife. The poor kid. It's hard to live with the fact that if I'd only done my job none of this would've happened."

"He'd still be in his mom's care if this hadn't happened. Don't forget that." Joel had a way of cutting to the chase.

When I ventured a glance at him, my stomach was aflutter. Even if he wanted nothing to do with me, Joel had a rugged gentleness to him that made me feel as if everything would be all right. Maybe that's all I was attracted to, his sense of calm.

The zoo had a new entrance from the one when I was a child. Now it was on the ocean side and the brisk, damp fog rushed right though me as I stepped out of the car. I went around to the passenger side and pulled out the portable wheelchair, then opened the door. Joel had grown quite agile getting into his chair, and it was clear that he was ready to dispose of it altogether.

"You really didn't need to come with me," I told him.

"Actually, Quinn insisted."

"I'll never get my new family. Quinn is always pawning off her fiancé on me when it's clear he doesn't want to be pawned off."

He stopped his movements in the chair and looked up at me. It was if he could see straight through to my heart. "You have no idea what I want, Sophia. Nor how much I want it."

I felt breathless for a moment.

"Won't Quinn be embarrassed when this engagement is broken? I mean, I would think it will be in all the newspapers."

"Quinn couldn't care less about what people think. That's the beauty of her. She has one image for the newspapers and then there's the real her."

I felt a tinge of the green-eyed monster surface. "You have the benefit of knowing the truth about us, but I don't even know what it is you actually do. Are you a cop? A lawyer? A hobo?"

He laughed, "All of the above."

"You still can't tell me why you're in the mansion, really? You trusted me enough to tell me this engagement wasn't real."

"Shh," he looked around him. "I can't tell you yet, but I can tell you that Quinn is incredible, and she saw me struggling. Quinn is something. Her sacrifice in all this has been significant."

"You're a fan, I get it." I tried to keep the bitterness out of my voice.

"You will be too when the truth comes out, Sophia. I promise."

I felt defeated. "You're not going to tell me the truth, are you?"

"Not yet." He stared up at me. "You'll understand soon enough."

I pushed his chair up to the zoo's entrance and paid for two.

"Why the zoo?" Joel asked on our way in.

I worked to heave him up the small hill to the Lemur cages, and he took over with his muscular arms. "I assume so Oliver has something to do while they discuss his behavior."

"I don't know why everyone expects a child who is going through the trauma of kidnapping, divorce and mom's violent roommate to behave decently. Does that seem reasonable to you?"

"They don't, but they want to make sure we nip it in the bud to make it easier on him. I'm really excited to see him. I miss all my kids so much."

We passed the lemurs and veered to the left. "They haven't moved the carousel."

"It was easier to move the giraffes," he quipped.

"Is that a joke, Joel Edgerton?"

"It is. A dad joke. Seemed appropriate." He shrugged his wide shoulders, and I smiled. The world felt happier with Joel around. *Safer.* I reminded myself of my promise to myself. I wouldn't be led astray by his charms.

When we arrived at the merry-go-round, we walked inside the historic glass structure. Oliver was there on a large, colorfully painted horse, but he didn't wear a smile. A man, who must have been his foster father, stood beside him and they both looked austere, as if waiting for the fun to begin.

I found Bobbi and the woman on an evergreen bench already deep in conversation. I left the wheelchair near the entrance and walked toward the red iron gate that surrounded the carousel. I watched Oliver as he whizzed by, and I was struck again by guilt. This little boy's life had been turned upside down. He was so adorable with his ruddy-red cherub cheeks and bright blue eyes. Except for the frown on his face, one would never know he wasn't a happy-go-lucky boy out for the day with his grandpa.

Before he spotted me, I went and met Bobbi at the bench.

She looked up at me. "Karen Winslow, this is Sophia Campelli."

Recognition crossed the woman's face. She knew my name, of course. I could nearly see the recognition flash through her brain:

The woman who allowed Oliver to be kidnapped. The idiot who got beaten by a man named Beef. The brain trust who wanted to be a full-time social worker.

Karen Winslow was nondescript. If she were a color, she'd be beige, but as it was, she wore an eggplant-colored tunic over matching leggings and comfort sandals—without the benefit of a pedicure. "I should let you know, Sophia, that I did not want you here. I believe you're more concerned with your career than Oliver's welfare and that will not serve us today."

"You can believe what you want, Karen. Bobbi knows it's in Oliver's best interest that I'm here, and on some level, I'm sure you do too. I'm not being paid nor am I on the payroll, so if I didn't care about the boy's welfare, I wouldn't be here."

She frowned and turned toward Bobbi as if to keep me from their conversation. Joel stayed by the entrance, and for that, I was grateful. The last thing I needed was for Karen to know that Joel had been hit by a car while serving me legal paperwork. It didn't exactly help my case.

"I asked Sophia here because she knows Oliver and his father well," Bobbi said.

"Obviously she doesn't if she thought Mr. Jessup was no risk. Clearly, he's a man who can't be trusted, or he wouldn't have had supervised visits."

"We've all made mistakes in this business, as you know. It's not an exact science. People can surprise you. For what it's worth, I think Sophia is right about Mr. Jessup. He wanted what was best for Oliver and that's why he kidnapped the boy. His living condition wasn't the best and his father was worried. "

"We'll have to agree to disagree on that point," Karen said. "As I've told you, Oliver's behavior is unacceptable. He's jumping off the walls and does not do as he's told. The other day, he turned on the oven for no reason whatsoever."

I can't stand this woman.

"He's a very clever little boy," I interjected.

"Oh? Is it clever to turn on an appliance that could kill the entire household?" Karen rolled her beige eyes. I knew she sacrificed having Oliver in her home, but she seemed to hate him and all children in general. I wanted nothing more than to get him out of her mousy clutches.

"Oliver has had a lot of trauma in the last six months."

"You don't think I know that?" Karen asked. "I've seen him every day since the kidnapping. He's very troubled. Parents who have children without consideration for the consequences have no right to keep those children."

"You should know, Karen, that Mr. and Mrs. Jessup have expressed the desire to try and make a go of it. The state will do what it can to restore Oliver to his parents' home when they can prove they have provided a stable environment for him," Bobbi said.

"Ridiculous!" she shouted. "Both of them belong in jail and that little boy should get farmed out to the next-of-kin. The sooner you can make that happen, the better we'll all be."

Bobbi's voice lowered. "The courts tend to be lenient when it comes to a parents' desire to do what it best for the child. Mrs. Jessup isn't pressing charges against Mr. Jessup and neither is the state at this point. His kidnapping charge will be reduced to a misdemeanor and nothing more than a miscommunication. He will have to reimburse the San Francisco Police Department for the chase, but other than that—"

"Utterly ridiculous!" Karen stood. "William! Oliver, let's go!"

Oliver clung to the horse's golden pole, and it was clear he didn't want to go anywhere with Karen. As she walked toward the red metal fence, my eyes pleaded with Bobbi. "You can't let him leave with her. She's a monster."

"She's currently his legal guardian," she whispered.

Joel rolled his wheelchair toward the ride's operator and said something to him. The merry-go-round continued to spin.

"How can we get the emergency court date?" I asked desperately. "I want to apply for temporary custody."

"You?" Bobbi shook her head. "That's not going to happen."

For once I thought about the inheritance. "Can my money make it happen?"

"You can't buy children, Sophia. That's called trafficking."

"I want him out of her hands as soon as possible. I'm going to get Mr. and Mrs. Jessup the best lawyer money can buy."

Bobbi smiled.

"That's what you planned all along, isn't it?" I asked her. "That's why you invited me here."

"Of course I didn't," Bobbi said. But I didn't believe her.

When the ride finally slowed, the line to get on the carousel snaked around the building. Oliver stepped off the carousel and clung to his foster father's hand. When he saw me, he let go and ran toward me.

I stood and he clung to my knees. "Where's my daddy, Miss Sophie? I want my mommy and daddy."

I bent down and put my face to his. "Your mommy and daddy love you something fierce, Oliver. They're going to be back soon. You be good for Mr. and Mrs. Winslow for now. I promise you Mommy and Daddy are doing everything to get you back home as soon as they can."

He shook his little head. "Don't want to go."

I knelt beside him. "I want you to see your mommy and daddy more than I can say. Miss Sophia is working on it, okay?"

"Don't want to go!"

Karen grabbed his hand, and he squeezed and kicked as she took him out of the carousel's glass structure. My heart grieved for how adults made children's lives so difficult—even the ones called in to be the supposed cavalry.

I tore my gaze from Oliver. "I can't believe Charlie is willing to get back with his ex. They don't seem to belong as a couple. He's so clean-cut and normal looking. And she's like something that stepped out of an all-night tattoo parlor above the bar."

"It's not like you to judge, Sophia."

"I just don't get it," I shrugged as I stared off at Joel. "I can't even get a date, and tattoo Sally pulls Charlie back to her like he's on a golden rope."

"One never knows the glue that holds two people together," Bobbi said. "But you have to admit, Oliver is a pretty good reason. He's a love."

I felt sick to my stomach watching Oliver leave with his foster parents. The little boy cried because he wanted to go see the animals, and it was clear that his day of joy was over.

"How can he go back to her?" I was dumbfounded. "She's a complete mess."

"He loves her, and love don't make no sense."

"That's for darn sure."

"I'll work on my end for the emergency court date," Bobbi said. "Find the Jessups a good lawyer." Bobbi strode past Joel but bent down and whispered something to him before she exited.

He smiled at me broadly when I caught his eye, and it felt as if the sun had just come out.

"Are you ready?" I asked him.

"I don't even get to see the gorillas?"

"They're all the way across the zoo. You up for it?"

"I have nowhere to be. Just for your information, I caught sight of the local society page photographer. He must have followed us here so be prepared for the headline. He pasted his invisible words across the sky, "First sister tries to kill sister's fiancé, then steal his affections."

"You're loving this."

He grinned. "I mean, how awful is it to have two gorgeous women fighting over you? Even if it's all made up. I'm going to bask in it. The whole thing ups my street cred."

"I hope you're right about Quinn being a peach." I pushed his wheelchair past the lemur walk toward the gorillas. "I do need to get home and find the family a lawyer."

"I can get you an attorney," Joel said. "The best."

"How can I know that's true. I don't even know what you do."

"I'm a lawyer. Sort of."

"Well, I'm a social worker. Sort of."

"See? It's complicated."

I parked Joel next to a bench by the gorillas' environment. They were so human-like. I wondered what they all thought staring back at us with their big brown watchful eyes. *Do they think Joel is out of my league?*

Just as I was about to sit on the bench, Joel swung his arm around me and plopped me on his lap. "Joel!"

I met his eyes. *What was I saying again?*

He softly moved my hair behind my shoulder and stared at me so intensely that I had no choice but to go towards him. As I was about to press my lips to his, my heart full of heated anticipation, I heard the shutter of the camera click. Joel sat up straight, nearly knocking me off his chair. I recovered quickly and stood up as if nothing happened.

Nothing had happened.

Chapter Twenty-One

Despite my hair styling event with Quinn and Gia's connection with Alisa, the five of us sisters ceased to bond in any meaningful way over the five days since I'd returned. We stuck to business conversations. Together, we'd decided on a traditional remodel to highlight the classic revival architecture while updating the finishes. We'd keep the mahogany staircase and lighten the walls, fixtures and add a cream stair runner with gold carpet rods at the base of each step.

After that decision was made together, Quinn took over the bidding process, and we awaited word from high-end contractors capable of restoring a mansion with quality modern finishes.

Other than design agreement, the sisterly bonding was cordial at best. We'd walk past each other in the hallways and smile, but if one of us was in the backyard or the gym, the other would immediately withdraw their presence and seek the quiet of their room.

The bids were finally collected, and tonight was the Sunday Dinner when we would decide who would do the work and what Wentworth Manor would become in its rebirth.

I slipped into a Marc Jacobs' dress with my Chanel flats, as I'd discovered no dinner in this mausoleum was worth the pain of heels. After being sidelined from running, my calves weren't what they used to be. There was a quiet knock on my door, and I opened it to see Gia standing with the *San Francisco Chronicle*.

She didn't look pleased. "Sophia, you do realize your grandparents' only activity aside from eating is watching the news and reading the newspaper."

"They watch *Jeopardy* too." I opened the door so she could come inside, then shut the door behind her and followed her to the window seats.

Gia looked like a million bucks in sleek heels and a yellow Derek Lam jumpsuit that clung to her in all the right places. It flowed around her ankles and made it look like she walked on the wings of angels with the clouds beneath her feet. While I managed to make the designer looks seem as if they were Marshall's copies, Gia took to elegance like a swan in the Fine Arts Palace pond.

"The society page today." Gia held up the newspaper to show a picture of me on a bench at the zoo in front of the gorilla enclosure, my feet casually crossed at the ankles and perched in Joel's lap in the wheelchair. My head was thrown back in laughter and seeing Joel's infectious smile made me laugh all over again.

"He said the funniest thing—"

"Sophia. This is your sister's fiancé. Look at the headline."

She held the paper towards me. "Lawyer Trades One Heiress for Her Sister?"

I bit my lip. "Did Papa see this?"

"What do you think?"

A door slammed hard, and we heard shouts echo throughout the cavernous house. "I said get out of my house!"

Muffled sounds came.

"Did you hear me? Get out of my house now before I have you thrown out!"

We opened the door and rushed to look over the banister where we saw our father screaming at someone, we couldn't see from our vantage point.

"Come on," Gia whispered.

We scrambled down the stairs to get a better view, and all of our sisters joined us along the route, like a dysfunctional Pied Piper of family drama. When we got to the second story landing, we could see that it was poor old Mr. Trunkett being yelled at.

He held his broken old briefcase in front of his chest and fiddled with his glasses with the other hand. "I cannot do that."

Quinn flew down the stairs. "Daddy, what are you doing?"

"Trunkett has always hated me, but now he's gone too far! You've gone too far!" He screamed at the old man, who swayed as if the words hit him physically.

Quinn stepped between them. "Daddy, stop this."

"Do you know what he's saying, Quinn?"

"I know what he's saying. You're not a Wentworth. None of us are."

Our father looked up at us staring over the bannister. "These are lies! You just know you'll lose in court, Trunkett!"

"I won't," Mr. Trunkett said calmly. "The girls are protected as the full inheritors of Mr. Wyatt Wentworth's estate. I'm telling you this for your own benefit, Bradley."

"You've never been a friend to this family. You did everything to turn my father from me, but it didn't work! I'm still on the board of Wentworth Industries and that's where I'll stay!"

"Daddy," Quinn said quietly. "He's telling you the truth. The DNA—"

"You knew this?" Bradley looked at each and every one of us to see if we were all traitors, but he was especially focused on Brinn, who was his golden child. "You knew this, Brinn, and you didn't tell me?"

"I couldn't, Daddy." She slunk behind us on the bannister. "Mr. Trunkett forbade me."

"I expected it from the others, but you, Brinn? You're my girl."

"Daddy, you were his son," Brinn shouted down the stairs and it echoed off the walls. "Test results make no difference. Grandfather loved you as his own, and that's all that matters."

Bradley scoffed. "He loved me enough to bypass me in his will and make me a laughingstock to my girls and the entire world. Is that how much he loved me?"

Brinn rushed down the steps and tried to hug our father, but he stiffened and stepped back. "You've all deceived me like I was unwanted paparazzi or an interloper. I'm your father, for crying out loud! Do you understand what the Bible has to say about your kind of betrayal? Honor your father! You're all Judases!"

My eyes widened. *Suddenly, Bradley Wentworth is religious?*

"I won't forget this. Quinn. Brinn. You should have known better. I'm not leaving this house. You want me out of here? Both of you can take me to court. Go ahead, break your mother's heart and take us to court as if your greed hasn't broken her heart already." He looked upward at me. "And *you*! It's not bad enough you made a play for your sister's fiancé? Now you have to betray me too? I guess your strong Catholic upbringing gave you moral relativity?" He shook his head. "Just like your alley cat mother."

I started to run down the steps when I saw Joel roll in from the elevator. "Bradley, I've had it with you. A real man protects his daughters. He doesn't lash out with vile words of hatred. You're a bitter, angry man, and your veneered smile doesn't fool me." Joel had a crutch with him and forced himself out of the chair. He stood and wobbled in front of Bradley. "It gives your daughters no pleasure to tell you this truth, and Mr. Trunkett is doing his job. It's not personal."

"You're going to defend these girls trying to throw their own parents under the bus? You make a perfect lawyer, Edgerton. One set of rules for you and an entirely different set for others."

"Don't say anything you'll regret, Mr. Wentworth. Your girls had nothing to do with what your father wrote in his will. You're out because of your own actions."

"I brought you into my house to recover and this is the thanks I get? Gallivanting in a public place with the wrong daughter?"

"Wrong daughter?" Something in his words sent me over the edge. It was as if he'd said my mother wasn't relevant, that we didn't matter, simply because we were inconvenient. "I didn't ask to be born to a lowlife, loser deadbeat dad!"

"Your mother hedged her bet and lost," Bradley sneered.

I flew at my father and nearly knocked Joel to the ground where he stood between us on his wobbly legs. "You're not fit to say my mother's name!"

"I never liked you, Joel," Bradley's eerie, calm demeanor returned as if a switch had turned on. "I know why you're here, and I also know why you're really here. You're after my daughter's money and how much easier is it to manipulate this one, right? With her innocent eyes and budget fashion choices."

I looked down at my dress. *Budget? This thing cost a fortune.*

"Careful Bradley, don't speak out of ignorance. I can and will use it against you in court," Mr. Trunkett said.

"Court?" Bradley said. "You'll never be in a courtroom with me."

"Daddy, never mind!" Quinn said. "Joel is here because I want him here and this is my house now. Everyone needs to calm down."

"Oh, it is, is it?" Bradley's eyes thinned. "We'll see about that, Quinn. When my lawyers get done with you, all of you." He waved his hand around to all of the sisters. "You won't have a penny left to live in this house. I'll keep you mired in lawsuits until I'm dead. That's a promise."

"You know full well I'm not your daughter's fiancé." Joel spoke calmly. Then he looked toward me. "Not yet anyway."

I felt chills run down my back and suddenly all the arguing ceased to matter.

"You know I'm here because of your father's hastened death," Joel said.

Bradly flinched. "I don't know what you're talking about. Quinn, is this true? You let this man in our house, and he's not your fiancé? What have I always told you about trusting outsiders?"

"I have to know what happened to Grandfather. I promised him on his deathbed."

"You think I killed my own father? Quinn, you can't possibly think I had anything to do with your grandfather's death. He was old, for heavens' sake. And sick."

"All the more reason no one would check into his death, but he died from a morphine overdose. Didn't you read his death certificate?"

He shrugged. "I didn't. I was too upset about losing my father. He was my father, no matter what that bogus piece of paper says. Quinn, I can't believe this—"

"Don't get upset, Daddy," Brinn said. This will all work out, you'll see."

Joel looked at Bradley. "When it's anything but a natural death, an investigation is prompted. Your father had too much morphine in his system, and there were vials missing from his medical kit in hospice. Inquiries are always made in these cases."

"You're a cop?" Bradley asked. "Quinn, you took up with a cop against your flesh and blood? You let him into our home?"

It fascinated me that Bradley wasn't interested in the fact that perhaps his father died from unnatural causes. He was still only concerned about himself. What on earth did my mother ever see in this freak? I had to hope he'd gotten worse with age.

"I know it wasn't you, Daddy. Naturally, I assumed it was someone on the staff." Quinn's voice wobbled.

Not that this family had ever been a beacon of hope for any casual observer, but to see it in the shambles proved that my mother had been right all along. Money was a powerful force. It could destroy so easily. As much as I thought my father was a walking, talking douchebag, in no way did I think he was capable of hastening his father into the next realm.

I glanced around the mansion's residents. Could it be true that someone hastened Wyatt into the next world? Part of me felt they were all capable and another part felt none of them were. It could have been an accident. Morphine wasn't a perfect science.

I was still rocked by Joel's true purpose here. A cop. A lawyer? I struggled to make sense of it all.

Bradley slunk down to the third step from the bottom and sat. "I loved my father. I know he did this for my benefit. He wanted to see me rise up and make something of myself without him."

"Then let it go," Joel said. "Take what stock he gave you in the company and leave these girls to figure out their future and this house. They have enough on their plate without your threats of lawsuits. Have some dignity, man."

Bradley's face went red and he stood again. "How dare you lecture me."

"Aren't you even interested in what my investigation has uncovered?" Joel asked.

"No, because my father is gone regardless. I'm going to dinner. Chelsea!" He shouted up the bannister. "Let's go. Our reservations are in an hour." He looked back at Joel in a false smile that didn't reach his eyes. "That woman has never been on time for anything in her life."

The doorbell rang, and Mrs. Chen went to answer it. Two men wearing ties and sport coats entered the foyer. One of them flashed their badge. "Steve Kendall, San Francisco homicide unit."

Bradley grabbed the thick mahogany bannister. "What's going on, Officers?"

"We have a warrant for Mrs. Chelsea Wentworth."

Quinn gasped and sank to the floor. Our father made no move to pick her up. "This is ridiculous. My wife would never— she had nothing to do with this. My father died of natural causes; do you understand me?

Chelsea? I exchanged a glance with Gia, and I saw the same acceptance in my twin's eyes. Neither of us were surprised. Money and prestige were clearly all our dear stepmother cared about.

More officers in uniforms came in, and this time they had guns. "Step aside."

Before being an heiress, I'd only seen a police officer when they ate at my mother's restaurant. Now I was becoming intimately acquainted with the entire force. The two officers in uniform stayed with us while the one named Steve Kendall climbed the stairs after directions from Mrs. Chen.

After a few seconds, he emerged and called over the bannister. "Where is she?"

"She's in there," Bradley said. "We have dinner reservations in less than an hour."

"She's not in here." He motioned to the other officers. "Search the grounds."

Quinn had risen by now. Brinn was still crying. Bradley pointed a finger at Quinn. "This is how you treat your mother? You invite cops in here to falsely accuse her of God knows what! Your grandfather died of natural causes, Quinn. I don't ever want to see your face again; do you understand me? You're a traitor of the worst sort.

Brinn followed her father out to the formal living room, and Quinn stared at Joel and then me. "It can't be my mother."

Joel's jaw flexed, but he said nothing.

She grabbed his arm. "Joel, it can't be my mother. Grandfather was one hundred years old. My dad is right, it was natural causes."

Joel's jaw was locked, and it flinched, but he still said nothing. He didn't offer Quinn any words of comfort nor did he tell her it wasn't true. He stood, stoic as any sculpture in the mansion.

At his lack of reaction, Quinn took a step back and put a hand to her throat. "Get out of my house. Get out of my house and don't ever come back! Joel, you're a monster!"

Mrs. Chen walked in the room, tone deaf as ever to the situation. "Dinner is served."

Chapter Twenty-Two

Wentworth Manor's walls were closing in. The massive space suddenly felt tight in the midst of the heady conflict—and now our very own *Dateline* episode played out before us.

The homicide detectives had been everywhere in the house and had ceased to emerge with Chelsea. We all stood in our original positions as if waiting for the theater lights to dim and the show to begin.

Two uniformed officers stood with us while the detectives searched every room, no small task in the mausoleum. Joel wouldn't look at me while all this was going on. I was left to wonder if he'd ever had feelings for me or it was all part of the convoluted plot to bring Chelsea Wentworth to justice. Why had Bradley gone to Joel's room the night he'd fallen, and why hadn't Joel told him to come in, or asked for help? Something didn't add up. Was he a police officer or a lawyer? Who was he? Was that photo op at the zoo all a part of some bigger plan?

The only noise in the house was the marching of boots when an officer would come out of a room. It was all so surreal and made me wonder what would happen if Chelsea and Bradley just watched *Jeopardy* at night. Quinn and Brinn both had visible tears on their faces. It was as if they'd lost their grandfather all over again, and no one in this room knew who to trust.

Mrs. Chen sat in the corner chair clearly annoyed that her dinner announcement was not only ignored but treated with disdain.

We waited silently while the homicide detectives entered the conservatory and went out into the backyard. No doubt if Chelsea was in the yard, she would have hopped the hedge and been on her merry way to one of her socialite friends' homes. I imagined her having a good laugh over the bumbling police department while she sipped her glass of pinot grigio.

"Does he have to be here?" Quinn said about Joel to the standing officers.

One of the officers glanced slowly down to Joel, who was now back in his wheelchair, and then at Quinn, "The gentlemen stays."

"Gentleman!" Quinn shouted. "He set me up. I only wanted to know what happened to my grandfather!"

"And now you do," Joel said plainly. "But Quinn, I did not set you up. I got the coroner to look into the cause of death as you requested. The toxicology reports showed exactly what you suspected; your grandfather died of a morphine overdose. Anyone who lost a loved one in this way would want answers."

"You set your own family up," Bradley said to Quinn. "I've told you since you could talk not to trust outsiders. This is what happens. They always turn on you."

It dawned on me why this family never solved anything. They only seemed to look for someone to blame; once someone was at fault, the conversation was over, and they moved on. This wasn't going to be something they'd move on from easily.

"I'm sorry if I'm not as paranoid as you'd like," Quinn said. "I wanted to know what happened to my Grandfather. I had a right to know. One day he was fine, the next he was incoherent, and then dead. I thought it was that awful nurse of his and I wanted her to pay!"

"I'm sure it was," Bradley said evenly. "I know for a fact it was not your mother. She couldn't hurt a fly."

Exactly what Norman Bates said at the end of Psycho. It was a suspicious choice of words, and I couldn't decipher what it meant. Bradley and Chelsea had a strange relationship that made no sense to me. Bradley didn't seem concerned about his wife's possible arrest, but he also wasn't too interested in the fact that his father had been murdered. I wondered if he looked forward to Chelsea's absence, however short. If history proved reliable, we might have a new sister in the near future.

While I contemplated my father's cool demeanor, the front door burst open and men in full SWAT regalia barged in and split into several different directions, swarming the house. Alisa, who I hadn't noticed before, snuggled up next to Gia. Gia held her tightly and whispered something in her ear.

I noticed that Joel didn't seem the least bit surprised by the SWAT team's presence. *Clearly, I have my mother's taste in men: handsome, secretive and cagey.* Not everyone was a deep pool of invisible insight—some people were exactly as they seemed.

Since I'd met him, I'd imagined Joel to be a heroic, angelic Prince Charming who swept me off my feet while serving me a lawsuit. But now I saw the human shards of emotions littered around his feet and his chilling lack of responsibility for the damage. Even if he was right about Grandfather's murder, the way he'd gone about it was so deceptive and cold. Quinn trusted him implicitly. She'd allowed him to become her faux fiancé to get answers. If I ever had any discernment, I'd been stripped and cured of it after the kidnapping of Oliver and now my false view of Joel as a protective, sensitive soul. Some men aren't misunderstood. Some men, like my father, are just jerks.

The scent of the Bay air infiltrated the house as the front door stood ajar to the portico.

The two homicide detectives came in from the yard. Chelsea was in front of them with her hands clasped behind her back. She wore a full face of makeup and a dark navy, almost black pantsuit that fit her like a glove. How anyone managed to look that elegant while getting arrested baffled me, but with one look she let us all know she'd be back soon. Since there was a different set of justice for the rich, I had no doubts about her being right.

"I'm right behind you, Chels!" Our father called out to her. "I love you, Babe! Don't you worry about this. We'll own the City for this false arrest."

Chelsea turned around and took one last look at him, and if looks could kill, Bradley Wentworth would be lying beside his father in the grave.

After the homicide detectives marched out with my step-mother, the SWAT team appeared from every crevice and doorway in the mansion. *There's something about a man in uniform.* Alisa approached a few of the younger, handsome members. "Can you do the Renegade with me on TikTok? It would so go viral!"

One of the men spoke into a speaker on his chest. "Not while on duty, young lady."

"I'm TikTok famous," she said as if this would mean something to the SWAT team. They laughed and surrounded her.

"From the shoulders down," one of them said.

Alisa posed and snapped a short video showing only her face. "Got my very own SWAT team, y'all! Hashtag heiress life!" she said with a peace sign.

With Marine precision, the men emptied out onto the porch, with the last one shutting the door and leaving what was left of our ragtag stepfamily alone.

"I need to go take a shower," Bradley said.

"You need to go get mom out of jail!" Quinn shouted.

"They have to process her, Quinn. It will take hours. Don't worry, I've got the lawyer on speed dial." He gazed down at Brinn with a sneer. "Your mother had nothing to do with this."

"I know that!" Brinn blasted back at him.

And I thought we Italians yelled a lot.

Bradley took the stairs two at a time and disappeared into his room with a loud slam.

The eerie quiet left in the foyer was broken by Mrs. Chen. "I said dinner is ready."

We all looked at her as if she'd lost her mind.

"You need to eat and there's an agenda that must be followed. Mr. Trunkett will want his answers by tomorrow." Mrs. Chen clapped her hands twice.

Somehow, I imagined life as an heiress differently.

"Mrs. Chen, I think Mr. Trunkett will understand," Quinn said. Then she pulled her long blonde hair behind her and wrapped it into a ponytail knot. "Joel, I'd like you to get your things packed and get out of this house."

He nodded and looked up at me with those mesmerizing sapphire eyes. I turned away so I wouldn't be confused by his angelic good looks.

My heart betrayed me because I didn't want to help him pack. I didn't want to gaze into those eyes again and relive my humiliation. I had a crush on a myth. Here I thought I'd been so fortunate that he wasn't Quinn's fiancé—that I hadn't fallen for someone who was in love with someone else. But I had no idea who he really was.

"Are you a lawyer? Or a cop?" I turned toward Joel, but I refused to look into his eyes.

"Does it make a difference?"

I shrugged. "No, I suppose it doesn't. Except that I trusted you, no questions asked. I took your advice about Mr. Jessup and Quinn."

Quinn glared at the two of us.

"It was an educated opinion," he answered. "On both counts. The Jessups from my legal background and Quinn from personal experience."

"Don't talk about me," Quinn said. "In fact, don't ever let me hear my name on your lips again, is that clear?"

"Please Sophia, help me pack up my stuff. I want to explain—"

"You said you were here to keep us safe!"

He said nothing, but by his expression I instinctively understood that maybe he had kept us safe. Maybe he couldn't tell me more, but then again, maybe I was perpetuating the fantasy that my mother kept alive for years. Maybe Joel was exactly who he seemed to be. Someone who manipulated Quinn and got into the house for an investigation and now he'd walk off into the sunset with whatever kind of accolades he expected.

Joel nodded his head slowly and rolled his wheelchair toward the elevator.

I called after him. "You went with me to the zoo on purpose. So, you could get out of this engagement without any public scrutiny as to your real cause for being here."

"Maybe," he admitted.

I died a little at his answer. I walked in front of his chair. And I got a flash of those Lake Tahoe eyes. My resolve to be angry and self-righteous weakened. It's soul-crushing when you believe you're somebody special to a man like Joel Edgerton, only to find out he doesn't really exist. Now more than ever I wanted to go home and end this heiress fiasco.

"I don't want to do this," I stated to the room. "I want to go home and back to my old life."

"That's impossible now that you've lost your job," Gia reminded me. "Your student loans, remember? You'll have to go back to a different life, but I think I agree with you."

"I don't want to be here anymore," I said again. "There's something toxic in this household. Dark."

"I have an idea," Brinn said. "We all need to get away from this guided cage. The house is ours, not the money, but the house. We can sell it as is. We'll get a court-appointed realtor to give us an estimate and sell our prison."

"That's brilliant!" Gia said.

"We won't have the lifestyle forever, but we'll all be able to live well on what we collect. It will be millions for each of us, even after taxes," Brinn said. "I'll go back to finance school. Sophia and Gia can go back to their grandparents' house and Alisa can set her mother up in a nice house and continue her social media career."

We all looked at Quinn. She was the only one who'd really depended on the lifestyle. Her days consisted of riding a fifty-thousand-dollar horse and competing in the horsey circuit.

"Don't be ridiculous, Brinn," Quinn said. "Your education is going to cost a fortune, and who knows what it will cost to get Mother out of this false accusation!" She turned to me. "Sophia, you don't have a job and the way you make that designer dress look like a sack, you're not going to be modeling the heiress life-style anytime soon."

I looked down at my dress. "Mean. Was that necessary?"

She ignored me and turned to Gia. "I mean, sure Gia, you can go to work at the museum, steal all the rugs from the house if you want, but ultimately, you can't afford to stay in San Francisco without fixing up your grandparents' home and you know it. The money from the house will dwindle in no time. Don't forget, my father is still suing all of us. Nothing has changed." She pointed her finger at each of us. "Nothing."

This family was no day at the beach, but like sand in your underpants, they weren't going anywhere.

Chapter Twenty-Three

Joel wheeled himself into the elevator and my heart was in my throat. What he'd said to me hurt immensely and at the same time, I grieved the thought of him leaving the mansion. Somehow, instinctively, I understood that he'd told me the truth, and he'd been in the house to protect us. Did it really matter how he'd gotten there? Then I remembered that sounded exactly like my mother's excuses for Bradley's abandonment.

How is Joel any different?

I felt safer with him in the house for one thing. Clearly, Joel had the cops on speed dial, and though my stepmother was locked away in that moment, with her connections and money, she'd be back soon enough. She was most likely a *murderess.* I'd seen enough *Dateline* to know the police couldn't arrest someone for murder without evidence. Which Joel had provided.

My head pounded. We'd be expected to live with a perpetrator because she'd been sly enough to fool my father into marrying her decades ago? How was that fair? And my father had been sly enough to remain in the house even when he had no business here other than to intimidate his daughters. I wanted Joel in the house. I *needed* him there, even if it was for no other reason than to let others know someone from the outside was watching.

"Joel's not leaving the mansion," I said to my sisters from the base of the grand staircase. My voice held more conviction than I'd ever mustered before.

Everyone stopped moving about and stared at me.

"Honestly, Sophia, you'll find another boyfriend," Gia said. "Don't be like Mom. Stop seeing the good in people that isn't there."

"This isn't about me," I snapped. "It's about all of us."

"He was here to do a job. He did it." Gia clicked her tongue. "You're just collateral damage, Sophia."

Of all my sister's traits, the ability to make me feel small and ridiculous was by far the worst. Gia and I weren't connected like other twins. We didn't have our own language. I didn't understand her most of the time, but on this she was dead wrong, and I wasn't about to let her step all over me like she normally did.

"Joel is not my boyfriend and I'm not attached," I hissed. "In fact, he probably only used my desperate and pathetic nature to take everyone's eyes off of what he was really up to. I've accepted that, but he's still the best defense against living with a murderer."

My sisters nodded and mumbled to the effect that this was probably true. Neither Quinn nor Brinn defended the use of that term against their mother. I supposed Joel wasn't on their radar as they had bigger fish to fry—like a mother in jail for murder and a dad who thought this was an appropriate time to take another shower.

"I don't know how you can trust him, Sophia," Quinn said. "He screwed with both of us. Have you forgotten what the society pages are saying about us both? Keeping him here will only give them more dirt, and trust me, we haven't seen anything yet. When they get ahold of my mother's story, all protections are gone."

"Think about it, Quinn. If your mother didn't do this, and there's a good chance she didn't, then someone else in the home might be responsible. Isn't a little humiliation worth the extra protection? It only matters if you care what strangers think and we have more important things to think about."

"I'm no fan of Joel's," Brinn said. "But I think Sophia's right. She's the one the papers are calling a tramp, so if she's willing to have him here, I don't see any reason he should bother you. You're the innocent victim in all the stories."

"Joel put our mother in jail. That doesn't bother you?" Quinn asked.

"Not if she did it," Brinn said honestly.

"How can you even think that?"

"I don't think it, but if she didn't, she'll be back home soon enough."

"Father isn't going to want him here," Quinn said.

"It's time for Dad to go," Brinn said. "We should have had Mr. Trunkett take care of things already. This is an awkward arrangement as it is. All of us sisters here with the man who stole a normal childhood from every single one of us. I'm not hating on Dad, but he's not helping the five of us get the trust's requirements done, is he? Every time we try to have a meeting, some sort of parental anarchy starts, and we don't meet. We don't get this money until the house is in full renovation, and we haven't been able to sit down to one mandated dinner without his interruptions and chaos. It's time to think about us as a team."

"None of us think Chelsea did this." Alisa finally spoke up. "She may be a prize witch, but she's no murderer. So that means, the person who did may still have access to us." Alisa proved to be very astute for as idiotic as she acted. "I, for one, think keeping Joel in the house is just smart. Plus, they love him on my social media. It pulls in an older crowd, which helps my numbers."

"I said, dinner is served!" Mrs. Chen shouted.

"Mrs. Chen," Quinn said softly. "There is no dinner tonight. Do you understand? Pack up the food and take it to our rooms. We've had a crisis, and we must deal with that first. I'll deal with Mr. Trunkett. Do as you've been told, Mrs. Chen. I won't ask again."

Mrs. Chen's eyebrows raised and she huffed off to the kitchen.

I wondered when Quinn and Brinn would realize the pain of watching their mother hauled off in handcuffs. For now, there seemed to be no other reaction than to get to business and decide what had to be done next, but eventually, they were going to take in the full extent of the day. Their mother was arrested for the murder of their beloved grandfather. Honestly, as rough as it was to leave Nonna and Papa and my mother, I now believed that Gia and I had it better than all of our sisters put together.

"I'm going to the police station," Quinn said. "Are you coming with me, Brinn?"

"Yes," Brinn said.

"The rest of you, eat and we'll talk about the renovations tomorrow. The sooner we get this started, the better. In the meantime, if you all vote for Joel to stay, that's fine with me, but keep him out of my sight."

"I'll tell him he can stay," I said too readily.

"Tomorrow, we'll have our official dinner and plan the gala," Quinn said emphatically. "We're not canceling it, and we're not running from the press. This is the hand the Wentworth sisters have been dealt and this is the hand we will play."

Joel had been right about Quinn. She continued to surprise me.

* * *

Once everyone had gone to their separate places to deal with the latest agony that reigned in Wentworth Manor, I climbed up the stairs to Joel's room. I wanted the truth. I knocked softly on the door.

"Who is it?" he called.

"It's me, Sophia."

There was a long pause.

"Can I come in?" I asked.

"Just a minute," he replied.

I waited in the hallway like some loser waiting for a text. I hoped against hope that my sisters wouldn't see me, pathetically standing outside Joel's door, rejected once again.

Joel finally opened the door. He stood on a single crutch with his free arm stretched up on the top of the door. His still-buff body stood as an impenetrable barrier between the room and me. He wouldn't look directly at me, but instead, looked toward the bay window at the top of the stairs while he spoke. "What do you need Sophia?"

"I want to talk to you."

"Now is not a good time. I have to pack."

"That's what I wanted to talk to you about. Move out of my way, please."

He stepped aside and stared at me with his arm still looped on top of the door.

"I'm not leaving anytime soon, so you may as well shut the door. Unless you want everyone to know our business."

"We have business?"

"We do," I said.

He shoved the door shut and hobbled over to a leather wing-backed chair in front of the heavy wooden fireplace. He sat down and dropped the crutch to the floor. "You want my full attention. Here it is."

"I want the truth."

"You want the truth? Your stepmother is a murderer. That's the truth."

"Why are you so angry?"

"I was asked to do a job. I did it. I stopped studying for the bar, put my life on hold and did what Mr. Trunkett asked of me. I did what the San Francisco Police Department asked of me. I found your murderer, but who is the bad guy here?" He shook his head and stared down at his lap.

"Does that bother you?"

"Not really," he said. "I did what I had to do. What bothers me is that you and Quinn are so quick to believe I had this outcome in mind. I had no idea who administered that extra morphine when I came here. I didn't know if it was an accident, incompetence or premeditated murder. Like Quinn, I assumed it was some flippant nurse who was ready to move on to her next assignment and she'd had enough of being in this creepy mansion."

"Chelsea has only been accused," I reminded him. "She hasn't been convicted yet."

"She did it, Sophia. You can search for your rainbow and gumdrops, but some people are just bad news and Chelsea is one of them. She's used her money and designer clothes to cover it up all these years, but what Chelsea wants, she gets. Your father looks like the bad guy because he had affairs and lives a separate life, but he's been trying to escape her for well over a decade and she won't let him divorce her." Joel shrugged. "She must have something on him."

"My dad has been trying to leave Chelsea? Are you sure?"

"I've done my research. The affairs . . . Alisa . . . he thought they would buy him his freedom."

I had to sit down. "It doesn't make any sense. Why would Chelsea threaten her lifestyle to get a few extra months, maybe a year free of my grandfather? He was one hundred years old, for crying out loud. How long could he have lasted?"

"Longer than she wanted him to, I guess. Motive isn't my job. That's the district attorney's job. I was about the investigation, and what I turned up wasn't pretty. Don't get me wrong, your father is a piece of work himself, but he's bitten off more than he can chew here."

"We want you to stay in the house. The girls and I voted."

He grimaced. "You do, do you?"

"Tell me who you are," I begged him. I got down on my knees under his chair. "The truth."

"I'm Joel Edgerton."

"I mean, how did you come to be here? Who are you, really?"

"After college, I was a rookie cop working under the investigative team for San Francisco homicide. After an incident, I thought my services would be better utilized as an attorney, so I went back to school at night and got my JD. While I was studying to pass the bar, Mr. Trunkett approached me with this assignment in return for his mentorship." He looked toward the window. "Plus a lot of cash. That's how things are done in this household. If someone says no, you up the offer. I have enough money now to go back home and practice law. It's time to get back to my responsibilities."

I ignored his swipe at the family. It was earned. "Like me, you're not done with your credentials."

"Nope. And now I might not get them because I'm burned out. I've had two full careers and I haven't mastered either of them. Essentially, I'm a thirty-two-year-old failure with a lot of cash."

"We have that in common. Well, minus your two years on me. And that fact that you wouldn't make this dress look like a sack," I laughed.

Joel turned more serious. "You do not look like a sack, and you'll have to protect yourself against those digs. That is common here, being reduced to a quip and being told who you supposedly are." He finally met my gaze. "You look gorgeous as always, but I prefer you in jeans and that sparkle Disney sweatshirt of yours. It highlights your eyes and makes them shine, too. Don't let them steal who you are. Do you promise?"

"Don't flirt with me, Joel. I'm not sophisticated like my sisters. I don't walk away from my feelings easily. I'm Italian, and I wear my heart on my sleeve. While that time in your lap at the zoo was a photo op for you, just a part of the job, it—" *Broke my heart.* I refused to speak it aloud and lose all dignity.

He placed his palm on my cheek and I backed away. I knew that I was naive and inexperienced, and maybe he hadn't said anything to imply we had a future, but I thought our relationship transcended words. I thought he'd said he saw the future with only me when he looked deeply into my eyes at the zoo. At that very moment, I felt he had so much more to say to me, but he said nothing, which could only mean I'd written a false script for Joel in my head, one that he had no intention of ever repeating.

"It's humiliating that you're going to walk out of this mansion like there was nothing between us. I didn't make it all up in my head!" I stared directly into his dark expression. "You're telling me I imagined it all?"

"I never said I was walking from you, but—"

"Why are you in such a hurry to pack then? You told me you were going back home. You're rich enough to do that now, remember what you said five seconds ago?"

"My job is done, Sophia. There's no reason for me to be here, and if this is meant to be, it will be."

It pained me that I wasn't a reason, but there it was, laid out bare. "You still live on the second floor without an elevator. How will you get around? What if you fall again?"

He reached for my hand while he stared into my eyes. My body shivered at his touch. "I won't fall."

"Your eyes are the color of Lake Tahoe," I said absently, lost in their intensity.

"That's where I was born," he said.

"In Lake Tahoe?"

"Not quite," he laughed. "Truckee."

"God must have been inspired and kissed your eyes with the color of the lake."

"You are a romantic."

"I'm worried you're going to leave and I'll never see you again." There. I'd said it. My truth as I knew it.

"I would never let that happen, Sophia." He placed both his hands on my face and cradled it in hands. "Kiss me, Sophia. I've wanted you to kiss me from the moment I laid eyes on you at your Nonna's house."

I rose up to meet his face and softly touched my lips to his. His kiss was firm and searching. Our passion quickly ignited to dangerous levels, and I felt lost in his touch, immune to anything anyone thought or said about me. I simply wanted to be in his arms and nothing else mattered. He pulled away first and left me seeking him like a blind baby bird pecking for its mother.

As I reached for him again, he twitched as if my touch burned him and suddenly his gaze, so deeply in connection with my own, had disappeared and gone vacant. "I shouldn't have kissed you. I'm sorry." He shook his head. "So unprofessional."

"Unprofessional?" I gasped. "This is about your job again?"

"I'm here to do a job. This isn't my life, Sophia. We can't pretend this is real. I shouldn't have kissed you," he said again. "I have responsibilities back home and I had no business falling for you or even staying on this one so long. If I hadn't been laid up—"

"If you hadn't been laid up, I would have navigated this strange new world alone, so I appreciate the time we had." I wasn't going to let him minimize what was between us.

"This isn't real," he repeated.

"What exactly do you mean by that? This is as real as it gets for me, Joel." I hadn't kissed him out of pure lust or his proximity. I'd kissed him because I felt there was nothing else I could do.

"Sophia, this—" He lifted his hand in the air. "All this. You need someone who is accustomed to this lifestyle. You're going to change and to grow. Don't limit yourself to me."

The sting of his comment brought out the bitterness in me. "I didn't ask you to marry me. No need to feel guilty. It was a simple kiss, Joel. Nothing more."

But it was more. My heart blossomed in his kiss and made me feel things I'd never felt before. I pulled my glasses off and rubbed the bridge of my nose. It was better not to see his expression. Whatever his duty was that he'd left behind in Truckee, it was more important than our connection.

"I'm sorry you feel that way," he said. "I lost myself. I have commitments back home. It's why I took the job in the first place."

I wanted to shake him and make his stoic self disappear, but then my rational self took hold and I exhaled. His words about Chelsea resonated. She'd done whatever she had to do to keep my father in her clutches. I wouldn't do the same to Joel. I cared about him too much for that. I wouldn't blame him for giving into the temptation of kissing me. We'd been involved in an emotionally charged situation. Naturally, he felt like kissing me. What else would he do with all that energy before he moved on to his next case? We were simply letting off steam.

"I understand," I told him, and, on some level, I did. I rose and left his room without looking back. "Stay here in the mansion," I said as I faced the door. "You need the help and the meals anyway. I won't bother you again. We'll forget this ever happened."

Well, I won't, but I'll do my level best to put on a good show of it.

Chapter Twenty-Four

Bail had been set at thirty-five million for my stepmother. *And she paid it.* Mr. Trunkett warned us she'd be home that afternoon and suggested that we find "something to do with ourselves" while he had the difficult discussion with Chelsea and Bradley and told them there was no room at the inn. It was time for them to take shelter in their Nob Hill penthouse and leave Wentworth Manor. For an old codger, Mr. Trunkett had a lot of moxie to face the woman who'd allegedly killed his friend.

Every one of us was going to be happy to see them go. Even Quinn and Brinn, which said a lot. After the news broke of their mother's arrest, Pacific Street was flooded with press. They were like crabs in a net, crawling all over each other to get the best shot of Wentworth Manor. It wasn't the typical, local press that had positioned one photographer/writer in a bush while he tried to earn his keep with a snippet from what the San Francisco socialites were doing for their Thanksgiving dinner. Or what went on behind the hedge that separated them from the home. This was an international press pool with tricked-out vans topped with satellites and cameras with lenses as long as my arms. They loved the salacious details of a murderess socialite possibly ending the life of her wealthier father-in-law. The story had everything but sex. We hoped anyway.

Mr. Trunkett arrived early that morning with his beat-up brief case and his haggard demeanor. He wanted to make sure we were all out of the house before Chelsea and Bradley arrived home. A connection at the police station promised to give him a heads-up on Chelsea's release. I wondered if it was the same informant that Bobbi had, and the guy was one big gossip.

The foyer was chaotic as we all scattered to find somewhere to be that day. Quinn and Brinn went to the stables and would lunch at the country club. They'd have dinner if her parents put up a fight. The police were on standby to escort them off the premises as Mr. Trunkett had secured a court order. One thing was certain, things were about to get ugly.

Gia went to work as was her normal routine, so I piled Joel and Alisa in the Prius and headed to my grandparents' home until the drama of the day had passed. Joel didn't want to leave the house, but Mr. Trunkett insisted. He scoffed and grabbed his cane before limping to the underground garage with a scowl on his face. I refused to acknowledge our kiss and decided we'd go right back to where we'd been when I thought he was engaged to Quinn. No harm, no foul. Simple mistake in the moment, that was all.

"I would rather be here to face them when they get home," Joel said as he struggled to climb into the passenger seat. "It would let them know a line has been drawn, and I'll be here if they give Mr. Trunkett any funny business."

"I'd rather you not tick off a might-be murderer," I told him over the hood of the car. "Live to fight another day and all that."

"She's the insidious type, that Chelsea. You can never be too careful with the likes of them."

"All the more reason to fear her. Don't you watch *Deadly Women*?"

He laughed. "I don't. For someone so naive of the world's dark side, you sure watch a lot of ghoulish stuff."

"Well, you should watch it. It might spare you from becoming the victim of a black widow."

"Duly noted," he said.

Once in the car, Alisa reached up from the backseat and plugged her phone in so we could listen to her incessant, upbeat pop. "My mom says she bets it's true about Chelsea. Bradley tried to leave Chelsea a bunch of times, and she threatened him if he ever left her, he'd live to regret it. The woman makes me shudder."

My mouth gaped open as I thought about Alisa's mother sharing such inappropriate material with her daughter. Did anyone in this family have boundaries? Or decency for that matter?

One lonely van followed us as we left the house. The bigger story was at Wentworth Manor, so we got some lackey intern. The regal face of Chelsea Whitman Wentworth coming home in a walk of shame—that was where the drama lay.

We drove the short distance to Papa's, and he stood with the garage door opened when we arrived. I pulled into the tiny garage, but it was too small for Joel to finagle his way out of the car, so I pulled back out, let him exit and pulled back into the dark, dank underground cement box that was the garage.

Papa dropped the garage door the minute we were in and stood at the doorway up the small staircase to the house. His face was alight at my presence, and it made me smile. He wasn't one for physical displays of emotion, but he hugged me hard and kissed my ear.

"Bella, we are so happy to have you home. So happy." He put his meaty hands on each side of my face and looked at Joel and Alisa. "She so beautiful, no? *Bellisima. Bellisima,*" Papa repeated.

"If only I could find a man who loved me as much as my Papa, I'd be set in life," I quipped.

Joel avoided my gaze and stuck his hand out. "Joel Edgerton," he introduced himself. "Former San Francisco P.D. I've been providing security for the heiresses in the house."

It bothered me that he'd introduced himself this way, especially after what my Papa said. It was as if he went out of his way to make sure there was no connection between us, to cast me off quickly like yesterday's dirty shirt.

"We appreciate you, no?" Papa said. "You keep my girls safe. They are everything to us." Papa focused his attention on Alisa. "Who is this little beauty?"

"Papa, this is our half-sister, Alisa Alton."

"Very nice to meet you, Alisa." He gestured to me. "Come in, eat. Your Nonna has been chomping at the bit to get some food in you. She says you look way too skinny in your newspaper pictures."

"Actually, I've gained weight," I told him. "Not being able to run these hills has really taken its toll."

Nonna greeted us all at the door and kissed everyone's cheek as they entered the house. She mumbled a prayer over each one of us and crossed herself and the doorway, especially when she saw Joel. It was clear she recognized him from the newspaper. Papa had moved the spaghetti rack from the kitchen, so for our house, it looked quite reasonable for a tired, 1940s kitchen that was still in use. Alisa looked around the house and went straight for the living room. "Oh my gosh, this vintage television is to die for. Can I take some pics?"

While Joel probably saw the house as a rundown shack worth millions, Alisa saw an Instagram playground filled with fresh backdrops and new textures for her TikTok videos and fashion shots.

"Have at it, Alisa. You can go anywhere in the house. There's a lot of great vintage stuff upstairs too. Go explore."

Papa stood, hunched over with his arm around Nonna. "We cook for you. You hungry?"

"It's 9:30 in the morning."

"You'll have eggs in a nest," Papa said. "You like bacon?" he asked Joel.

"Don't worry about me. I had some coffee this morning."

"Coffee." Papa waved a hand in disgust. "I'll make you espresso."

"Where's Mom?" I asked.

"At the restaurant. Working late tonight so I do not think you will see her unless you walk down there," Papa said.

I couldn't hide my disappointment, but I thought about the press outside and tried to be happy that I was at home with my Nonna and Papa. They were going to make breakfast and for one blessed morning my life was going to be the normal, stable world I craved.

Joel had treated me with eerie silence since our kiss and subsequent break-up. Truth be told, I was happy the kiss happened first. Otherwise, I would have wondered. Had I imagined it all? Was the chemistry only one-sided? But it hadn't been no matter how he tried to wiggle out of its impact on both of us.

Nonna pointed at Joel. "*San Michele Arcangelo?*" She nodded her head up and down and took his face in her hands briefly. "*Così bello.*"

"I thought so too, Nonna. He does look like the archangel." I looked to Joel. "Nonna thinks you look like the archangel Michael as well. And she says you're handsome."

He nodded at Nonna. "*Grazie.*"

She beamed when he spoke to her in Italian, and it dawned on me I wasn't the only one he had that charm over.

"We are selling the house," Papa said abruptly.

I nearly choked. "What? Why?"

"It's too much to keep up. Nonna and I are tired. We want to go somewhere simpler. We'll find a place with a nice kitchen. Maybe a view. Wouldn't that be nice?"

"In the City though, right? You're staying in the City."

"It is not the same place, Sophia. There is no place here for us now. Everything has been bought up and remodeled to look like the same old white boxes inside. This is not our home anymore."

"Papa, you can't leave Mom. Where will Mom go?"

"Your mama, she come with," Papa said. "She going to sell the restaurant. Some Greeks want to buy it."

"But it's in North Beach."

"Nothing left of North Beach no more. Your mama, she sell the place and come with."

I had to sit down, and the kitchen table was closest. "Papa, you can't. This is the only stable thing left in my life. My job is gone. I don't have my room anymore. Nothing is the same, Papa. This has to stay the same."

"Change is good," Papa said as he patted my cheek. "You go off, you'll get married. Change."

"No," I told him. "No change." Now I was talking in half sentences, but I could hardly believe my ears. My whole life had been about creating stability. Stability for families because I didn't have a father growing up. For some reason, God thought it was time to pull the rug out from under me in every facet of my life. Because I had a crush on my sister's fake fiancé? Is that what started this nightmare in motion?

My mom walked in the door, with two loaves of bread sticking out of her tote bag. I accosted her. "What's this about you selling the restaurant?"

"Oh, you heard. Yes, the Greek restaurant around the corner made me an offer. He's going to keep the staff."

"They always say that. Buyers say whatever you want to hear and then, they do as they like."

"Everyone is settled, Sophia. The staff will find something new if it's not to their liking. They're good at what they do. Who's your friend?"

"Joel," I answered absently. "Mom, Gia and I need this stability of home when this is all over. Let us buy it. We'll buy this house when we get the settlement, and then you and Papa, you won't have to worry about anything."

"What do you want this crumbling piece of brick for? It's falling apart."

"So is Wentworth Manor, but we're fixing that up. This place just needs some TLC and look at the comps around us. This place is worth four million without doing a thing to it. Do you really want to move Nonna and Papa at this stage in life?"

"You girls need to move on with your life—that's healthy. Papa and I went and looked on the peninsula for some places. We found some beautiful homes that are all one floor. There's enough room for—"

"The peninsula? You may as well move to SoCal! With traffic, it will take us forty-five minutes to get to you. What about the Italian market? Where's Papa going to get his sausage? His pecorino?"

"We can order it, Sophia. What's this about? I thought you'd be happy for us. You're always telling us this house is such a burden."

I thought I would be happy for them. But now it feels like such a betrayal.

"It's just so much change. More change and I can't handle it."

Joel put his hand on my shoulder, and his touch went through me like a bolt of lightning. I could tell myself it was a simple flirtation all I wanted, but that's not what I felt for Joel. I felt a magnetic pull towards him like a force that I could not control. A runaway train on a downward Sierra mountain track. I looked into those Lake Tahoe eyes and my own snowpack around my heart melted.

"You can have a driver take you to your family any time you want," Joel said helpfully.

I hadn't gotten used to the fact that people were now at my beck and call. I doubted I'd ever get used to that because it felt wrong. Insipid. "You're not going to be there, so please stay out of it!" I snapped at him.

"Where's your family, Joel?" my mother asked him as she tried to lower the tension.

"Truckee. Up by Tahoe," he answered.

"See Sophia? Joel lives here on his own here in San Francisco."

"I should hope so. He's a grown man."

"I meant he most likely still sees his family and yet he doesn't live with them. This is what's best for you, trust me."

"Joel, in Italian families, men usually live with their Mamas until they get married. Am I right, Mom?" The sizzling scent of bacon took over the kitchen.

"Sophia, behave yourself. What's gotten into you?"

I couldn't answer that question. Was it Joel's rejection? Or the idea of my childhood home being sold and leaving me with no escape from Wentworth Manor?

"Well, my mom should be thankful we're of jolly old English stock," Joel said "I don't think she'd be willing to wait that long. In fact, when I moved out, my room promptly became the den, so there's no going back now."

"Sophia tells us you're a lawyer."

"Breakfast ready!" Nonna called in her broken English. She looked at Joel and motioned for him to come to the table. "You come. Eat. Mangia!" She made a motion with her fork.

"What's it like in that mansion?" My mother asked. "Have you ever lived with clients before?"

"Joel is moving out soon, Mom. He's a cop, and his job is done."

"I thought he was a lawyer?" Mom said.

"He can't make up his mind what he is. He's both a cop and a lawyer. You have to ask him what he is today."

"Sophia! Don't be rude."

Perhaps I'm a wee bit edgy.

"You should come see where we're living, Mom. It doesn't feel right that you haven't seen it. It's only a few blocks, and we feel like a we're a world away. I know both Gia and I would feel so much better if you came and checked it out. Bradley is moving out, so it will be perfectly safe."

"I don't know, Sophia. I think it's best for me to not enter the lion's den."

"You're going to come to the gala," I said without giving her a chance to say no. "We're having a gala to announce our sisterhood and the plans for the mansion."

"Not while their mother is fighting this crazy accusation. Surely you're not having a party?"

"Take everything you know about family, Mom, and throw it out the window. These people don't operate like a normal family. What is happening to one of them seems to have no effect on the others. The gala was planned. The show must go on."

"I should say not."

"It's settled, you're coming to the Gala. Get something nice for Nonna and Papa to wear, and you too. Bradley and Chelsea won't be around, and this is your girls' celebration, Mama. You have every right to be there and you can't miss it." She looked to Joel, as if for permission.

He shoved a piece of bacon in his mouth while he nodded. "She's right. This is their celebration. Bradley has nothing to do with this gala. His inheritance is separate through the company, and he's not connected to the house. I agree it would look strange if you weren't there."

I could see my mother's inner turmoil brewing on her face. She didn't know how she felt about showing up in Bradley's lair. About being pulled back into his world. The world that rejected and vilified her though she hadn't been present in his life for more than two decades. I felt like if we could break her out of that fear, she could move on with her life. Maybe get a boyfriend or, ultimately, a husband. Maybe she could get unstuck and find a life that didn't include penance for her long-ago sin. She didn't look a day over thirty, and I wanted to see her dressed like the woman I knew hid beneath her overwrought, overworked surface.

"There's a letter for you there from your work. On the kitchen counter," Mom said.

I walked into the kitchen around the exposed water heater and grabbed the letter. I sliced into it with one finger and read the contents.

"It's my official termination letter. I've been fired, which I guess is good. I can get back to grad school full-time. Maybe go the psychologist route if social work isn't for me."

"Just leave that job off your resume," Mom said practically. "You were too low on the totem pole for it to matter anyway."

Shame crept over me like an afternoon fog. Joel seemed to recognize my humiliation and did me the favor of looking away. It wouldn't do any good to complain about it. No one felt sorry for an heiress. Nonna kept putting food in front of Joel, and he politely ate while my mother shot continuously invasive questions at him like a rapid-fire machine gun. I almost felt sorry for him. *Almost.*

Chapter Twenty-Five

After breakfast ended and Papa had taken away all the plates, Joel wanted a tour of the house. I warned him that three floors on a crutch sporting a few broken bones was highly impractical, but he was your typical male and determined to prove himself.

"What good are these metal plates in my leg if I can't get up a few steps?"

"Okay, Superman," I told him.

But he was relieved to see my grandparents had installed a gliding chair lift. It took forever, but he got up to the second floor and grinned. "I never would have made it up all that without falling." His brows rose, "But you knew that and wanted to spring the old man chair on me."

"Maybe." I smiled.

I showed him my room and then Gia's. "I can see why you didn't want to leave here. This is a great room. You're in the middle of everything."

I watched him grimace. "I think we should skip the rest of the house and get you downstairs."

"No, please. Your Nonna will feed me more and I'm going to pop. You want that chair rail to come off the wall?"

I laughed. "We'll skip my mom's floor. Suffice it to say, it looks like Gia's and my floor only neater."

I followed behind the chair lift as it ascended to the rooftop deck. "This is the only modern convenience my Papa has allowed in the house because my Nonna likes to come up here and drink wine with him. She says it reminds her of their courting days in Calabria, and her arthritis made it harder and harder."

When the chair stopped, I squeezed around Joel and opened the door to the patio where sunlight met us. The clip-clomp of his cast followed by his cane on the wooden planks echoed over the traffic below.

"We made it." The view from the deck was unimpressive. Nothing more than the surrounding buildings and tacky billboards, but it was home. I settled into one of the zero-gravity chairs Papa brought up during some past decade when they'd been popular. I motioned for Joel to sit in the more stable Adirondack chair and he did so.

Alisa came from out of nowhere behind a chimney and sat at the old table which probably came over on the Italian equivalent of the Mayflower. "This place is so cool. No wonder you didn't want to move."

"Are you hungry?" I asked her. "My Nonna lives to shove food down people, especially skinny ones like you."

"That's so sweet. Do you know how sweet that is?" she asked. "I called my mom and she's coming to get me."

"Do you need the address?"

She held up her phone. "No thanks, I pinned my location. She'll be here soon enough, said she was on her way. Seriously, I'd much rather live here than in Wentworth. This location is the bomb!"

"It's pretty cool," I agreed.

"We want to be together and watch when Chelsea gets home and gets kicked out."

"Did your mom say anything else about Chelsea's arrest?" I

asked her, interested in what someone who'd known Bradley more recently had thought.

"She always said Chelsea was a sociopath, so she wasn't even surprised. You know, Mom had been hurt so I thought maybe she was just jealous. Maybe bitter, too. I love my mom, but she's pretty insane at times, especially where my father is concerned. Here it turns out she might have been right about Chelsea all along. When I first heard that word, I had to look it up."

"You looked up the word "sociopath?""

"Yeah, I was eight."

It's getting harder to believe Alisa was never in state custody.

Alisa's phone dinged. "She's here. See you two back at the mansion. We're going to get pizza on the wharf. My mom knows a place that has the news on twenty-four seven." Alisa skipped toward the door to the stairs and disappeared behind it.

How I wished I had her youthful zeal and the ability to see our current circumstances as some great adventure to be cataloged on Instagram. I felt ancient for my years.

An awkward silence stretched between Joel and me, marked by his robotic movements as he tried to get comfortable in the wooden beach chair. He looked at his watch and likely lamented how much time we still had to kill.

"Do you want to go for a walk, maybe?" I looked at his cast propped up on the table. "Ah, never mind."

"The press is out there anyway. We should turn on the news and see if your father has come back to Wentworth Manor."

"Should we though? I mean, do we really want to watch his forlorn face when he exits? As much as the man probably deserves all he's getting, he has to actually leave his house and live with the woman who probably killed his father. No matter how you slice it, that sucks."

Joel shook his head. "It's this type of event that made me decide to go back to private defense work. Trunkett never rests, and he has to do the dirty work for others. At least in the investigative role I can use both of my strengths.

"Trunkett loves you. He'll be disappointed."

"He agrees I don't have the stomach for family law. He's found me something in Placer County that uses both of my skillsets."

"Placer County. You mean by Tahoe?"

"Yeah. I'll come down here now and again if Trunkett needs me, but he found me a good position. I'll help law enforcement when they've been accused of a crime anywhere in California. I'll help abuse victims prove their abuse in court—not easy to do. I'll work remotely from Truckee and fly out of Reno or Sacramento when I'm needed on a case."

"That's great," I lied. "Were you planning to tell me?"

"I'm telling you now."

"Wow. You don't pull any punches, do you?"

"Listen, I'm sorry about yesterday—you know, kissing you."

"I knew what you meant." *Rub it in why don't you?*

"I don't know what came over me. It was completely unprofessional. Scared me that I gave in so easily. I took a much harder look at Trunkett's offer after last night."

"I chased you away, is that what you're saying?"

"Don't mix my words up. I don't know what I'm saying. I'm trying to do the right thing. I'm a terrible choice for you, so how far can this thing go? I'm being practical and ripping off the Band-Aid."

"Really? Is it practical to leave an international city job and go to some Podunk county sheriff's office? That's a brilliant career move now, is it?"

"I can't stick around and watch you get swallowed by the heiress lifestyle. It will happen. Money makes it happen. Then, you'll see me for who I am, a blue-collar guy who got lucky in law school and can't stop a case to go to the opera opening."

I rose and swept my hand out over the City. "This *is* my heiress life, Joel. Look at my surroundings. Check out the erectile dysfunction billboard that is my view from this patio. This is who I am. A second-generation Italian-American, runner and social worker who wants to reunite families and craves stability. I never asked for any of this."

"And I'm a cop slash lawyer. What's your point? I can hardly do investigations with an heiress on my arm, can I?"

I'm not going to chase him. Nor was I going to beg him. We'd shared a kiss and a connection. In the long run, it was nothing more than an online hook-up to today's generation. It meant nothing, and my romantic notions weren't going to change that. I wouldn't fall into my mother's trap of believing there was one man for me. There was a plethora of men out there. All I had to do was get over this one and start my search. How hard could it be when you were worth a few billion?

Though it did make it fairly obvious that being an heiress didn't stop rejection, and this one made me feel slightly empty inside, as if I couldn't imagine a life without him. But I would.

"You're right, Joel. You have a calling. I have a calling. They're different. I will say that I'm incredibly happy our paths crossed at all. I am grateful you were in Wentworth Manor when I arrived."

He took my hand and lifted it to his lips. "Me too, Sophia." I couldn't take my eyes off of his.

Finally, I blinked and the spell was broken. I wanted to ask him why he had to be the blasted hero and leave. Men confounded me. I suppose that was genetic.

"Hello?" The door to the stairs opened, and my mother came out with a tray full of lemonade and Italian wedding cookies my Nonna had made. "I thought you might need a snack."

"Mom, we just had a lumberjack breakfast."

"I know, but you're too thin. Both of you are wasting away in that mansion. Don't they feed you?"

Joel laughed. "They don't feed us enough. Can I move in here?"

My mother grinned, "You protected my daughters. You can live here any time you'd like, and that's not just politeness, it's the truth."

I rolled my eyes. Of course my mother would fall in love with Joel. He was as emotionally checked out as my father. "Joel's moving. He's just told me that he's accepted a job near Tahoe."

"Tahoe?" Mom exclaimed. "Such beautiful country. You know, it used to take us three hours to get to Tahoe. Now it's about six with all the traffic." She clicked her tongue. "San Francisco isn't the same place it was, that's for sure." My mom focused her eyes on me, "You're not moving?"

"I can't move, remember? I'm stuck in the mausoleum for a year. Hopefully, I make it out alive."

"Now Sophia, that isn't funny. I'm sure there's a rational explanation for what Chelsea has been accused of."

"There is," Joel said. "She wanted her father-in-law dead."

My mom gulped. As much as I loved my mother, she wasn't great at believing people harbored bad intent. She always seemed to think they were unable to do good and the evil was forced upon them. Maybe it was that naïveté that kept her single all these years.

"If that's the case, Joel, you've got no business starting a new job now. This one isn't done."

Now it was Joel who visibly gulped. "Chelsea and Bradley are moving out. Your daughters will be fine once I leave."

"I'm sure whomever left Chelsea alone with Wyatt Wentworth assumed the same thing. I always knew there was something not right about that woman."

Now you think that. "What happened to 'that's who your father chose and like it or not, we are better off for it?'"

"We are better off for it. If a father can't be there, you should know it's better to have him out of the picture than to come in and out and disrupt your lives. It gives a child false hope."

"We certainly never had any of that," I said.

My mother's Pollyanna view of life humiliated me. I didn't want Joel to bear witness to it. I didn't want him to know she never spoke ill of Bradley Wentworth, nor had she ever done anything to keep him away. He simply hadn't bothered to show up in our lives. Nor did he ever acknowledge he had two daughters in the old Italian section of town. It still shamed me to my core.

Mom came and sat beside me in the other zero-gravity chair and nearly fell out of it while she tried to balance. She giggled at her own klutziness. "Papa got a deal on these chairs. You take your life in your hands trying to sit in them, but by golly, they were cheap."

"They look comfortable. If I could get into one without breaking the other leg, I would have tried it," Joel said.

"You need to get healthy. You're a strapping young man and you're fortunate you were hit by such a small car."

"I was fortunate your daughter was there. Did she tell you she stayed with me and kept me awake?"

"No. I don't think she did." Mom glared at me and sighed. "She doesn't tell us a lot. I think she tries to protect me. I don't know if she's told you, but I avoid bad news with a vengeance. The world has so much bad news, why do I need to hear about it? It doesn't talk about the homeless man at my shop who picks up garbage and smiles through the day. Nor the woman who feeds twenty-five people a day on her small pension. No, the news chooses to focus on the negative, and I can't take that. Mr. Rogers used to say whenever there is bad news to look to the helpers. I can't tell you how good I feel to know that my daughters are the helpers."

"You raised them well, Ms. Campelli. They're so polite to the staff at the manor, and they took in Alisa like she was one of their own because her mom couldn't come with her. You have a right to be enormously proud of your girls."

"I do, don't I?" Mom rose from the chair. "Well, if you're leaving soon for Tahoe, I'll let you and Sophia have your time. It's a shame there wasn't more than friendship here. You two make a striking couple."

"Really, Mom? I think I'm out of his league."

Joel spit lemonade on the porch while he erupted in laughter. "She is, Ms. Campelli. She's completely out of my league."

Mom's expression lost her mirth. "That's what they told me about Bradley, but now his wife is in jail for murder. Don't listen to anyone who tries to put you in a box, Joel."

"No, I wouldn't," he said. "Mrs. Campelli, do you mind if I ask you about Bradley? Not the one I know obviously, but the one you knew?"

Mother sat down again, this time more gracefully, in the zero-gravity chair. "Well, what do you want to know?"

"What was he like when you knew him?"

"Let's see." She pursed her lips together while she thought. "He was tall and gangly in high school. He couldn't play sports, and the kids made fun of him for wearing glasses. You know, beat on him in dodge ball, tackled him in flag football, that kind of thing. Kids are so mean."

"That's where I got my bad eyes," I exclaimed.

"He must wear contacts now or maybe had that surgery they do. You know, the one where they laser your eyeballs?" Mom said. "But back in the day, he couldn't see two feet in front of him, and his glasses made him look like one of those stuffed animals with the googly eyes."

"Mom, what on earth did you see in him? He sounds abhorrent."

"He was so sweet back then. He'd carry my books to class. He'd take them to my locker after school. And he loved to treat me to nice things. Ice cream in the soda shop. French fries at the little cafe in the theater district. He made me laugh like no one else because he was so genuinely smart. I shined when he was near." Mom's face was lit up like the Bay Bridge at night, then her reality set in. "Then we graduated and he went off to college and I never heard from him again." She stood. "End of story."

"Did he know you were pregnant?"

"He knew. He accused me of trapping him. Said it was someone else's, but he didn't even have the decency to say that to my face. He had it printed in the newspaper. It wasn't like it is today. In the 80s, having a baby out of wedlock, especially in North Beach, was humiliating. There was a lot of shame, and people talked about me on the street. It was awful, and of course, I was as big as a house with you two."

"You didn't deserve that Ms. Campelli. I'm so sorry that happened to you and the girls."

"Ah, we were better for it. Who wants a man around who thinks it's a chore to stay? You want a man who takes pleasure in providing and protecting. I don't know where the Bradley I fell in love with went, but who he turned out to be was someone who took pleasure in my downfall. Trust me, being alone and raising these girls alone is the best gift he ever gave me."

My mom patted me on the shoulder and left the rooftop. "That's the most I've ever heard about my father in this lifetime."

"Sometimes you have to ask the right questions," he said.

"The story depressed me something awful. I'll never understand love. It's only gotten more confusing since moving into the house and being with my dad and my sisters . . . and you. All this time, I thought my calling was to put families back together. How can I do that when I have no understanding of how love works?"

"What makes you say that?"

"My mother. If anyone knows how to love, Joel, I'm convinced it's her. She's sacrificed her whole life to love her parents well and bring my sister and me up in one of the most expensive markets in the world. She never stops and she never complains."

"Well, that's love."

"But why didn't Bradley love her? Why did he marry that dreadful woman? Why does he stay married to that dreadful woman? She may have killed his father."

"She *did* kill his father," he said emphatically.

"I thought innocent until proven guilty."

"You're right," he said. "I want you prepared is all."

"I was raised to think that God is just, and that's not just.

Nothing about this situation is just. How is it fair that women like Tanya get to walk all over the people who love them, let their kids get beat on by some drug-addicted dude, and men like poor Charlie Jessup take her back at her first apologetic word? Women like her love their drugs more than their own children. I see it every day. Those kids still love their parents and want to be with them, no matter what has been done to them."

Joel shrugged. "I bet no matter what you did in this lifetime, your mother would never stop loving you. Kids are wired to love their parents. Some people are wired to love more than others."

"That kind of love is everywhere in my life. I'm so grateful for it, don't get me wrong, but why did my mother have to spend her life alone?"

"She didn't. That was her choice. I imagine your mother listened to her gut while Chelsea made a business decision to stay with a man who doesn't seem capable of monogamy."

"I feel as if the veil has been torn and the world is a much uglier place than I imagined."

Joel put his hand gently on my knee. "Chelsea made a choice every day to stay with Bradley. She might tell herself it's for the kids or the family, but ultimately she's made her choice, and now it seems the worst choice of all. She chose to play God in a situation that wasn't hers to control. That's what it cost her to keep Bradley and now she may lose her freedom."

I was astonished Joel had so much to say about Chelsea's choices. It didn't seem like his nature at all to judge, and yet I felt his rage under his calm demeanor. "You hate Chelsea."

"I don't like to think of myself as a hateful person, but she comes close," he said. "I did a lot of research on Wyatt during this investigation, and he didn't deserve this. No one would."

I wondered why so many innocent people had to come into contact with those who wished to do harm. "Do you think my mother made a conscious choice?" I asked him. "I don't know that she did. I think she never recovered when my father betrayed her in the way that he did. There are some hurts that you just can't seem to get past."

"You have to get past them. Life doesn't give us other options. You either learn from mistakes and grow, or stagnate." Joel stared off into the distance. "It probably sounds cold to you, but I see a lot in my line of work, the worst human beings have to offer. You have to get beyond it to be effective."

I felt sick at his comment. I knew he was right. It's what my mother had done. She'd stayed in the same place her whole life rather than accept God's forgiveness of her sin and move on. *What's the point of praying every day and believing in forgiveness if you aren't willing to accept it?* I'll admit, I struggled with her brand of faith.

"Maybe moving out of this house will give my mother a new perspective." It never dawned on me that keeping things the same is what kept us all in the stagnant energy of old-school Italia when San Francisco was changing before our very eyes. Maybe mom was supposed to get on with her life—maybe we all were.

"Sometimes, it's important to move on. Don't let the grass grow under your feet and all."

"So that's it. I have no say in the fact that this is over, and it was just a dalliance. Something to pass the time while you—"

"You make it sound dirty. You're safe. My job was to keep you safe and I did that. I can't help it if I fell for you in the process. You're gorgeous with the personality of an angel, so why wouldn't I fall for you?"

Something about his false compliment and the word *safe* lit a fire in me. "I don't have any such thing! The personality of an angel? Have we met? And I'm safe? You mean, like my mother has been safe her whole life?" I equated his version of safe with alone. "Maybe I don't want to be safe. Did that ever occur to you?"

"Well no—"

"Maybe I look at Charlie Jessup and I think what a man he is. Everyone on earth calls him an enabler and weak, but he fought for the woman he loves. He fought hard, and now his family will be back together again. He didn't care who thought he was a fool. He did what he had to do, and I'll admit it, I want a man like that. I don't want some wuss like my father who stays married for decades and cheats because he doesn't have the guts to file for divorce. I want a man who fights for me, and I'm not afraid to admit it. So, you're right, we're done here."

"I'm doing you a favor, Sophia. You think that you want what we have together, but you'll get past that. You need a man who doesn't have so much baggage. One who has a solid career by my age."

"What baggage?" I asked him. "It's not like you've shared a lot with me. Why don't you share what makes you such bad boyfriend material? So I'll feel better about being safe." I bat my eyelashes like an impish cartoon character.

"I don't want to discuss this."

"Tough. We're going to discuss it. I mean, it's fine to dump me, say that we never had anything more than an attraction to each other. Whatever. But you owe me the truth on who you are and why you're leaving because you kissed me and that's like a pinkie promise."

His mouth went ajar. "You sound like Alisa."

"And? The baggage please."

"We both need to focus on our careers," he said.

"I have a career now," I told him. "It's called being a billionaire. My plan is to work for children and families in San Francisco. I'll set up charities and group homes. I have a career, Joel. Don't you worry about me."

"I'm not worried about you. That's just it. I know you're fine without me. You're right. You have a career. You have a life. It's me—"

"I want to go home," I told him.

"We can't yet," he looked at his watch.

"I'm not afraid to see my father. I'm not afraid to see the murderess. I want to go home." I really wanted *him* to go home, but that didn't seem polite. Everything that mattered to me had disappeared, my mom, my grandparents, my job . . . and sadly, the one that currently hurt the most . . . Joel.

It dawned on me that I could ask Mr. Trunkett to rescind the job offer, and I worried maybe I had more of my father in me than just my bad vision.

Chapter Twenty-Six

Gia rushed at me when I arrived home at Wentworth Manor. "You've heard about Mama?"

"You mean that she's moving?"

She nodded. "Selling the restaurant? What is she thinking? She claims there's no reason to stay here, like we've made some kind of choice to be here and she's wiped her hands clean of us."

"She probably feels rejected. She isn't going to walk away from us. We're her world." I didn't want Gia's dredged up drama. I had enough of my own to think about. "We can go live near Mom when all this is over."

"We can't just leave the City," Gia said. "We need to get back to work." She lowered her voice. "Or we might become miserable like our sisters."

"They're not miserable," I told her. "They're stressed."

"They're stressed because their mother is a psycho and their dad is a wimp," Gia whispered.

"Our dad," I reminded her. "I can't worry about this right now. I need to think about other things."

"What other things?" Gia asked.

"Things," I said flatly. I walked through the conservatory and toward the backyard so I could get some air. Maybe some time under the stars would help me to organize everything in my monkey mind. That's what I called it when I couldn't get the kids to stop running long enough to meet with their parents. There was so much to think about—going back to school and getting my doctorate seemed the best option. School would take my mind off of everything and take me back to my focus—restoring families, creating the new normal with my own brand of stability. Relying on myself and not my childhood home. . . .

When I reached the end of the opened glass doors in the conservatory, I heard people talking. Frightened after living in the family *Dateline* episode, I ducked behind a camellia bush and listened. I tried to discern who was speaking, but the hushed whispers were barely audible. My body felt like it lived in fight-or-flight mode ever since I'd moved into the mansion. Rather than step back into the safety of the mansion and get help, something kept my feet firmly planted on the red bricks beneath the camellia. As my heart rate slowed, the words took shape and separated.

"Quinn, please hear me out." It was our father—who was supposed to be out of the house by now.

My legs shook, and my hands trembled against the green leaves, but I made no effort to leave. I had to know what he had to say for himself—how he felt about his father being possibly murdered by the woman he married. I clasped my eyes shut tightly as if I'd hear better.

"Dad, this is so much worse than you told me. I need you to be honest with me, the whole truth!" Quinn said. "You can't protect me from it any longer, is that clear?" Her voice cracked. "I won't help you anymore unless you tell me the whole truth."

"I promise," he said.

I needed to calm down so they wouldn't hear my heartbeat, which was thunderous. I breathed shallowly so I wouldn't be found out, and waited.

"You promised before," she said. "I did everything that you asked of me. I brought Joel into the house. I let him do his job and search for the empty vials. You basically turned me against my own mother without warning me. What more could you possibly ask of me?"

"I never should have asked that of you. I didn't think I'd be right. It was a hunch. I thought—"

"What happens now, Daddy? You were right. It appears that Mom gave Grandfather more morphine than was necessary. Certainly more than he needed since he wasn't in pain," Quinn snapped. "You took him away from me."

"I didn't."

"You did," she said. "You knew she was capable of it or you wouldn't have hired Joel in the first place. The question is why didn't you hire Joel before she did it? Why after? How am I supposed to believe you're innocent in all this?"

"I couldn't have known she was capable of that. It was after because I never foresaw anything like this. Your mother, she's self-absorbed, lacking all maternal instincts as well as the ability to connect with other human beings, but a murderer? How could I have thought my wife capable of such evil?"

"Because you of all people knew who she was." Quinn hadn't backed down.

A long silence formed, and I held my breath as I waited.

"You're right," Bradley conceded. "I'm as guilty as if I injected the morphine myself."

"Grandfather is gone, and now we're ruined in this town. We might have gotten over you pollinating the entire mistress realm of San Francisco, but this? Never."

I gritted my teeth tightly. My mother was no mistress, just a misguided soul who saw the best in everyone, even when it wasn't there.

"We are finished," he agreed. "But you have to separate yourselves from this scandal. You need to have the gala regardless of what happens with your mother's case. You can't back down or these hyenas will eat you and your sisters alive. This isn't your sin. You shouldn't pay the price for it."

"But we will."

"The best way to handle scandal is to face them down. We'll get your sisters media training as soon as possible. I'll text Anne at the office as soon as we're done. Remember, don't deny it, don't engage the subject. You'll have the gala next month in December rather than January before the ballet opening."

"People are so booked at Christmas. What if it's too fresh and no one shows up? We'll be shunned and ruined."

"You've got your sisters as a siren call for the press. San Francisco urchins become heiresses overnight. They won't be able to resist the deliciousness of that gossip. Society will show up, I promise."

Quinn's breathing became shallow. "I'm hyperventilating. I don't think I can do this, Daddy."

"We'll get some press stories planted about how Grandfather Wentworth would have wanted you to soldier on, how you can't comment on the case, but get them to admire you for your backbone and fearlessness."

"That's the first time I've heard you acknowledge my sisters, as in more than one."

"They're your sisters." He said this with a softness, a humility that I'd never heard in the man before. In fact, I hadn't thought he was capable of it. "I loved Mary." His voice seemed to crack as he spoke of my mother, and I struggled for air, so fearful I'd be caught eavesdropping. "I'd forgotten how much I loved her until I saw Sophia and Gia—they're her very image. Mary was such a light and happy soul. All the guys at school thought she was the perfect catch, but she chose me and my Ichabod Crane self. You can't know what that did for me back then."

"I can't imagine you being anything but the Homecoming King, Dad."

"Hah! I was so awkward. All spindly limbs with a concave chest and bony horse knees." He chuckled. "I didn't fit in at public school, but my father felt it would be good for my character. But Mary . . . she invited me into her friend group and suddenly I was cooler than I had been before. People took notice of me, and they stopped making fun of me because Mary would ignore them when they did."

"You were a geek?" Quinn asked with a giggle. "I can't even picture it, so if you were so in love, how did you meet Mom?"

It was obvious that Quinn wanted to hear her own parents' love story, but I ached deeply to hear more about my mother when she was a perpetual light and a popular cheerleader.

Bradley's voice began again. "That's a dark tale," he said. "My mother told me Mary wasn't worthy of being a Wentworth. She didn't have the proper family background, nor the finishing school upbringing my mother felt was necessary for a wife and hostess in San Francisco society. She told me I was doing Mary a favor, that I'd only embarrass her and make her miserable in such a role. It was much more formal back then than it is now, if you can believe that."

"But when did you meet Mom?"

"Mother said I was too young to be married and tied down. I asked her to marry me, you know."

"Mom?"

"No, Mary. My parents were livid. They sent me off to college at USC and forbade me to talk to her again. I heard through some mutual friends that she tried to get word to my parents when she was pregnant with my child—well children—but they shut the door in her face. Mrs. Chen told me that part many years later."

"She's been here that long?"

"Yes, and she seemed old back then, so how she still manages to run everything as tightly as she still does, I'll never understand. The irony of my mother saying Mary wasn't worthy to be called a Wentworth, when I was never a Wentworth to begin with—her godliness act—I wonder if that great faith came before or after her affair. One thing is certain, our family is a mess. No wonder Grandfather wanted us to fix it."

"Daddy, I'm truly sorry you're not his son. Grandpa Wyatt loved you."

"I'm sure he never knew. If he had, he would have made sure

to cover his tracks somehow. He would have never let my mother be found out. He loved her too much for that. But like most men in his business, he was never present enough to love her in person. It was always from afar. Some grand gesture, some great gift—like this house, but never what she wanted, never his whole heart."

"Daddy, I've never heard you talk this way. Do you think that's why he structured his will the way he did?"

"I don't want to make any more mistakes, Quinn. If your mother finds out that I'm the one who outed her, so be it. You need to do what you have to and protect yourself from here on out. I'll even testify against her if it's necessary, but I can't pretend anymore. I can't be the one who makes her look normal in society. It's not who she really is."

My pulse quickened again. I could hardly believe what I was hearing, what I was witnessing. The conversation sounded as if it was coming to an end, and I sank deeper into the camellia bush and begged God to not be found out.

"You never answered me. What about Mom? Did you ever love her?"

"I did in my own way, but it was never easy with us. She always wanted more than I could give, and I struggled my entire life to be worthy of her love, but it was never enough. She wanted complete obedience and sole surrender, and I couldn't make myself small enough."

"Mom needed to know she was your one and only. That's just how she is. Obviously, she loved you Daddy."

"Not as much as she hated my father."

"Maybe not," Quinn said. "But you won't stand by her?"

"Not after this," he said.

"What about Alisa's mother?" Quinn asked him. "She stood by you after the affair. You say you loved Mary; did you love Jennifer too?"

"I loved her for what she gave me, unconditional acceptance that I didn't deserve. She loved me. I'm sure of it, but I was only substituting her for your mother. I wanted your mother to love me, and I'd run myself ragged trying to make it happen, but she wasn't capable of loving me. No matter who I became or what I was, I wasn't what Chelsea needed or wanted."

"You don't think it's because maybe Mom is incapable of love?"

"Quinn!"

"Dad, everyone covers for her. Everyone around her makes her look like a normal human being and loving wife and mother. But you and I both know that she was never that. It's time this family faced some hard truths."

"I'm not ready for that. I have to regroup. Think about what I'm going to do."

"She forgave you for the affair," Quinn reminded him.

"I had that affair publicly on purpose. I'd asked her for a divorce, and she wouldn't give me one. Oh Quinn, I shouldn't be telling you any of this."

An icy chill ran down my spine, and I shuddered at Bradley's confession. *He was trying to get a divorce? The photos of the happy family were all staged?* I struggled to understand the mindset of pretending at life for other people's benefit.

"I need to know the whole truth," Quinn pleaded. "This is what Grandfather wanted. He wanted us to face our demons and be a real family, so you're not helping me by keeping me in the dark."

Bradley paused as if he considered remaining quiet. I waited breathlessly before he started to expand on his confession. "I figured the humiliation of the affairs would be enough to force her into signing the papers, but I underestimated your mother. My affairs only made her look like more of a saint because she chose to publicly forgive me," Bradley said. "Nothing that woman does isn't carefully weighed out and measured. I should have known she'd play her full hand, and I'd be left defeated."

"I hate that you cheated, Dad. It was humiliating for us too. Did you ever think of that?" Quinn asked.

"I didn't," he admitted. "I thought of my escape. Anyway, I

shouldn't be talking like that about your mother, but she said if I pursued the divorce I'd never see you girls again. It's been an all-out war and I'm battle weary."

"It's going to be hard, but I think you have to do the right thing and let her pay for what she's done. If she really did it."

"She's already got the press on her side. I can almost guarantee you that it's going to get turned around on me. San Francisco loves your mother. I can see the headlines now, 'Socialite and beloved benefactor faces unsubstantiated murder charges.'"

"I'm scared, Daddy. People have no idea—"

"I won't let her anywhere near you girls. That's a promise and I hope Joel is as clean as he claims because any skeletons he has are coming out to play if Chelsea has her way."

"If we all stand together, maybe—"

"She's thought of that, trust me. She thinks years in advance, and she's livid. She threw a tantrum like I've never seen before at the penthouse tonight. No vase or piece of glass was safe. I'll have to clean it up because I don't trust her with anyone just yet."

"Why didn't she stay in jail?" Quinn asked.

It was obvious Quinn didn't feel protective over her mother at all, which made me wonder what kind of mother Chelsea was. Were they right? *Is anyone really incapable of love?*

"She put the penthouse and the Napa house up for collateral. I thought you couldn't bail yourself out, but apparently, when you have that kind of money, you can do what you like. She is wearing an ankle bracelet so she can't leave the penthouse. I'm safe here for now."

My legs were shaking so that the trellis and leaves in front of me quivered from the movement.

"You can't stay here though, Dad. There's a court order that you're not supposed to be here, but I'm afraid for you to go back. I don't want her to know that you did this, that you hired Joel. You have to let her think it was me, and it was an accident that we found out it was her. That part is true on my part. I never guessed she was this bitter, this hateful."

"I've sheltered you and Brinn over the years. Now I know I didn't do you any favors. I do believe she's dangerous. I lied to myself long enough, but when you tell Chelsea Whitman Wentworth *no*, a nuclear fallout is coming. She was in the kitchen finding things to throw when I escaped. That's why I texted you that I was down here. I had nowhere to go. Our name will never be the same in this town, and it makes me think of places I might escape to."

"I'm sorry it was true, Daddy."

"Your grandfather didn't deserve to die like that. I keep thinking of the fear he must have had on his face when Chelsea entered into his chambers. Did he scream? Did he call out for anyone? Or did he accept his fate like the stoic man I knew him to be?"

"Dad, stop torturing yourself. Grandfather is at peace now."

"I wish Grandfather never brought Brinn back home to this house with his ridiculous inheritance scheme. Brinn should have stayed at school. You all could have had your life and the money. This house is haunted with the memories of times gone by. Times that we all pretended were good but never were." Bradley screamed out an expletive. "My brother Wyatt's death was only the tip of the frigid iceberg. I want you girls to have your freedom."

I stumbled against the brick exterior wall and hit right where the hairline fracture was in my rib. A whimper escaped my lips.

"Who's here?"

Within seconds, Quinn and Bradley were standing over me. I clutched my side as the air evaporated from my lungs. I couldn't breathe. My body convulsed, and the harder I tried to settle myself, the more my body protested. Everything I'd been tamping down exploded, and I trembled like an earthquake from the unyielding agony inside.

"Quinn, call 911." Bradley stood over me and lifted me off the patio. "Sophia, what's happening?"

I shook my head frantically, but I couldn't answer.

"Are you diabetic?"

I shook my head again and searched for more words that didn't crystallize.

"Sophia!" Quinn gasped. "Stay calm. The ambulance is on its way." She looked to our father. "Dad, you need to get out of here. The cops are coming and the last thing we need is more press."

"I'm not leaving. They'll have to arrest me." He looked down at me, and I saw warmth in his eyes, and I understood. I understood so much. He loved my mother and it was in his eyes. "It's all right, Sophia. You're going to be all right. You've had a scare, that's all."

"Sophia, I don't know how long you were listening," Quinn said. "Can you hear me?"

I nodded.

"You can't let people know my father hired Joel," Quinn said. "It's not safe for him. Nod if you understand."

I couldn't feel my body. I heard everything Quinn and Bradley said, saw his pale form as it hovered over me and cradled my head in his hands off the cold, hard ground. It all felt like a nightmare, which I watched at the end of a long tunnel from another realm.

Marred from the discovery of his secrets, Bradley appeared blanched and broken under the patio's pale light. I took no pleasure in his wounds—instead, I finally saw the humanity in my father. He was neither hero nor villain. He was simply a sinner—no better or worse than me.

Chapter Twenty-Seven

Days at Wentworth Manor seemed to stretch on forever. We were living in the movie *Groundhog Day* with better accommodations and a view. The EMTs said I suffered a panic attack brought on by acute stress, and I needed to rest. The pain was most likely psychosomatic. *Honestly, how humiliating.* I'd woken up inside the conservatory with everyone in the household standing over me, leering down at me like I was the latest episode of *American Idol*.

I knew I should go to bed and make the horrible day end as soon as possible, but my heart was still high up in my throat. It pounded hard at the words I'd overheard. *My dad loved my mother once.* I couldn't get past the admission. I thought my mother made up their relationship, that she'd romanticized the fleeting yet idealized time in her head—but I was wrong. Somehow, it changed everything for me.

Grandmother Wentworth, portrayed as this godly, ethereal human being above the rest of us, had stood between their relationship. She'd slammed the door in my mother's young face and torn her innocence away with her rejection of Mama's pregnancy.

She can keep that brand of religion, thank you very much.

Gia brought in a tray of soup and set it down on my bed. "Do you need to eat? Gosh, you were shaking. It was so scary."

"They said it wasn't the pain."

"What do they know? Did *they* feel the pain?" Gia asked. "I hate so-called experts."

"I'm glad we already had the X-rays. The last thing I wanted to do was go back to the hospital."

"Just so you know, we refused to press charges against Bradley for being here. I wanted to, but I got overruled." Gia shrugged.

I told her everything I'd overheard except for the revelation that it was Bradley who hired Joel. We both stared at the bowl of soup, unsure of why it mattered that our mother's fantasy had a basis in truth.

"I'm not hungry," I told Gia. "I was at Nonna's all day."

"Oh right," she said and lifted the tray to a nearby table.

"I wonder how Nonna and Papa reacted when Mom announced us. Did it happen before or after the great saint Amelie slammed the door in her face?"

"We could ask her," Gia said. "But I suppose when we came into the world, most of it was forgotten."

"It's hard for me to have much sympathy for Bradley, yet I do."

"He still seems like a shell of a human to me. Not man enough to protect the women in his life. He didn't stand up for our Mom in any way, shape or form. That's vile behavior."

"Well, he didn't know she was pregnant until later, and he was so young," I said.

"I've put up with your bleeding-heart nature for a lifetime. Let's get one thing straight. Bradley is no hero. He didn't stand up for Mom. He didn't protect her in any way, and he denied and abandoned his children—us! No matter what his mommy issues were, there's no excuse for that behavior," Gia said. "He's a grown man who had plenty of opportunity to come around and make things right. He left us out to dry. Then, when things got hard because he married an ice queen, he escaped to Alisa's mother and did the same thing all over again."

She has me there.

"Now the results of his passivity are deadly," Gia said. "His father is gone because he was too much of a pansy to protect anyone but himself. As much as I want to believe in his love for our mother, what did it matter? He treated those he loved no better than the homeless he ignored on the streets. His supposed loved is no more than empty words and promises. There is nothing to back it up, no actions taken. Empty words and smiling images. *Simulated humanity.* Gia walked to the bank of windows and stared at the lights below.

Once she left, I needed to confront Joel on his lies—even if I never saw him again. I needed closure because once he left, I was sure he'd change his phone number and escape for good.

* * *

It was nearly midnight when I inhaled a deep breath and knocked hard on Joel's door. I didn't wait for him to answer like a normal person. Instead, I unlatched the old door and pushed the heavy mahogany barrier to find him reading in his wheelchair. He sat beside the creepy four poster bed that harkened from another era when the Gold Rush was fresh.

"You lied to me," I accused. *So much for starting out soft and demure.*

"What?" He looked up with wide, blue eyes like I had the wrong room.

"You're one of them. You always were."

"One of them? I don't catch your drift." He shut the book and tossed it on the bed.

"You couldn't just leave for Truckee, but you had to make up a convoluted lie to spare my feelings?"

He wheeled over to me. "Sophia, what is happening?"

"I know the truth. You were hired by my father. Your fake engagement was planned all along by him so that he didn't have to man-up and do the right thing. He was too afraid to get rid of that awful woman himself, so he put his father and his own daughters in jeopardy. You helped him do that!"

"Honestly, I think you should have more compassion for your father. He was essentially the frog in the proverbial water—he didn't know anyone was in danger until it was too late."

"You're not even denying it."

"It's my job to keep client confidentiality."

"It's also your job to not fraternize with the people you're supposed to protect, isn't that true?"

"It is, but we needed the front with the press around. If we were found out, Chelsea could have lashed out at Quinn, and I wouldn't have gotten the proof I needed. In case you're unaware, Brinn has taken the brunt of Chelsea's abuse nearly her whole life. That's why this scenario only worked with Quinn. The engagement gave me a reason to be in the house." He looked down at his cast. "Until I had a permanent reason."

I wanted to be angry, but I was forcing tears away. Joel's cruelty of starting something with me and taking off as if I'd imagined it was more than I could bear. As an investigator, he had to know I had abandonment issues—that his leaving would cut me deeply.

"You didn't think one fake fiancé was enough?" I shook my head as I gazed into those glacial lake eyes one last time. "*Sono così stupida!* I'm such an imbecile. Men like you don't go after women like me, and here I thought it had nothing to do with my billions. That you were really concerned about me and wanted to help." I couldn't take that I'd fallen for the same kind of suave words that my mother had decades earlier.

"Sophia." He wheeled his chair so he faced me.

I tore my gaze away. *Don't look in his eyes. Don't look in his eyes.*

"I only had eyes for you from the first moment I saw you at the reading of the will. That's why I told Quinn we had to end the farce." He tried to take my hand, but I stepped away. "I couldn't help my attraction to you. It was as if I'd known you my whole life. Whether you like me right now or not, you can't deny what we have."

"Had. Isn't that what you said yesterday?" I crossed my arms. "Just stop with the dramatic unrequited love speech—you really needn't bother." I forced back tears. I wouldn't give him the pleasure of seeing how he'd hurt me. Anger was my shield. Rage, my fortress. "There's no reason to lie anymore. You're leaving town, and I suppose that's best. Maybe Bradley can hold a gala, and all the men of San Francisco can attend for my virtual glass slipper."

He looked as if I'd hit him. "I admit, I lied about the engagement, it was in my contract. I lied about Mr. Jessup because I worried about his mental state, and I didn't want him anywhere near you. When he said he was going to get back together with that wife of his, I thought all he needed was money. You had money, and you could make him go away. Then, I knew you'd be safe."

"Wait a minute. You lied about Mr. Jessup?" I couldn't wrap my mind around it.

"I called your boss and told her to have you hire him a lawyer."

"Why on earth would you—"

"I can't explain it. I had my reasons. I called Bobbi—and your mother."

I scratched at the back of my neck. "Doesn't anyone tell the truth in this house? Are conversations in this mansion all a strategic act of how to get what you want?"

"Mr. Jessup seemed like a nice guy sent over the edge by the crazy addict in his life. It triggered dark memories in me, and I didn't want more blood on my hands."

I felt as if a whirlwind of fog and sand blinded me. I normally had a good read on people. "*More* blood on your hands?"

"I had my reasons. You'll have to trust me."

"Joel, I *don't* have to trust you. You literally haven't told me a word of the truth since we met. One lie, understandable. Two lies, okay, I get it, you're in a sobering job. But three big lies! This is every red flag you read about on an ID Network murder show."

"You really need to turn that crap off, Sophia."

"Then, rather than apologize or deal with the falsehoods, you take a new job elsewhere, so no one has to hold you accountable. Are you sure you're not my father's son?"

"It looks bad, I get it."

"It doesn't look bad. It *is* bad. You've been sneaking around so long, you have no idea what the truth is, nor why it matters."

He nodded his head up and down. "You're right. And it wouldn't matter at all if I didn't want your good opinion. But Sophia, I *do* want it."

"Why? You're leaving. What does it matter what I think of you? You'll never see me again. Isn't that what you want?"

"No, it's not what I want." He looked down at his wheelchair. "But it matters."

"Then tell me the truth."

"I can't," he said.

"Moving to a new job won't fix this," I told him, my voice more pleading than angry. "Did you ever think maybe this is your calling? You're not going to escape it in Tahoe." I walked over to him and touched the stray curl off his face. "Why are you running from San Francisco? From the job you're already good at?"

"I'm not running. I'm taking the job created for me."

I hated the thought of him finding someone else to gaze at with those devastating blue eyes. They'd be even more even beautiful in Tahoe where they reflected Crystal Bay, more mesmerizing. I'd have all the money in the world, but not what I really wanted. I didn't even care that I looked pathetic like my mother had all those years ago, pressing the doorbell and announcing her pregnancy. Begging for acceptance from people who would never offer it. I simply wanted the truth, and it was in his eyes, regardless of what he said.

"You belong here, I don't."

I leaned over him and pressed my hands against the arms of

his wheelchair. I met his tantalizing gaze full force. "My father needs to man-up and testify against his wife, but I have no doubt he'll chicken out and let Quinn take the fall. Brinn was smart. She escaped this dark castle and got away, got herself an education despite being an heiress. But Quinn and Bradley stayed and perpetuated the myth that Chelsea is a decent human being and not the monster you know she is."

"I never said she was a monster."

I knew by the look on his face that he wanted to kiss me. I could feel the heat between us. "Alisa's mom called her that. She said she was a sociopath. Although I assumed Bradley told her all sorts of tales. Isn't that what men do to keep their mistresses?"

"I might agree," Joel said. "But Alisa's mom has her own motives, and Bradley's word won't mean anything since he's clearly trying to get a divorce."

"Joel, you're going to do exactly what my father would do in this situation. You'll run. You'll say that your work is done here, and you'll head to Tahoe never to be heard from again. Do you think it ever occurred to Wyatt that some families aren't worth restoring?"

"Did it ever occur to you?"

I stepped away from him before I did something I regretted. "Not before this. I discovered that there are people on this planet who truly want to hurt and control others for no other motive that their own emptiness. These people have a deep void that can't be filled by stuff."

"You really aren't happy being an heiress. Is that possible?"

"Wyatt's dead, and there's a scramble to grab everything he left. But when my Nonna and Papa leave this earth, they leave their investment in me. The love for who I am, the nourishing food that filled my soul. They leave kindness and caring for others at great sacrifice to themselves. My grandparents leave a giant, empty void when they go. That's a real legacy."

"You're right."

I struggled for breath. "Bradley is dropping the lawsuit. My sisters and I will probably sell this house, and the rest of the money can go to charity. I'll be able to pay off my school loans and fix my Papa's house. Maybe they'll stay put. Maybe I'll go back to everything I knew."

"I wouldn't take Bradley's word for it. Wait until you hear from the courts." Joel fought to rise from his wheelchair and plopped himself on the bench under the bay windows. "I wouldn't listen to a word that man says."

"But I should listen to you? You've lied to me more than my father has. It hurts more coming from you."

"I screwed everything up. I didn't mean to fall for you. That was real. Everything I felt for you was real, and the harder I tried to protect you, the more dishonest I became."

"Protect me? I don't need protection, Joel. I'm a grown woman and trust me, I've probably overcome more than you in this lifetime. I'll survive this. I'll live to fight another day, but I won't be swayed by a dashing detective who tells me what I want to hear. The man I love won't turn and run at the slightest barrier. He'll jump over it."

"I'm not leaving because I'm scared, Sophia. I'm leaving because I have a duty."

I took one last glimpse into his angelic eyes and I turned on my heel. I couldn't hire a realtor fast enough, and I prayed none of my sisters changed their minds about selling the mansion and moving forward. Quinn and Brinn never lived without billions as collateral. I wondered if they were strong enough to go through it, but in that moment, I didn't care. There were only so many times I could allow Joel to dump me. For my own sake, this had better be the last time.

Chapter Twenty-Eight

The distance between my sisters evaporated like the fog burned off the City by noon. We no longer harbored contempt for one other or competed in that insidious, underhanded way. Rather, we started to see each other as individuals with our own struggles and battles to wage. We all shared in the overwhelming responsibility of the inheritance and somehow, without our noticing, it built a semblance of family.

I hated to admit it, but maybe Wyatt Wentworth was right.

I still missed the life I left, the normalcy of running to Coit Tower and down the dirty sidewalks of North Beach. For all its homelessness and signs of lawlessness, San Francisco would always be my own. I'd use my inheritance to make it better. Whether that was the proceeds from Wentworth Manor or the billions after the stipulations, remained to be seen.

I wouldn't run like Joel had done. His absence weighed heavily on me. He'd left the mansion without saying goodbye, and it felt like I'd been ghosted in a personal, deeply cutting way.

"At least you didn't have his parents slam the door in your face," Gia said. "When it comes to getting ghosted, our mother was before her time."

"Is that supposed to make me feel better?"

Gia shrugged and left my room at that point. Was there anything worse than someone telling you that your pain wasn't legitimate? Other people had it worse? Of course they did, that didn't mean it didn't suck to get dropped by someone you felt such a deep and abiding connection with. There was always the fear you'd never feel that way again. That you might have to settle. Now I had the added burden of being worth money. How would I know if a guy was interested in me or my Wentworth stock?

Joel's vitality, even while in a wheelchair, haunted the mansion like an unseen force. I missed him terribly, even if I'd done the right thing by not begging him to stay. What self-respecting woman would have done that? If a guy wants to break up with you, have the courtesy to allow him to do it. The emptiness I felt didn't compare to the pride I'd gained letting him go without chasing him. No woman deserved to be with a liar. Whatever his motives, Joel proved himself dishonest, and there was too much at stake to trust a liar.

On a Wednesday evening after the New Year, my sisters and I met for a family dinner to discuss the final plans for the gala before the ballet opening. The unspoken reason for the meeting was that we needed to decide on selling the house or finishing the family farce of redecorating.

The holidays had come and gone with relatively little attention paid to them. I thought the house would be decorated in grand, ornate style for Christmas, but that didn't happen. It wasn't even worthy of a Hallmark movie with its fake Christmas tree farms and cotton snow. The day came and went like any other. If my Nonna hadn't sent over packages and pasta with her homemade gravy, we may have forgotten it was Christmas. One more way that the Wentworths lived an emaciated, empty existence.

The dining room table was set in opulence with hurricane glass candle holders. Crystals draped from golden chains, and they sparkled in the candlelight. The china was a pattern I'd never seen before with baroque, gold chargers set underneath the vintage pink and gold plates. I picked up a dish and read the back: *L. R. L. Limoges France*. It meant nothing to me, of course, but I imagined it to be very expensive, and I challenged myself to remember the name so I could look it up on eBay later. It dawned on me if we sold the house, we'd have to host an auction to sell all the collectibles as well. Even the easy way out of selling wasn't simple. The house, for all intents and purposes, owned us.

At the table, I looked with genuine love at each of my sisters. None of us had an easy time with the last few months. Quinn bore the worst of it because she'd have to testify against her mother in court. She'd told me privately that she and Brinn loved to be in public because that's when "Mommy was good."

Chelsea's public persona was warm and nurturing. Quinn and Brinn lived for those glimpses of their mother at her affectionate best. "When all the guests left and the photographers dissipated," Quinn told me, "the scary monster Mommy would reappear and mentally torture us for some terrible misstep we'd made that evening." She had twisted her hair nervously when recounting her childhood. "Brinn and I always had friends come to the house. Whenever possible, we invited them to play. Then we begged them to stay overnight so our mother would behave herself."

As more stories came to light, it was clear Chelsea's true dark nature lurked somewhere beneath her stunning exterior.

Of all of the sisters, Quinn was most torn about selling the house. On one hand, she didn't think on her childhood fondly, and a fresh start held infinite possibilities. On the other hand, her horse would probably have to be sold. Dressage horses like her Avery Lane required obscene amounts of money. The country club costs alone would eat away at mere millions from the home sale fairly quickly.

Quinn nestled herself at the head of the table and braced for whatever we decided as a group. Today she had her blonde hair in an elegant updo with dubious amounts of contour under her cheekbones to make her wide face appear slimmer. In the candlelight, it appeared as a straight brown line drawn on by a russet charcoal crayon. In case this was a practice session, I vowed to tell her of this epic fail before the gala. She wore a pale pink dress that hugged her every curve and set a sketch book before her place on the table. Everything she did came naturally to her with a dainty gentility. It was hard to believe she wasn't the ballerina.

Quinn held up photos from a promotional folder. "The gala's Cinderella theme is coming along wonderfully. I thought the Fairmont's Laurel Court room where they host teas might be more public, but the catering manager convinced me the Crown Room would offer more prestige. Sweeping views of the Bay, two hundred and fifty seating max. We'll have tables of ten with a head table where we will all sit and speak."

"Speak?" my voice cracked when I asked.

"We're simply going to introduce ourselves and announce our causes. Sophia, I'm sure for you that would be something to do with children's issues."

"Why would anyone care what I had to say? I got fired from working with children."

"People will care because you have the means to make things happen. This gala is all about convincing the City we're here and we're making the most of the inheritance we received, that it will benefit the community in various ways." Quinn showed a schematic for how the tables would be laid out in the ballroom. "Whether we sell the house or inherit the billions, we're going to discuss how we'll be responsible with it."

"Will we?" Brinn rolled her eyes.

She still resented being home for the inheritance requirements and her attitude showed it. She wore a hand-ripped, black T-shirt with holes in it that wasn't from any designer even Gia could name. Black denim pants, and as a nod to her upbringing, a single strand of pearls.

"Before we discuss this gala's attributes, we need to decide," Brinn said. She was seated beside Alisa who had her Ear Pods still injected. "The deadline is looming, and we've been putting it off for months. We either need to start on the renovation or get a realtor and sell this place."

Brinn hopped up and handed out a glossy real estate folder with pictures of the house. "I've already secured a high-end Sotheby's agent for the sale. It should come as no surprise I'd like to leave the billions on the table and move on with our lives."

Brinn's bitterness at being a "kept" woman inside the dark recesses of her childhood was growing. As the black sheep of her family, she took the full force of her mother's emotional torment and the longer her mother escaped due punishment, the more Brinn's resentment grew. The sting of Chelsea's icy coldness had marked Brinn deeply. She'd thrown herself into ballet and other forms of physical torture to escape. And she thought she *had* escaped until Wyatt's crazy will pulled her back into the fold.

Alisa was on the fence about selling the house. She'd actually grown her TikTok and Instagram pages so that she made her own money. The amount bought her anything her teen heart could desire, so she hardly cared if we sold the house except it gave her good backgrounds for daily photo opportunities. Alisa's mother had moved into her room with her after Christmas, and now our house was starting to feel like some kind of socialite nunnery.

Gia had voted to keep the house, which surprised me. She now dressed like a billionaire and bought the best fabrics and the latest styles. She slipped into fancy shoes on a daily basis, but her heart hadn't changed. She still went to see Nonna and Papa on her way home from work and paid the restaurant's rent with her extra money. She'd already had design ideas for our bedrooms and had swatches of color and fabrics everywhere in everyone's quarters. I think she wanted to witness the transformation of the house—to leave it more beautiful than she'd found it. The first thing she'd done was take down the family portrait in Bradley and Chelsea's quarters. Chelsea leaving it behind spoke volumes about her maternal nature.

As I looked at my sister with her reading glasses on as she perused the gala and real estate packets, I realized that Gia was always meant to have money. Granted, I thought she'd get it being some snobby professor's trophy wife, but I was wrong. She took to money and independence as if it she'd been raised at the Olympic Club.

"It seems like everyone is ready to sell Wentworth Manor." Quinn's eyes teared. "Brinn, I'm sorry. I know this house doesn't mean the same thing to you, but did you notice how everything changed when Mother and Father left?"

Brinn's eyes widened as if she couldn't believe what she was hearing. "I did notice, but that doesn't mean I want to be stuck here for another ten months."

"I thought if we remodeled maybe it would continue to get lighter for all of us. I mean, we'd have our freedom." Quinn's voice wavered.

"You had a different upbringing than I did, Quinn."

"I'm trying to make it right though. I'm going to testify against Mother if that's what it takes. I'm trying to do the right thing."

"Don't do that for my sake. You won't win anyway. She'll buy her way out, and you'll be left out in the cold. She'll destroy you in the City. It's not worth it. You won't get justice; you'll only be the target of her wrath."

Quinn set the design boards on the surrounding old-world cabinets that lined the dining room. Brinn set the real estate packets beside them, and they both looked to the rest of us. I had no idea how to pick a realtor. I imagined you went for the shiniest ones with the biggest teeth.

"Once we decide to sell, we can't go backwards," Quinn said. "The money will be dispersed to charity, and we'll be left with whatever proceeds come from the house. After taxes. I figure that will be between three and a half to seven million apiece."

The money from selling the house put it into perspective how much we had really inherited. Seven million dollars felt like enough to live any dream we imagined for ourselves. But billions? It was unfathomable and pointless. Who needed that much money in life? I felt terrified to wait things out and take on that kind of responsibility.

However, dreams flowed like a river in my mind. I could buy Bobbi her own private building. She could service more kids and take the government's long arm out of the equation when deciding what was best for the kids of San Francisco. We could set up nationwide services and offer solid financial help for those women in abusive marriages who couldn't afford safety. My mind started to whirl with possibilities.

Brinn held out her hands, palms up. "Let it go. It's enough to pay off my schooling. Ballet is dead to me now, so what more do I need? Our full-time job will be managing this money, making sure we're giving enough to charity and the like. It's not going to be as it has been with Grandfather managing the cash and we all do as we like. We'll have to pay attention."

Quinn looked around and caught my eye. "I can't fight all of you. Maybe my horse doesn't need to be at the club. Maybe I could take her down to Woodside. Find her something more affordable."

Sympathy for her stirred my heart. This would affect her in ways I couldn't understand. That horse had been all the warmth she'd had under a roof with cold-hearted parents who always put their own needs first. I could see it wasn't the money that she'd miss. It was the one friend who'd stood by her.

Alisa pulled the Ear Pods from her ears and set them on the table beside the gold charger. "I think we should keep the house. I think it shows we're a family, and that we're not part of what Chelsea did to Wyatt. I say we remodel in the classic revival motif." She plucked a design board off the cabinets and set it down in the middle of the table. "We'll get Mr. Trunkett to find us quality money managers, and when this is all over the mansion is in all of our names. Even if our dad decides not to drop his lawsuits, we're safe."

Gia's eyes widened. "You want to keep this place?"

"I don't want Quinn to have to give up her horse," Alisa said.

"She's already lost her parents in this mess. I mean, they're not allowed to come back here."

Quinn popped up from her place at the head of the table and hugged Alisa. "I'll do whatever we decide but thank you for thinking about Avery Lane."

Gia, Brinn and I joined the group hug, and in that motion it was decided we'd keep Wentworth Manor. We'd keep it and we'd host the gala ourselves at home—with a Victorian theme.

Chapter Twenty-Nine

The evening of the gala came quickly since we changed the venue. We had a lot to do to ready Wentworth Manor for its official "before" showing. Since we'd decided on a Victorian theme, the party planner had arranged for all guests to select costumes at a shop in the Haight District.

The invitations were on thick embossed stock, hand-addressed in calligraphy and delivered by an official "page messenger boy" in full regalia. He looked like the doorman at the Mark Hopkins hotel, but I said nothing about my opinion. Official decor and arrangements were definitely Quinn and Brinn's department.

The evening of the gala, the house looked amazing. We'd hired horse-drawn carriages to pick up guests from a nearby parking lot we'd rented, along with a few golf carts, and people would be shuttled in when the clock struck 7 p.m., with dinner to follow at 8.

Quinn and Brinn came up with the guest list. The only people Gia and I invited were our coworkers and Mom. Nonna and Papa didn't want anything to do with the Wentworth Mansion and they stayed home for *Jeopardy* like it was any other night of the week.

My "date" showed up at 6:30. A blind date was really a test of how people who set you up felt about you. Apparently, Quinn did not have high regard for me at the point when she set me up. James Beardman was a husky man, a chef by day who'd been raised in a nearby mansion and had known my sisters since they were children. He had a full beard and dark, wavy hair slicked back by what appeared to be mayonnaise. Maybe olive oil? Whatever it was, it didn't smell right. I'd say he was the same age as my sisters—maybe twenty-six at the oldest. So not only did my date smell like a salad, but he officially made me a cougar. He wore tails with a burgundy silk brocade vest that was stretched to capacity.

All of us sisters had Victorian gowns made with full hoop skirts and ruffled sleeves in some variation of crimson red. When we stood together, we looked like a bad bridesmaid advertisement, but the costumes allowed us to step into another world and play a part, which was exactly what we needed as we faced strangers to tell them of our good fortune and share our plans for the house and the inheritance. Quinn had been practicing what to say about her mother's arrest and charges while Brinn would make the introductions of the added three sisters and how we came to be co-inheritors in this massive fortune.

I simply reminded myself it would all be over soon. My date brought me a wrist corsage and wrote his name on my dance card. Yes, we had dance cards that dangled off our arms on a small braided cord. Once he'd made his introductions and attended to the niceties, James went to check out the food spread and see if it was up to his standards, since he seemed perturbed about not being asked to cater the party.

"Ms. Campelli, you have a visitor and he doesn't have a costume, nor an official invitation."

"Then tell him to leave," Gia said, like we were suddenly royalty.

"Wait a minute, who is it?"

"His name is Charlie Jessup. He claims he's here to thank your mother."

"My mother?" I questioned. "Charlie Jessup doesn't—you know what, never mind. It must have slipped my mind to send his invitation. Please send him in."

It was then that a collective gasp rose among the crowd. At the door, dressed like Prince Albert himself, was our father grinning from ear to ear. He shook hands with everyone who dared to come near him and loudly boasted, "Welcome one and all to Wentworth Manor!"

"Our father is suddenly P.T. Barnum," Gia said. "Of course he ignores the court order and has the nerve to act like he's host of this party."

Quinn started for the front door when she heard his voice, but Gia stopped her. "Enjoy your guests," Gia told her. "I'll handle him. Sophia and I don't know anyone anyway." Then she looked toward the buffet table under the giant ice sculpture of two swans. "I'll grab up Sophia's date before he eats all the shrimp."

"Hey," I snapped. "At least I have a date."

She stopped and her laced sleeve fell as she raised her wrist. "Do you? Because it looks like that chocolate fountain has a date, but you? I'm not so sure."

"Sophia!" James called. "Come here, I want you to meet someone."

Charlie Jessup would have to wait a few minutes. I walked toward the chocolate fountain where an array of elegant truffles in exotic flavors like lavender honey and green tea were displayed.

"Hello," I said to the brunette behind the table. "Your work is beautiful."

James beamed as if he'd conjured her up himself. "This is Vivien Thorn. She's Evie Thorn's daughter. You've heard of her, right?"

"Your mother is the Chief of Protocol for the City. I've seen her in the paper."

Vivien smiled, but rolled her eyes towards James. "Yes, that's her."

"I didn't know she had a daughter," I said. One would think the socialite would have paraded her daughter out at least once.

"She has two," Vivien said. "We're not quite ready for prime time." She winked. I vowed to get to the bottom of that story with James later.

Gia gestured to me from the front doors.

"Excuse me, Vivien," I said. "I hope we meet again."

"Count on it," she said.

I hurried to join Gia and we went toward the commotion being made by our boasting father. As we drew closer, his attention came toward us, "Here they are, my beautiful firstborn girls. Let me introduce you to— "

Gia took him by the elbow. "May we speak to you for a minute please?" She led him to the portico outside, and I followed dutifully.

Once under the hollowed dome of the porch, Bradley's cocky smile disappeared, and he looked a sickly shade of green. Instinctively, we both followed his gaze and down at the base of the steps.

Emerging from the horse-drawn carriage was our mother in a pale pink gown that followed her slender figure to the ground. Rather than a full skirt like we wore, Mother's dress only had a bustle in the back. Her décolletage was framed in rose silk flowers, and her waist was cinched so tightly, she might have been a teenager. Around her slender neck, she wore a simple cameo choker, and she looked so breathtaking that the entire party seemed to freeze in place. Like Cinderella arriving at the ball.

As Mom ascended the stairs, the tiny ruffles on her fitted skirt moved like liquid. Gia and I gaped at each other as we realized what was about to happen. Our mother and father were about to meet for the first time since they'd parted before we were born. I held my breath and prayed silently, fervently and worthy of Nonna.

When she reached the top step, she barely glanced at Bradley. "Sophia, Gia," she said in her gentle voice while everything was silent around us. "You both look impeccable, and I'm so happy to be here. What an exciting night this is."

"Mary," Bradley stammered. "It's me. Bradley Wentworth."

She smiled nearly imperceptibly. "I know who you are, Bradley. I raised the best things you ever did in this lifetime. You'll excuse me, won't you? Girls, I'll see you inside."

And with that small statement, she walked inside as if she'd never known Bradley Wentworth in this lifetime. If I could have stood and applauded her there on the steps, I might have. As I watched her walk in, our mother was quickly surrounded by every San Francisco divorcee and widower on the hunt for his next trophy wife. They descended like lions on fresh meat.

"Bradley, you don't belong here," Gia said to our father. "There's an order of protection, and you can't be here. Tonight is for your daughters. It's for the future of the Wentworth legacy in San Francisco."

He glared at her. "This is my family. I am the legacy."

"Not any longer. Please leave so that we don't have to call the police. Quinn and Brinn have enough on their minds tonight. This is their night."

"Sophia." Charlie Jessup moved to my side in a modern suit, and Oliver was beside him in a matching little boy version.

"Oliver!" I bent down and hugged the little boy. He'd never been much of a hugger in our past sessions, but he clung to me as if he'd never let go.

"Miss Sophia, you brought me my daddy."

"I'm sorry to show up unannounced," Charlie said. "I wanted to thank your mother and your grandfather told me I could find her here. He didn't say anything about a shindig. This is quite a party."

"Thank my mother?" I shook my head. "What are you talking about?"

"The lawyer you found? Your mother gave him the retainer fee."

"How on earth—"

"It's a long story, but your family put my family back together," Charlie said. "I'll never forget it, and neither will Oliver."

"Where's Mrs. Jessup?"

He leaned in close to whisper. "She's still in rehab, but she'll be home soon. We're a family again." He beamed proudly.

How Charlie Jessup found out my mother was an easy mark, I had no idea, but wonders never ceased with Mary Campelli.

He looked over my shoulder at the party. "Well, we should be going. It looks like you have a big night here. I wanted to personally thank your mother—and you, of course." He held up Oliver's hand. "We both did. But I'll find your mother at the restaurant."

"I think that's best." I smiled. "She's got enough on her plate tonight."

Charlie and Oliver were a deliberate picture of what the Wentworth money could do for the world. I recalled my mother's ominous words about how we could use the money better than the Wentworth family. From her thoughts to God's ears.

When I walked back into the party, people of all ages milled about in their costumes, and I looked for some place that I might belong in the grand rooms, but I didn't know anyone. My date was now behind the buffet helping the staff and speaking to the guests as if he made everything. At least he wasn't annoying me.

"Nice date Quinn got you," Gia said. "Did you see the guy by the conservatory doors? He looks like your type."

"I have a type?" I asked her.

"Buff, stoic, maybe slightly emotionally unavailable?"

"You should mingle. Maybe find yourself a date. Mom's got more game tonight than both of us put together."

Quinn rang a bell, and the cocktail hour ended. She stood on the stairs where everyone could see her, and she looked amazing in the candlelight. Her gown made her look like a Civil War belle more than a Victorian lady, but her up do did indeed highlight her long, graceful neck, and even if she weren't worth billions, Quinn garnered attention like a swan in a tea party.

"Thank you all for coming tonight. It's with great privilege that we welcome you into Wentworth Manor, the before edition, in the hopes that you'll appreciate the final renovation when it's finished and we have another event here. Now, if you'll please follow me to the ballroom, it's time for us to have dinner and make our introductions." She rang the bell again and raised her parasol up so the crowd could follow her to the dining tables.

The ballroom, adjacent to the kitchen, had inlaid marble floors and a hand-painted ceiling. We'd all decided that it wouldn't be touched in the renovation. Stepping into the room was like stepping back in time to a more opulent era when people behaved better. Looking at my father walk into the room uninvited, I'd wished he'd behaved better and stayed home with his jailbird wife.

I lifted a brow Gia's way, but she shook her head when I mouthed *police*. Maybe she was right. Officers swarming the place would ruin the night.

The ballroom had a parquet floor stage, and the head table was set to perfection for my sisters and all of our dates. Gia's date was our mother and Alisa's date was her mother—which should have given Bradley Wentworth pause—but he moved a place card from someone's seat and sat down in the front row of round tables set to match the head table in the luxurious rose and gold motif. I wondered what Chelsea would think of him having a front row seat to the exes he'd tossed aside like garbage. Both my mother and Alisa's mother sat to each end of the long table. Both of them well out of his league.

Bradley hadn't taken his eyes off of my mother since he'd sat down, and I wanted to walk down the steps and smack him. *See what you missed?* I hoped it hurt him desperately to know what he'd traded in for the woman who murdered his father. Bradley's leering at Mom felt predatory, and I didn't know how I'd make it through speeches with him in someone else's seat—acting as if nothing had happened to bring us all here together.

He tried to talk to the people next to him, but they seemed upset that their place card was missing, and he was in their chair.

Soon, a security guard came and whispered in his ear. Bradley shook his head and remained seated and another place setting was quickly squeezed into the table while he sat there alone and stared at Mom.

I squeezed Gia's hand. "Do you think we should get involved?"

"She's had so many offers tonight that I don't think he's had any effect on her whatsoever. She's literally the belle of this ball. It's her demographic."

I hoped that was true.

I missed Joel. It didn't seem right to celebrate our inheritance and the elimination of Chelsea in our lives without the man responsible for making it happen. I told myself it was about the right thing to do, but I missed him desperately. I missed his sexy smile meant only for me and our stolen moments in the elevator. I missed what I thought we had together.

The double doorways to the ballroom opened, and my mouth dropped as the man I'd just been daydreaming about appeared in the arched entrance to the ballroom. Joel. Was he really there? I blinked and looked again at the devastatingly handsome man in a striking black tuxedo with tails. It really was Joel Edgerton.

He removed a top hat to reveal his cropped curls. I could see the blue of his eyes from across the room and I knew I'd fall right back in it again. All he had to do was call and I'd come running. I squeezed Gia's hand again for support.

"It's fine, Sophia. You'll be fine."

With that, Joel disappeared from view. I clasped my eyes shut and rehearsed my speech in my head rather than get lost in dreams of old.

Chapter Thirty

Bradley hadn't spoken to anyone throughout all of dinner, but he sat perched in his chair with his direct line of sight view of our mother. It creeped me out to be honest. All of the years he could have reached out at any time and he had no interest. Now all of a sudden he was obsessed and couldn't take his eyes off of her. It enraged me, as if Mom being out of his sight made her a nonentity.

Dinner was served to the head table first, and James commented on everything with his expert opinion. I was grateful for the diversion and asked him questions about the food's consistency even though I didn't care. It kept me from wondering where Joel had disappeared to and if he'd planned to speak to me while he was in the mansion. Or would he disappear into the world again without so much as a text as if I'd never existed? Maybe that was the attraction. He'd left without a word just like my father had done.

After dinner, Quinn stood up at the podium and turned on the microphone. *It's time.* My nerves made it impossible to eat, so I simply watched my date as he picked off my plate as well as his own. The scent of expensive vinegar filled my nostrils as I waited.

"Good evening everyone and thank you all so much for

coming. Allow me to introduce myself. I am Quinn Wentworth, the oldest child of Bradley and Chelsea Wentworth."

Murmurs could be heard throughout the ballroom and Bradley, undeterred by any sense of shame, waved his hand and half-stood to introduce himself. As if anyone needed an introduction.

"That's my girl!" he yelled.

Quinn ignored him. "I hope everyone is enjoying this fine Victorian feast and getting dressed up to indulge my sisters and me in our eccentricity. We wanted to do something fun and different to introduce ourselves to San Francisco society as a family. We'll be announcing our individual plans for the Wentworth fortune going forward. Everyone here looks so dashing and it feels as if we've stepped back into another era when this magnificent house was built. We planned this gala to celebrate the renovation of this Victorian mansion as we create a modern dwelling space without ruining its Victorian splendor."

Quinn paused for a polite round of applause.

"There have been a lot of questions and I'm here to fill you in on how my sisters and I came to inherit the Wentworth fortune. I know there is obviously a bigger story happening around my family, but we would all appreciate if you'd understand our silence in an ongoing and very painful legal case for us."

Society offered one benefit that I could see. People were careful to gossip in private and maintain a sense of decorum in public. I was elated that the guests exercised a certain propriety. It was easier on Quinn and Brinn. However, Quinn continued to surprise me.

"Brinn and I have known the rumors of secret siblings for a long time. When I first found out that my father had twins from his first love in high school, I didn't believe it. I'd threaten bodily harm to anyone who said something different to my face. However, it was true, and after meeting Mary Campelli, it isn't hard to see why. Mary is here tonight and she's the mother of my new sisters, Sophia and Gia."

I squeezed Gia's hand hard, but our mom held her head high. As the crowd stared at her, I could see the appreciation in their eyes. They were enamored and mystified by her as if this gorgeous creature had been unfairly kept from them. It felt impossible not to imagine Mary's beauty from days gone by if she looked this good now. I felt the sting of tears behind my nose as I watched the recognition she deserved. How long she had waited for this redemption and how gracefully she owned it by smiling gently at Quinn.

"It seems not only were Sophia and Gia part of our family, but we also learned of another younger sister, Alisa Alton. She's here with her mother Jennifer Alton, as well." People clapped courteously, but many eyes were still affixed to my mother. "We learned that our father is quite. . . ." She looked down at the podium. "Shall we say prolific."

Uncomfortable laughter ensued. Our father flinched in his chair. Still, he made no effort to rise or acknowledge the awkward circumstance that his presence brought. As far as I knew, neither Quinn nor Brinn had told him to leave or threatened him with the order of protection. I wondered why.

"I'm kidding, Daddy." Quinn said to Bradley. "You know how much we love you."

Bradley gave her an over-enthusiastic chuckle and saluted Quinn from his chair.

"My grandfather, as you well know, was a business mogul. Some would say both a legend and an icon, but to Brinn and me he was simply Grandpa. On his last day on earth, he told me that I'd be the executor of his will. I begged him to reconsider, but he said when I saw the will, I'd know why he chose me." Quinn suddenly stopped speaking. A long moment of silence stretched while she composed herself. "Little did I know that I'd be sharing his fortune with three added sisters. And before any terrible scandal gets started, let me explain that I'm not sharing my fiancé with my sisters. Joel Edgerton was in fact our bodyguard and not my fiancé."

She waited for the chatter to die down while I felt all eyes upon me. I wished I'd worn contacts, so at the very least, half the eyes could have fallen on my innocent twin. Gia wouldn't have cared what people thought.

"Grandfather's sole purpose in this choice was to honor his beloved wife, Amelie, and make sure that all of the Wentworth heirs—or in this case heiresses—were rightfully restored to the family tree and his legacy." She paused again while people clapped. "Now, without any further ado, I'd like to introduce you to my sisters and their charities of choice. We're all excited going forward in this new and wonderful venture. Please welcome my sister Brinn Wentworth."

Another round of applause with a few raucous whistles. "We might need to cut off table nine! Sounds like they've had enough," Brinn joked as she rose to the podium. "We want to get the band going and this party started, so I'll keep it short. My name is Brinn Wentworth. I also will not be commenting on my mother's absence from this party. We love both our parents, and we appreciate your sensitivity to this obviously stressful situation."

Our father fiddled with his knife at the table.

"I want to reiterate how wonderful it's been to have not one, but four sisters. At first, we were very leery of one other, but the longer they've been here, the more grateful I am that our grandfather had the forethought to put us together as a family." Brinn cleared her throat. "My charity is going to be for domestic violence and abuse victims. I'd like to use my share of the money to help women who cannot afford good counsel to escape from bad situations with their children. I'll be working closely with San Francisco's women's shelters while concurrently finishing my master's in finance. Thank you." She took her sheet of notes and sat down promptly.

Our turn. Gia was introduced and I loved that she was seen as the oldest, but technically, I was six minutes older than she.

Gia lifted the microphone up. "Many of you might know me from the de Young Museum of Fine Arts. I'm the curator for textiles so if any of you have an antique rug or clothing collection of merit, please be sure and call me. The textile arts are one of the oldest on our planet and a great contributor to pollution, so it's important to maintain the integrity of the art rather than use cheap, disposable materials that pollute our earth further. I'd love to share your art collections with the public, and I can guarantee their safety during the exhibition." A slight rupture of laughter. "My charity will be working with micro loans in America and abroad to help creatives support their art businesses. Thank you."

When it came my turn to stand, I glanced at my mother who beamed at Gia's speech. Mother still held the entire soiree enraptured, and I wondered if she'd known she'd had this power over people, would her life have turned out differently?

"Good evening," I said into the microphone as it squealed. I stepped backward, "I'm Sophia Campelli, Gia's twin sister. I am a social worker by trade, and I'll be using my inheritance to revamp the protective services for children and families in the great city of San Francisco."

There were whoops and hollers not unlike a college football game, so I sat while Alisa stood, unafraid of anyone or anything, this girl.

"Hey, I'm Alisa Alton. Jennifer is my mother. When I was growing up, we didn't have a lot of money—or any, really. There were many nights we slept in our car. My mom is my hero. She had made friends with the security guard at her work and he'd let us shower inside and also park on the property without telling anyone."

There were audible gasps as Alisa told her story.

"This money that I've inherited is unreal, but we're going to use it to help the homeless of San Francisco." It was the first time I'd ever heard Alisa speak without plugging her social media channels. "There are a ton of homeless here and lots of people who are one paycheck away from homelessness. I never thought it could happen to us, but my mom and me want to use the money to help people get off the streets." She lifted her hands up to the hand painted, ornately carved ceiling. "No one needs all this when someone outside simply needs a blanket. Thank you for listening. And follow me on TikTok and Instagram—thank you."

Quinn stood back up. "When you're finished with dinner, please make your way into the other rooms. The tables will be cleared for the band and dance floor. Thank you all again for coming."

I lifted my heavy skirt and made my way gingerly down the staircase.

Bradley was there to meet us, as he hadn't taken his eyes off of our mother through the whole of the introductions, "Mary, please. A word."

Mother lifted her dance card to show him. "I'm terribly sorry, Bradley. All booked up for this evening."

"Mary, I—you're so stunning, exquisite," he stuttered. "You look as young and fresh as the day—"

"As the day you . . . what is it they say nowadays? Ghosted me. Thank you for the compliments, Bradley. Do have a lovely evening."

Some man I'd never seen before took my mother's gloved hand and off she went into the crowd.

"Well, one of us has been accepted into this world," Gia whispered.

"How lovely that it should be the most deserving of us," I said.

"Sophia?"

I felt Joel's voice in my chest when he spoke, but I was afraid to look up at him. To hear his accounting of how he was only here for a brief time, but he must get back to his new responsibilities. I couldn't bear to watch him leave again. By looking down, I noticed he still wore a walking boot. However, he walked without a cane, and the image of him standing at the end of the ballroom in his tux and tails was not one I'd forget.

It was better for my peace of mind if I didn't look at him again.

"Will you look at me?" he asked, his voice still resonating in my chest.

I shook my head childishly.

"All right, well, will you listen to my explanation at least?"

"I suppose I don't have a choice," I told the floor.

"Years ago, when I was training to be a full-time homicide detective, something traumatic happened."

I sneaked a glance at him, but quickly averted my gaze before those amazing blue eyes could snag me.

"My mentor was shot while going to court. When you were involved with the Jessups and court, all those old fears were triggered. I remembered how I didn't protect Casey. She deserved better."

"She?" I couldn't help myself. I never expected his mentor was a woman. "Was she killed?"

"No, she's alive and well, no thanks to me."

This was all so confusing. He'd said this happened years ago, so why would he run off now? I didn't understand.

"You went to see her?" I asked.

He nodded. "She's undercover now, and I heard someone was stalking her. She's a single mother. I didn't protect her the first time, and I knew I had to get to her this time. I had to redeem myself and protect her this time."

I still wasn't tracking very well with his explanation, and I couldn't help the surge of jealousy that he'd left me to help someone else. Another woman.

"So, you didn't go to Truckee? Or is that where Casey lives?"

"I didn't go there yet," he admitted.

"So it was all another lie. If you'll excuse me." I tried to pass him without looking up, but he blocked my path. "So fine. Why are you back now? Nothing has changed."

"Everything has changed. Sophia, I love you. I didn't know how much until I left."

"But Casey's still there, right? With her child and needing help?" I couldn't focus on what he'd said. Love meant nothing to Joel. It was all about duty and honor, and he didn't have enough of either to ever tell me the truth.

Who knows if this is the truth now?

"Casey doesn't need my help. She was livid that I'd tracked her down. It made her feel I didn't think she was a good enough cop. She's a great cop, the best. So I left her to handle her stalker, and I heard earlier today that she has him in custody."

"What does any of this have to do with me?"

"You're not safe. Your stepmother is probably going to get off on these charges of drug-assisted murder.

I nodded. "Then we'll hire a new bodyguard if necessary."

James came behind me. "Let's get out of here so they can get the dance floor going. We're going to boogie!" He did some awkward dance move and laughed at himself. "Maybe we'll be good enough to make Alisa's TikTok page, do you think?"

"James, can you give us a minute, please." Joel said.

"Find your own date," James said sternly and led me by the elbow until Joel was in my virtual rear-view mirror.

Chapter Thirty-One

Joel didn't come after me. I felt forlorn and stunned as I stared at the chocolate truffle in my hand.

James had steered us through the crowd straight to the chocolate fountain. If I didn't know better, I'd think he was more in love with the chocolatier than the actual truffles themselves. When he was near her, his eyes sparkled and his personality came alive.

"You missed a lovely dinner," James told Vivien, the chocolatier. Her station was now surrounded by guests, and she worked hard to focus on James amidst all the excitement.

I felt a hand come around my waist, and I tried to disengage myself from James's grip before realizing he was deep in conversation with Vivien about the truffles' ingredients.

A breath tickled my ear, and I heard the warm resonance of Joel's voice. "Meet me in the yard." His grip fell away from my waist.

My heart skipped a beat, but my head kept yelling the word, *liar, liar, liar. If you end up with Joel, you'll get what you deserve. He's shown you who he is.*

But was that really true? Had I given him a chance?

My feet in their tiny Victorian boots, had a mind of their own, and I could no more keep myself from following after Joel than if Zac Efron himself had invited me to the garden. I made my apologies to James and walked through the throngs of guests in the conservatory. I emerged into the brisk San Francisco night air. It had rained earlier, and the sky was now clear and brilliant with the few bright stars powerful enough to dot the lit sky against the galaxy's midnight blue.

Joel leaned against his smart Victorian walking stick and smiled at me under the twinkle lights of the far patio. The scene felt magical, as if everything around me was an Instagram dream and I'd stepped back into another era when chivalry ruled. *I mustn't lose my head.*

"So, she sent you back, this mentor of yours. That's the only reason you're here."

"I would have come anyway. As soon as I was gone, I knew I'd been stupid. And the court case with Chelsea is going to last a long time."

"As I said, if we need security, we will hire it. That's a dumb reason to come back."

"I told you the real reason I came back. I love you, Sophia. I'm here because I love you and for no other reason. I didn't know until I'd left how empty my life was without you. Can't you understand that?" He stepped toward me, and I instinctively retreated.

My heart was trying to rebound out of my chest, but I made one last attempt to parry his attack on my defenses. "I can't have a man who walks out on me when the going gets tough. You can understand that given my history."

He leaned on his cane as he walked toward me. I felt breathless at the sight of his Tahoe-blue eyes affixed upon me with a gaze so powerful I withered under their strength. He took my hand in his and shimmied off the glove I wore so that my bare hand was nestled into his. His touch sent shivers through my spine, and my resolve weakened.

"You have no reason to trust me." His thumb moved gently

along the inside edge of my hand. "But I'm going to give you no reason to mistrust me. I'll tell you about every case I'm working on, and you'll have full access to my phone."

"But I don't want that. I don't want to mistrust the man I love so that he has to do those things for me. Don't you get it?"

"I know now that I took the easy way out, and I ran when I should have told you how I felt. I thought you'd think I was a weirdo, or worse yet, after your money. So I went away rather than face the rejection."

"And the rejection that I felt? Being left alone with the gossip sheets to discuss how the cheating sister had also lost her man? That I'd gotten everything I deserved for being such a wanton snake? It made my mother relive her days of humiliation all over again."

"They simply want to sell papers. You and I know the truth. Your sisters know the truth." He came closer and tossed his cane into the bushes beside us. "Will you at least kiss me goodbye?"

"One kiss," I said bravely as if I'd volunteered to be sacrificial lamb and not kissed by the most gorgeous man I'd ever known in my lifetime.

He placed both his hands on my cheeks, and I felt the warm touch of his words when he spoke. "One last kiss."

He came close and I shut my eyes and dwelled in the splendor of his soft touch. As his lips materialized on my own, it was as if we'd never been apart. As if we were never meant to be apart. His kiss grew deeper and more insistent, and I felt his love resonate in my soul. . . . *He loves me. Joel Edgerton loves me.* His secrets, his loyalty to his work and his duty were no match for the truth that was in his kiss.

I tore my mouth away. "I love you, Joel."

He pulled away from me and smiled so that his eyes mirrored the midnight violet of the sky. "Not the last kiss then?"

I cupped his face in my hands and stared into those amazing eyes. "Joel, we're only just getting started."

About the Author

Kristin Billerbeck is a best-selling, award-winning author of over forty published novels. Her work has been featured in The New York Times and on "The Today Show." When not writing, she enjoys good handbags, bad reality television and annoying her adult children on social media.

Also by Kristin Billerbeck

Kristin Billerbeck Author Page

Swimming to the Surface

PACIFIC AVENUE SERIES

Room at the Top

The View From Above

ASHLEY STOCKINGDALE SERIES

What a Girl Wants

She's Out of Control

With this Ring, I'm Confused

SPA GIRLS SERIES

She's All That

A Girl's Best Friend

Calm, Cool & Adjusted

STAND-ALONE TITLES

A Billion Reasons Why

The Scent of Rain

Split Ends

The Theory of Happily Ever After

Made in the USA
Monee, IL
27 March 2023

30614194R00166